CODE TEAL

A MINA KANE NOVEL
BOOK FIVE

AMANDA CARLSON

Even crafty ex-marshals need help in 2105.

Agent Mina Kane discovers that her pal, ex-marshal Norm Webb, is missing. It's unusual for a highly trained agent to disappear into thin air, but that's exactly what he does. Mina tracks down an old case, a likely candidate who was recently sprung from a box and happens to be a deviant who enjoys cruelty. But waiting the mandatory forty-eight hours to make this op official might prove too deadly for Norm.

While investigating the ex-marshal's whereabouts, Mina and Lee, with help from a certain colonel from France, discover that the suspect has ties to the Syndicate, and things get hotter than a comet trailing toward Earth. Before any action takes place, Mina and Lee get called back to headquarters to participate in an audit. The higher-ups are suspicious of their recent headlining cases, so they've launched an inquiry. But it quickly becomes clear that their intentions are not on the up and up.

It's not every day your rookie partner gets a commendation. Go, Lee!

Other Books by Amanda Carlson

Jessica McClain Series
Urban Fantasy
BLOODED
FULL BLOODED
HOT BLOODED
COLD BLOODED
RED BLOODED
PURE BLOODED
BLUE BLOODED

Sin City Collectors
Paranormal Romance
ACES WILD
ANTE UP
ALL IN

Phoebe Meadows
Contemporary Fantasy
STRUCK
FREED
EXILED

Holly Danger

Futuristic Dystopian

DANGER'S HALO

DANGER'S VICE

DANGER'S RACE

DANGER'S CURE

DANGER'S HUNT

DANGER'S FATE

Mina Kane

Futuristic Thriller

TOTAL ENHANCEMENT

PERFECT PLANT

CUPID'S BOW

VID STAR

CODE TEAL

DROP ZONE

Chapter 1

MINA CHECKED HER cuff a second time. She stood on the roof of Government One waiting on her partner, Lee Adams, to arrive. It was six forty a.m. They had five minutes to get to the interrogation rooms. "Where are you?" she muttered.

"What's that?" Agent Darian asked from her position a few meters away. She was there to escort them in. Government One was a maze of checkpoints and security scans, so it was easier to have someone on the inside who knew where the perpetrators were being held to lead them down.

"Nothing," Mina answered, managing to keep the grumble out of her voice. "Just wondering where my partner is. He should be here by now. I sent him a ping this morning. He pinged me back." Mina scanned the sky. It was mostly dark, the horizon just beginning to lighten. The start of a new day.

No craft. No Lee.

Anna Darian moved closer. "Can I ask you something while we wait?"

Mina's eyebrows rose. "Sure." She forced herself not to check her cuff again. She didn't want to nannybot the rookie, even though he might need it.

Mentoring was constant, like a mother chasing after an exuberant tot.

"What's it like to be involved in an op like the one you had last night?" Agent Darian blinked rapidly, her excitement easy to spot. She'd obviously been briefed on the basics of Mina's case by their mutual boss, Duncan McAllister, director of the CIU.

Mina didn't know much about Anna Darian, other than she was personable, competent, and smart. They'd worked together a few times, Agent Darian providing fieldwork assistance. But as far as Mina knew, this agent had never been assigned her own case. She was usually found at headquarters.

What did it feel like to be involved in a big case?

Mina had never analyzed it before. It's just what she did.

"It feels great when it all comes together," she started. "You know you're helping innocent victims, and at the end of the op, the perpetrator goes into a box where they can't harm anyone else. That's what matters to me the most." Mina shrugged. "So I guess I'd say it's pretty fantastic."

Agent Darian nodded.

During her last op, Mina had been able to help the people of Pormal, a group of individuals without access to bank borrows who lived on the border of the outskirts. The situation had been a happy chance, since that area wasn't in her jurisdiction. Most ops didn't go down like that. She and Lee had been assigned to investigate an extortion attempt against a vid star, and the two cases had overlapped in the best way possible.

Mina thought it'd been a coincidence, but Vincent Kramer had given her the idea that Norman Webb, an ex-marshal whom Mina had enlisted help from recently, might've been more involved than she'd originally thought.

She was planning to get to the bottom of that very soon.

Agent Darian hemmed for a second while Mina searched the sky again.

"But what about, like, going into the *actual* outskirts? That had to be scary, right? Were you worried something was going to happen?"

"Happen, as in bodily harm? Not really. We had escorts and SWAT doing the roundup. Our time on the ground was minimal. We were in and out in about twelve minutes. Not really much time to be worried."

Anna shuffled her feet, kicking a nonexistent pebble in front of her. "I don't think that'll ever be me," she lamented. No hint of a whine. "I don't have the courage it would take to do something like that. Or to jump off a ten-meter hydro-ship into the harbor. Or to be in the same room with a serial killer. You've done all of those things in, like, a week."

Mina heard wistfulness, not envy. "You're in your second year at the agency, correct? Once you pass that phase, you'll enter the field more often. It takes a while to get comfortable making tough choices, but then it becomes second nature."

She scanned the sky again. Where was Lee? Her euroboot began to tap on the syncrete roof.

Agent Darian blushed, shaking her head. "No, I've actually been here for four years. McAllister has offered me time in the field over the last few, but I've refused. I'm really great at researching, data filing, and assisting agents like you. But my stress levels would be up through the strato if I did what you do on a daily basis. Even though I love being part of the agency, and it's been a dream to work here, I'll never be that kind of agent."

Mina wasn't sure if that statement needed a reply. She settled on, "If you change your mind, you can always start small."

With relief, she heard props in the distance.

They watched as a government drone entered the airspace. They wouldn't know if it was Lee until the craft set down.

"Maybe," Agent Darian replied.

In an effort to be helpful while they waited, Mina offered, "I cut my agent teeth on catching petty criminals. Kiosks are notorious for break-ins."

Kiosks were small, one-room shops that printed specialty food items that contained hard-to-find trace elements. Those trace elements were essential to get the flavor and consistency perfect. Kiosks had been a part of their world for at least fifty years, and since they were usually stand-alone structures, they got broken into a lot.

Like, a lot.

But luckily, kiosk owners had gotten good at hooking up vid surveillance. Tracking down the unlucky assailants had never been overly difficult, just time-consuming. Those kind of crooks were usually nonviolent. Most of the time, petty thievery landed under the jurisdiction of Street Crime, but agents in the CIU, or Corruption Investigation Unit, were called in when they were overwhelmed.

It was a good place to start.

Agent Darian bit her lip. "Honestly, I'd jump into the field if I was lucky enough to be assigned a partner like you."

"There are plenty of agents out there like me."

"Oh, there's not." She shook her head. The ordered blonde knot at the base of her neck remained unmoving. "I can assure you."

The government drone set down, and a harried Lee hustled out.

Mina was relieved to see him in more ways than she could count. She sympathized with Agent Darian, but counseling her on her career path was not Mina's strong point. Or even a weak point. It was more of a moot point.

Lee appeared more rumpled and owlish than usual. Maybe not? He so often looked like that. "Sorry I'm late," he huffed, coming to a stop in front of them. "Right before I was ready to leave, I got a visit from a bot sent by my landlord. It took me a while to get rid of it."

Mina gestured for Agent Darian to lead the way. "Bots do what you say. They're unconfrontational for a reason."

If humans had to deal with confrontational bots, bots would cease to exist.

As it was, people were highly suspicious of them anyway.

"I know. But this one...wouldn't leave." Lee coughed, clearing his throat by thumping on his chest a few times. It'd been a *morning*, apparently. "I had to short-circuit its power. I didn't know what else to do."

They DNA-swabbed at the sky-screen-enclosed entrance and followed Agent Darian to a wall of tubes, where they offered their helix strands once again.

"Expedited entrance, interrogation level, no stops," Anna commanded.

The tube doors whisked open, and they stepped inside.

A sim intoned, "Expedited request accepted. Please grip the handrails. The ride may be unstable."

Mina grabbed on to one of the protruding polymold handholds. They were about to plunge down hundreds of stories in about five to seven seconds. "What do you mean you had to short-circuit the bot?" Mina asked Lee as the tube started its descent.

"I have a special tool. A remote power blast. It affects the bot's circuitry and takes them a few minutes to recover. Kind of like the hyppie trick, but it's not a memory thing, it's just a power thing. While it was sputtering, I snuck out." Lee frowned. "It told me I owe a bunch of back borrows and said I wouldn't be allowed to leave my residence until I settle the debt." He glanced at Mina, blinking. "Do you think that means I can't move into my new high-rise?"

Lee had just been assigned new government-approved housing, which was a major improvement over his current living conditions. He'd been occupying a super tiny, two-room, outdated residence since his mother had left him alone at age sixteen.

Mina was about to scoff at the mere thought, but seeing the genuine concern in her partner's face, she held off. Having basically been abandoned at the age of sixteen, Lee hadn't learned how to function inside their bureaucracy. Her mentoring process wasn't just about making him a good agent, it was about educating him about anything and everything. "You will absolutely be able to move into your new high-rise. We just have to figure out what this bot is talking about. You've been living there for, what, six or seven years? Why would they only mention something now? Legally, they have to inform you if your contract changes. When you enter into an agreement or Terms of Residence, borrows are deducted directly from your bank account. If you don't have approval from your bank, you can't get a residence." That's how people ended up in Pormal and the outskirts. "Do you have monthly borrows deducted out of your account?"

Lee scratched his head, his other hand gripping the bar next to hers. The ride hadn't been bad. Just a little stomach wobbly. The tube was already slowing.

"No. Nothing comes out of my borrow account. I'll have to talk to my mom. I thought everything was taken care of by my father's death benefits. I guess not."

The sim announced, "Arrival at underground level five. Have a nice day."

The door whooshed open, and they stepped out.

"Try not to worry about it," Mina suggested. "It'll work out." To Agent Darian, she asked, "Is McAllister in the building?"

"I'm not sure," Anna replied, moving to the right. "He was off-site at an investigation bright and early this morning. I know he wanted to make it down here at some point. Follow me."

They wove their way through several corridors, stopping at various checkpoints to give more DNA and complete retinal scans. They passed through another secured entryway, and as the doors opened inward, Mina spotted guards standing sentinel in front of four doors down a long hallway.

This was the place.

Last night, SWAT had apprehended four individuals at a location in the outskirts. Dominic Nesbit, Shauna Nesbit, Yolanda Terrin, and Jesse Guthrie. Shauna had tried to kill, or at least subdue and kidnap, Petra Pebbles, the pink-is-her-favorite-color, spoiled-above-borrows vid star they'd been trying to extort and Mina and Lee had been assigned to protect.

Mina had taken the industrial-strength tranq meant for Petra, receiving less than half the dose jabbed into her side while she'd wrestled with Shauna at a vid premiere.

Luckily, the needle had fallen out quickly.

Or she wouldn't be standing here.

"I want to start with Yolanda," Mina told Agent Darian.

"Is there a completed DNA match for Shauna yet?"

They were relatively certain that Shauna Nesbit had been using a DNA alias made from Dominic Nesbit's strands, so she wasn't actually Shauna Nesbit at all.

"Nothing conclusive," Anna answered.

Mina shot an inquisitive look at her partner. "Is that possible?"

Lee shook his head, looking equally dismayed. "DNA inside the body can't be manipulated," he said by way of explanation. "I mean, it can over a lengthy amount of time, involving the natural process or sped up slightly by a chemical process. But even if it shifts a little, you'd still get ninety-nine percent of the sequencing. It should show up with lifecheckable descendants, even if she paid a hacker to wipe her background completely clean. We should have received a definitive answer as to her real identity through her blood."

Agent Darian nodded, looking impressed by Lee's knowledge. That made two of them. "I totally agree. But the results came back inconclusive. Feel free to peruse the data yourself. I'll shoot it to your cuff. It came in about ten minutes ago."

"That means something unprecedented is happening here," Mina said.

"I'll assess the data while you start the interview," Lee suggested. "Maybe something will pop for me."

"Good plan," Mina replied. "Join me in Yolanda's room when you can."

Agent Darian gestured to a door on the right. "She's inside there. She's been read her rights. She's pretty haggard. Been here all night. Crying off and on. Refused food."

"Who's running lead?" Mina asked.

"That hasn't been decided yet, but if I had to guess, Banking, Borrows & Credits will get it. Their agents were in last night, and they were righteously angry. This was a big operation, lots of their people involved on the inside. A few corridors over, we have seventeen bankers and brokers in holding rooms. Had this plan launched, it would've been a fast-moving comet, hard to stop. Lots of currency lost. You know how they feel about that."

"The BB&C considers missing coin akin to murder," Mina replied wryly.

The rough idea of the scam, as Mina understood it, was that Dominic Nesbit and his cohorts were going to provide people in the outskirts with DNA aliases and fake identities. They would then be sent into the city to purchase goods funneled through fake bank accounts and resell or trade whatever they brought back for profit. The outskirts didn't run on borrows—it ran on hard coin and items of value. Trades were often extremely inflated because resources were scarce.

The gains would then be split between Nesbit and the bankers and brokers who'd set up the fake borrow accounts. The banks would shoulder the losses, because the payments from the fake aliases would never be paid back. Once an account was flagged as illegitimate, the corrupt banker would just create another, tagging a different fake DNA alias, and the scam would continue.

Because banks felt so strongly about being stripped of

currency, they would fight for max time in a box, which was equal to what Mina wanted. The more time the Nesbits spent in a box, the more time the people of Pormal would be free of them.

Whoever took lead would run this investigation, and they could allow or disallow access. Rather than letting Mina and Lee get caught up in that, McAllister had wrangled this interrogation first thing in the morning so they could shore up the extortion case involving Petra Pebbles. They owed the vid star that much. Not to mention, Mina wanted to know exactly why the Nesbits had been trying to murder Petra and assume her identity.

There was a lot to unravel here.

Mina headed to the door for her first interview, nodding at the guard to start the unlocking process, stopping when her cuff beeped. It was a holo alert.

"Engage," Mina ordered.

Director McAllister popped up, his image hovering above Mina's wrist. "Remains of a human body have been found."

CHAPTER 2

"THE DNA MATCH is to one Esther R. Rizzo," McAllister continued. "Former owner of Honeycomb Gelskin Inc."

"And Petra Pebbles' aunt," Mina added. "Has the body been aged yet?"

She knew McAllister would say Esther Rizzo had been dead for twelve years before he said it.

"Death was approximately twelve years ago. Remains were found under several layers of syncrete in one corner of the Honeycomb building."

That was the exact time frame in which a computer search had identified Dominic Nesbit, Shauna Nesbit, and Esther Rizzo in the same place together. However, the location had come up as unknown in the system, likely due to a hack.

Now they knew that location was Honeycomb.

"This confirms what Agent Adams and I found on Dominic Nesbit yesterday," Mina relayed. "He was released from a box twelve years ago. When Shauna tried to attack Petra, and I intercepted, she admitted she'd already taken a life. We can assume she meant Esther, but there could be more." Both Lee and Agent Darian were paying rapt attention. "I'm about to interview Yolanda Terrin now. I read her file before arriving and know she has no family ties to either Dominic or Shauna and no link to Honeycomb, at least from what's on file. I'll be interested to see where she came from. Agent Darian is betting the BB&C take lead. I'm not sure how much wiggle room I have, but if I can offer her less time in a box or make her a deal, we may get more."

"I have little authority in terms of offering a deal," McAllister said. "But I'm certain the BB&C will want to crack this open as far as it can go and would be willing to work with offers that sit within fair margins. You can hold out a treat, but don't promise anything until you get confirmation from lead."

"Understood. One more thing," Mina said. "DNA results have come back inconclusive on Shauna Nesbit. None of us have ever heard of that happening. Agent Adams is going to look into the report while I start the interview, just confirming that Tech is trying to figure out that mystery."

"Indeed, they are. They're in the process of reanalyzing the samples and are working to get to the bottom of it. The hypothesis at this time is that they have a good hacker on the payroll. That's as far as it's gone. Report in person to my office when you two are finished with all four interviews."

"Will do." He popped off Mina's wrist. She turned to Lee. "Do you agree with the hacker hypothesis?"

"I mean, it's a possibility." The rookie shrugged, appearing skeptical, which resembled a cross between an inquisitive fox and a confused panda. Mina did love her naturecasts. "But you'd need a hacker that could hack into every medical database in the world at the same time. We're talking about blood samples that are drawn and entered into an active system, one that updates its data based on human genetic matter gathered from around the planet minute by minute. I've never heard of a hacker being that prolific. Sure, they could gain entrance into a single static system, like the Medi Center comp, and mess with the results. But a uniformed wipe of thousands, if not hundreds of thousands, of active genetic database systems, all being alerted simultaneously to decode and cross-ref the blood sample? Unheard of. Plus, the hacker would have to be timely, monitoring the system right as the samples were being entered. An off-site hacker wouldn't have that kind of knowledge. Nobody flags their sample before it's entered."

Mina nodded. She thought the same thing. "I agree with you. Saying it's a hacker is the easiest way of explaining DNA being inconclusive. There has to be more to it. Once you're done examining the data, everything I do and say in that room will be on vid. Catch yourself up before you step inside. Agent Darian will show you where to do so. If I'm not getting anywhere, deliver dire news, like you just uncovered something extremely damaging, but you can't say what it is yet." Lee appeared unsure. "I'm asking you to act. Play a part. Make it seem like Yolanda is in for the worst and the government is ready to box her up tight. The goal is to keep her unsteady."

"Okay. I can do that."

Mina knew he could. These situations were new to him, but pretty soon they wouldn't be.

She walked over and placed her finger in a receptacle next to the door. When a green light issued overhead, the guard nodded and placed his own finger in the receptacle, retinal-scanned, and then opened the door.

The room was stark. One metal table, three simple chairs. White walls. Dim, yellowed ultras.

Yolanda glanced toward Mina as she came in, startled. Her diffracted emerald-green eyes were red and puffy. She'd been given clothing to wear, a basic drab-colored uni to replace the bright orange tube dress she'd worn to the vid premiere. Her hair was still tinted the same shade of orange. It'd fallen out of its snaky updo, tendrils dangling limply around her face.

She brought her fingers up to brush some of the pieces out of her eyes, her hyperglo nails giving a weak flutter. The best hyperglo on the market emitted lighted charges for only twenty-four hours, the chemical reaction fading over time. It'd been over twelve hours since Mina and Lee had picked up Yolanda and Petra at The Bella on the way to the vid premiere, with Vincent Kramer in tow.

It seemed like it'd been a lot longer. She was certain Yolanda would agree.

Mina pulled out a chair directly opposite of the beleaguered former assistant.

After Mina was situated, Yolanda leaned across the table, throwing her e-restrained hands out imploringly.

"Please. *Please* get me out of here. I haven't done anything wrong," Yolanda cried. "I worked for Ms. Pebbles for two years. I'm worried sick about her. There's been some kind of mistake. I was taken against my will. You have to help me get out of here."

The entirety of Mina's response was to cross her arms and sit back in her chair.

Yolanda began to panic. "You don't believe me! I can see it on your face. I swear I didn't do anything wrong! I was only trying to protect my employer. They took me prisoner. I was held against my will in the outskirts!"

Mina said nothing.

Petra Pebbles' ex-employee laid her forehead on the table, banging it a few times, fresh tears pouring out. "I shouldn't be here. I don't deserve this. I didn't do anything wrong. Help me! Help me! Help me!"

After a prolonged amount of drama, which was unsurprising, since Mina had discovered that Yola was a very talented actress who'd played the part of Petra's assistant while double-crossing her with laser precision, Yolanda snuck her head up a fraction of a centimeter to examine Mina's reaction to her theatrics.

Mina smirked. *You're going to have to do better than that.*

"Fine!" Yolanda hauled herself up, tears evaporating, replaced by a lick of hot anger. "I knew you were going to be trouble from the moment I saw you. Even before you ordered me to scan your badge." She narrowed her eyes, scowling. "Damn Petra and her stupid, useless vid comparisons. Who cares what Cuticle Cantrell thinks? If she'd let the PPF in, then the world would have a new, better Petra, and everything would be as it should be."

Now they were getting somewhere.

"Did you have someone inside the PPF?" Mina asked.

"No," Yolanda answered miserably, rubbing her face. "We were just counting on their incompetence, but then Petra insisted on hiring federal agents."

That's not the way it usually worked, but Mina left it alone. She was still reclined back in her seat, arms crossed. "You extorted Petra and accused her of murder. Even though the PPF should've been allowed to investigate first, federal agents would've been called in eventually. I mean, it was extortion and murder. We kind of specialize in that for a living." Mina shifted in her seat, dropping her arms and scooting closer. "Extortion was where this entire thing went south. Why choose that particular method? Why involve the PPF at all? If it were me, I'd just make the Shauna/Petra swap somewhere no one was watching, much less under the noses of a couple of federal agents and a hundred thousand witnesses." The alleged kill-Petra-and-make-a-swap plan had taken place at the Ultimax Dome during a vid premiere. "If you'd been stealthy about it, you might've pulled it off. Shauna's physical alts make her a dead ringer for the vid star." Mina wasn't kidding—the woman looked *exactly* like Petra Pebbles. "You had access to a lab to manufacture DNA. She could've impersonated Petra for years. Why risk it?"

Yolanda collapsed back in her seat, trying to cross her arms, but unable to do so because she was e-restrained. If she moved her hands around too much, she'd get a shock for her troubles.

She was petulant. She didn't want to tell Mina anything. But Mina recognized the anger, fear, and uncertainty that now fueled her. Mina would take it.

All she had to do was wait.

Finally, Yolanda groused, "Petra wouldn't give me the rotary safe combination, so we tried to scare her with the murder stuff. It was Dominic's idea. Go big, add in subtle clues, like the rose watermark, and she'd figure it out. She'd go running to the safe and open it herself. She'd likely call the PPF, which was fine, because the most they would do would be to take the ad plates in to examine them. When they found nothing, because they are terrible at investigative work, they would bring them back. And because I'm her air-breathing service bot, I would pick them up. One way or another, I would have had them."

"You were extorting Petra so she'd open her safe? And if that didn't work, the second plan was to knock her out and make the swap midpremiere?" A mighty terrible plan. "Why not just wait until after when no one was watching?"

Yolanda was clearly uncomfortable. Her gaze landed somewhere over Mina's shoulder, and she remained silent.

"You might as well tell me," Mina coaxed. "We have the ad plates. You clearly feature in some of them. There's no going back now. If you cooperate, whoever takes the lead in this investigation will go easier on you, which means less time in a box. I'm assuming that's what you want. I mean, that's what I would want." Mina paused, adding a bemused tone. "Why didn't you just make the Petra swap after you got home last night? So silly not to. Tots would've done a better job coming up with a plan."

"Because Petra can be incredibly dense, that's why!" Yolanda erupted. "Even though we hoped she'd open her safe, we didn't really think she would. She's insufferable! So we came up with the vid premiere plan and...sort of locked ourselves in." Yolanda visibly deflated. "There was an added bonus of doing it at the Ultimax. If we pulled off the swap in front of the PPF, there was no way anyone would *ever* question her identity. I mean, we had Police Protection officers with us the entire night." She thumped her back against the chair, frustrated. It was the most she could do. "But you got in the way of months of planning. You and the colonel-in-arms and your stupid partner. You wrecked everything."

Mina shrugged. "Being good at my job isn't the problem here. You should've called it off or changed your plan once we came on the scene. Proceeding when you knew federal agents were shadowing you was incredibly dumb."

"It wasn't my decision." Yolanda clacked her jaw shut with an audible snap, more tendrils of hair falling around her strained, tired face.

"Let me guess," Mina offered. "They kept the ill-conceived plan in place because the bankers and brokers that Dominic and Shauna have wooed over the years, who gave currency up front so they could build a lab in the outskirts, among other things, were demanding repayment, and time was running out."

Yolanda was done talking.

That's what she thought.

"Two years with Petra must've been mind-numbingly tedious," Mina offered casually, going with the insufferable thread Yolanda had given her, getting comfortable in her seat once again. "Bending over backward for an extremely spoiled vid star when you yourself came from almost nothing. All that waste. All that excess. Must've been hard to watch." Yolanda's eyes shot to Mina. "That's right. When you commit a crime, the government has access to everything about you. So we looked you up. You lived on the edge of a city in Illinois very close to what they call the Rambles. Just like the outskirts here." Cities had their own names for places where people went to live when they were out of borrows and could no longer live the typical way of life. "Since there were no records on how you arrived in this city, I'm assuming it was via private transpo." Yolanda wouldn't meet her gaze. "Once you got here, you were able to transform yourself. I'm wondering how you did that with very few borrows to your name. Seventy, in fact. Seventy is barely enough for a few printed meals and a day or two at a pay-a-day. Your first job was as an assistant to a prominent businessman. You were hired through a temp agency. How did you manage to get the references needed to secure that kind of a position?" A temp agency in charge of placing an assistant with a high-profile client would never take someone with a sketchy background. One DNA lifecheck was all it took to validate or invalidate a candidate. That was why it was so hard to climb out of poverty. "Don't worry. I actually don't need you to answer. I figured it out all by myself."

"Good on you," Yolanda sneered.

Mina waited.

Yolanda fidgeted. She wanted to know what Mina knew.

Mina stayed silent.

"You don't know anything!" the restrained former assistant finally snapped. "There's nothing in my lifecheck that would give away *any* details. You're just guessing. So what if you know I only had seventy borrows to my name? It was enough." She nodded, satisfied. Lots more hair bounced in her eyes. She brought up her fingers to swipe the irritating pieces away.

Mina shook her head. "It wasn't nearly enough. Who brought you to the city? I can only assume it was Shauna, although that's not her real name. Did she find you begging for food in a desolate alleyway? Were you pals? Maybe she was your caretaker. She must've promised you a lot to get your cooperation, and boy, did she deliver. Was your first DNA alias actually your own identity? So, not really an alias? More of a sidestep? That was extremely clever. I don't think I've ever come across anything like that before."

Yolanda's eyes widened.

Mina chuckled. "Don't be so surprised we figured it out. When you landed in this city, you DNA-swabbed as Yolanda Terrin. But the computer hiccupped a teensy bit.

It wasn't hard to catch. The first swipe within city limits was a ninety-nine-point-three percent DNA match. Not enough to register as an error. You were you, but not exactly. If questioned by any authority or bank, they would just take another DNA sample from you, a hair strand or from a different finger, then you would swab at a hundred percent. Like I said, it's brilliant. After you'd been working for a few months, your DNA magically went back to one hundred percent. Whoever was in charge of your alias did an excellent job. DNA manipulation is complicated. I'm assuming that zero-point-seven percentage point discrepancy, back twelve years ago, allowed a very talented hacker to alter your background momentarily, so you'd come up as the new and improved Yolanda Terrin, the one who swabs at ninety-nine-point-three. Enough for you to clear the temp agency lifecheck and get a job. From there, it was all you." Mina sighed while shaking her head, expressing her sorrow for the poor assistant and how she'd ended up. "You worked *so* hard. You made decent currency. You built a life for yourself here. A good one. Why allow them to strip you of it in the first place? Now it's all gone."

Yolanda slumped in her chair. There was defeat, but also lingering anger. She knew what she'd lost, but instead of accepting her part in it, she blamed Mina.

"Are you related to her?" Mina leaned forward. "Shauna's not coming up in the system even after a blood draw. We can't figure out who she is."

The assistant smirked, straightening a little as her eyes danced. "You'll never find out who she is."

"Do you want to bet currency on that?"

A beep sounded, and the door opened.

Lee came in, looking all business. He pulled out a chair next to Mina's and sat. He placed his hands on the table and causally wove them together. He even smiled.

Go, Lee!

Then he dropped a huge Yolanda-sized hive bomb. "No need to place any bets. Your aunt 'Shauna' is internationally recognized geneticist Fiona Fabion, and she's using DNA suppressors she invented to mask her own DNA, along with the DNA topical cream she invented to swipe as Shauna Nesbit."

Mina's eyes flicked to Yolanda. Then she smiled. "Judging by your sheer surprise and utter astonishment at my partner's revealing announcement, had you taken me up on my bet of coin, you would've lost *big-time.*"

"EXCELLENT WORK, AGENTS." Director McAllister praised them from behind his desk in his small, serviceable office. He was relaxed, with a hint of a smile, happy the case had been solved. It was always a great feeling. Mina wished she could bottle this up and show it to Agent Darian. "It took you less than an hour to put all the facts together and gain a confession from three out of the four parties. I just received confirmation that BB&C has taken lead. They're reviewing the interrogation vids and have sent their appreciation for a job well done."

"Honestly, as far as I'm concerned, all the accolades for this go to Agent Adams," Mina said, meaning it. "Figuring out that Shauna Nesbit was Fiona Fabion was brilliant investigative work. He put it together on the thinnest of filaments. The look on Yolanda's face confirmed everything in less than two seconds. After that, we just had to go through the motions."

"Don't minimize your part in this, Agent Kane. You

played a key role in garnering all the admissions. But I'm in agreement that Agent Adams discovered compelling facts that led to a swift conclusion of this case." McAllister shot a look at Lee. McAllister's inquisitive expression resembled a shrewd fox surveying its prey from its place concealed behind a tree. Honestly, naturecasts never failed to mirror real life. "I'm curious to understand how you pieced this together so quickly."

"I...um..." Lee stammered under the scrutiny. Mina wanted to urge him to relax, but instead stayed quiet as she rested her shoulder against the wall, waiting for him to spill his sharp, investigatory secrets. "When I reviewed the data, I was actually thinking about how Agent Kane would do things." He glanced down, blushing. Mina's eyebrows rose. Did that mean she was a better mentor than Kaylee? She couldn't wait to brag about it. "After Agent Darian sent me the inconclusive lab results, I began to search for the particular reasonings and verbiage of why they were inconclusive. The word 'masked' came up a few times. The DNA was there, but it was 'masked.' The interpretation was that it'd been masked sometime during the upload and was considered a hacking issue that had blurred the results. But then I remembered something I'd read a few years ago about the invention of *masking* DNA. Only a handful of people in the entire world had learned how to do it. It's done by ingesting a biogenerative material that encompasses cell matter at a very atomic level. The science behind it has been outlawed since its invention, at least fifteen years ago, by almost every government, because, you know, if there's a way to mask DNA, it would disrupt our entire system."

He was right. It would be unthinkably costly for the government to find a new way to identify people. DNA was unique to every individual and was the most reliable way to identify someone. Retinal scanning was a close second, but it wasn't infallible. Over the years, people had perfected printing high-res images on biolenses, which of course was illegal. But it was harder to detect.

"One US scientist by the name of Fiona Fabion refused to stop researching, so she was stripped of her credentials. After that, nothing more was said about her or masking in general." Lee ran a hand over the back of his neck. "After I read Shauna's report, I pulled up Yolanda's file. There was an aunt listed as Fiona F. Terrin. But when I went into Fiona's lifecheck, it was blank. No information listed other than her age, which is forty-one. The middle name didn't come up as Fabion either. Everything had been scrubbed." He shrugged. "So, um, Agent Kane wanted me to come into the interview with big news. I was guessing based on what I'd read a few years ago, but I felt like it was a pretty solid guess. Agent Kane is a master at reading people, so I figured if I was right, we would know."

Mina nodded, super impressed with the rookie. "It was perfect, actually. I'd just hit a wall with Yolanda. She was ecstatic we didn't know who Shauna was and was prepared to keep it that way, even if that meant longer in a box. Her face after Lee spilled was priceless. She knew we'd caught her, so she decided to talk. Turns out, Fiona was Yolanda's guardian for years. Her credentials weren't the only thing the renowned geneticist lost—she was stripped of her bank borrows and pretty much her entire life. They were forced to move to the edge of the Rambles. But even there, Fiona found a way to continue her genetic research." Mina moved to stand next to Lee. "Fiona was so stymied that we figured it all out and that Yolanda had flipped, she admitted that Yolanda had been routinely stealing Petra Pebbles' DNA, which Fiona had been *ingesting.*" Mina was dramatizing this story like Petra did with all the vids she starred in, with lots of inflections and hand gestures. She couldn't help it. This storyline was out of an *actual* vid. Though Mina didn't think Petra Pebbles would be very excited to star in this one. "The physical alt work Shauna had done to her face to look like the vid star was done by a very talented cosmetic transformationist, but that was aided by Petra's own DNA." Mina allowed a small squeal to escape. "That's why they look so much alike. Now that she's not taking the DNA cell maskers, she told us, her actual DNA will read like a crazy map between hers and Petra's. I'm sure scientists will be researching it for years to come." *Aaand...scene.*

"I'm sure they will be," McAllister answered thoughtfully. "Fiona's sole reason for taking over Petra's life was financial gain, or was there more?"

"Mostly for currency and security," Mina replied. "Even though Fiona is an expert geneticist, she isn't much of a criminal strategist. She and Yolanda came across Dominic by chance the day he was released. They were lunching near the jailing facility, hoping someone who fit their checklist would be released. Fiona decided that anyone of diminished circumstances just emerging from a box would be easy to control. Dangle a few borrows in front of them, use them for a handy DNA alias, tempt them with currency down the line—why wouldn't they do what she asked? With the alias in place, she figured she could remain undercover and continue her work. They chose Honeycomb Gelskin as a place to conduct their business because the air-breathing manager was an old pal of Dominic's. But Fiona miscalculated with Dominic. People who perpetrate crimes tend to like the criminal lifestyle and crave the power that comes with it. Dominic wasn't a passive follower in Fiona's plans. He had his own agenda and actually forced Fiona to do what he wanted for years, on the threat of turning her in for DNA manipulation and the death of Esther Rizzo."

"She told us," Lee added, "that they came to an agreement. Dominic would retain one hundred percent control of the new alias business, which Fiona created for him, and she would become Petra Pebbles, and they would part ways."

"By this time, she was desperate to be rid of him," Mina said. "She was twelve years in, and nothing had gone how she'd imagined it."

"They targeted Ms. Pebbles purposely?" McAllister asked.

Mina nodded. "Yes. They discovered that Esther Rizzo was related to the vid star on that very first day and that Petra would inherit Honeycomb upon her death. They murdered Esther and took over her business. Yolanda paid attention to how often Petra hired and fired new assistants. It took almost a decade, but she finally got into the right temp agency and got the job. Fiona and Dominic kept Honeycomb running all that time, but they didn't have access to Esther's borrows, and they didn't want to arouse any suspicion, so they were forced to wait. Once Fiona *became* Petra, they would announce Esther's death, and Honeycomb would become Fiona's underground laboratory once again. Or something close to that." Mina shook her head. "By the time I crossed paths with Shauna, aka Fiona, at the vid premiere with a gigantic syringe in her hand, she was beyond frantic. She knew this had to work. It was her only chance. We got in her way. The nerve of us." For a moment, Mina contemplated the fact that the PPF might never have uncovered all this. Then Petra would be gone, and Fiona and Dominic would've achieved all their goals. "Dominic was apoplectic. When we got into interview, he said next to nothing. He will be raging for a long time. Jesse Guthrie was their hacker. He was good at erasing lifecheck information, but was hardly prolific. He was doing it for the currency, trying to get himself out of the outskirts. He confessed everything almost immediately."

Lee said, "He was barely a Level VI."

McAllister nodded. "This was a complicated narrative that you both uncovered due to sound investigative work and intelligence. The perpetrators will be processed by the BB&C and boxed for a long time. Good work."

"Thank you," Mina said.

"Yeah, thanks," Lee agreed.

"Your next task is to head over to Ms. Pebbles' residence and let her know that her aunt's remains have been found. I want you to outline the details of the case and let her know she will be receiving a full report from my office. She can follow up using that report for clarity and legal purposes. She deserves to hear in person about the death of a family member at the hands of Dominic Nesbit and Fiona Fabion."

Mina had been expecting nothing less. "Of course."

"Then I assume you'd like to conclude your business in Pormal?"

"That would be optimal," Mina said. "With your permission, I'd like to deliver the payment personally for use of the safe house, in physical coin. I also have another request, which I'm hoping can be satisfied through our Tech Department. I owe an eleven-year-old girl payment for a service well done. I believe it will be in our best interest to keep the people of Pormal satisfied and willing to work with us again. I can see us continuing to utilize that safe house." It was a bunker four levels underground. In about a fifth of Mina's ops, escorting a victim or witness to safety was necessary. Fortified bunkers came in handy.

McAllister folded his hands on top of his desk. "The physical coin will be ready for pickup in an hour. I'm certain our Technology Department will fulfill your request, if it's filed within the parameters of the case. If you have any issues, let me know. I'm expecting your next op designation to come in soon."

"Also on the list is to schedule a meeting with Norm

Webb," Mina said. "Vincent Kramer indicated that perhaps the spider might've had something to do with our involvement in Pormal. He may be right. If that's what happened, I'd like to get to the bottom of it." Her boss would understand the implications of a former federal marshal manipulating an investigation. If what Vince had told her proved to be true, there would be more than just trust issues. Norm was well-connected among law enforcement, and if it came to light that he'd lied to a federal agent during an investigation, many would turn their backs on him.

McAllister nodded. "You have my permission to meet with Webb. I'd also like you to rendezvous with Mr. Hampburg and make sure he has plans to leave the city. Bliss Corp has been very clear about their intentions, welcoming him back and assuring us it was all a big misunderstanding, but I want confirmation of where he lands. I intend to set up a monitoring system with agents in that city, just to be sure."

Mina appreciated that. "Will do. I'm in the process of rounding up a few interviews for him, all government-asset jobs. HR should be sending me confirmation in the next thirty or so." She wasn't looking forward to breaking the news to Harri that he should leave town, but she felt good about the options she would be presenting him and hoped he took their advice to leave.

McAllister turned his attention to Lee. "You're moving into a new residence momentarily, correct?"

"I think so." Lee hesitated. McAllister inclined his head for Lee to explain, so Lee elaborated. "I ran into a slight issue today. The company who owns my building sent a bot to my door this morning. They told me I owe currency, and I'm not allowed to leave without paying it."

"Does your monthly residence cost come out of your bank borrows?" McAllister asked.

Like Mina, McAllister knew how the banks operated. No one lived anywhere for free.

Lee hesitated. "No. Nothing has ever been deducted from my account. I was pretty young when my mom left. She set it all up. She said that my dad's death benefits covered everything. I never questioned it. No one has ever come to my door until this morning. I'm not really sure what it all means."

"Death benefits are usually good for nine years," Mina said. "Your father died"—murdered by Veritus when Lee was three years old—"nineteen years ago. Your mother might've been mistaken. You'll have to get a hold of her. Start there." Mina addressed McAllister. "I can deal with Petra and make the delivery to Pormal by myself while the rookie deals with his housing issues. Then we can meet back here for the op designation. Does that work?"

"Fine by me," McAllister replied. "Depending on what the designation is, we might be able to do it by vid chat." Some cases were complicated. For others, a vid chat worked just fine. "Moving into this new residence is a high priority for you. Isn't that correct, Agent Adams?"

"Yes," Lee said, nodding quickly. "I'm looking forward to it. I'm sure I can figure out the issue with my landlord. My new residence will be ready for occupation tomorrow morning."

"No time to waste, then." McAllister pulled out a small board, glancing at it. "One more thing. I've arranged a recognition ceremony to be held in your honor tonight, Agent Adams. You will receive a commendation for your work bringing down Franco Tedesco the Third and ending the serial-killing ring Veritus."

McAllister had told Mina and Lee this would be happening. Mina was happy to hear it'd been planned. Recognition ceremonies held prestige by honoring the agent, but they also elevated them in status within the agency.

"It will be attended by agents from our department, held in the main Gala Room in Government Four at eight p.m. Food and beverages will be served. You are each entitled to invite one guest." To Lee, he clarified, "An invitation for the guest of honor can be extended to a family member. Their name must be cleared by me before they attend, and they may be required to sign a confidentiality agreement. Agents are under strict orders not to discuss anything about our department at these events. If your next op precludes attendance, the event will be rescheduled."

Ops often interrupted fun things. It was their way of life.

"The Gala Room is pretty spiffy," Mina commented. "It's right at the top." The four government buildings had lots of nice gathering places for ceremonies and such, but the Gala Room was the most upscale, with commanding views of the city, a full bar, lux furnishings, a small stage, and an array of gel-cush booths. The food was usually good, too. "It's been a while since we got together for a recognition ceremony." Noticing Lee's highly flushed face, she added, "It's a rite of passage for most agents, Lee. You just happen to be getting one early, which elevates your status from rookie to full agent. Congratulations."

Lee stood, shuffling his feet. "Thank you. I don't know what to say." His head tilted forward in a little bow. "I...I...think I'll ask Harmony Biggins. If that's okay? I don't have any family members in town. You know, if she's not already invited. She might be, which is fine. I really don't have anyone else to ask."

McAllister exuded nothing but professionalism. "Good choice. I'll add her to the list. Two crafts will be waiting on the roof to escort each of you to your destinations. If you have any more issues with your landlord, contact the housing department," he instructed Lee. "If they can't solve it, they will contact me. I'll be in touch about your next op designation. You two are excused."

CHAPTER 4

ON THE TUBE ride up to the roof, Lee was quiet. Mina knew he was overwhelmed. Once they stepped outside, she said, "If you need help figuring out your residence issues, give me a call. I'll check in with you after I'm finished with my stop in Pormal. I don't think either of my tasks will take too long."

"Okay," Lee said. "Can I ask you something before you go?"

He stopped, so Mina stopped.

"Sure. What?"

"Do people usually ask family to recognition ceremonies?"

Mina could see the emotion churning behind his eyes. His father was gone, and his mother had left him at a young age. Going by what he'd just said, he didn't have any family close by. She knew he had a cousin named Penny, because his home sim had been modeled after her voice, but that was about it.

"No. They don't," she assured him. "If our department wasn't so secretive, maybe people would opt to bring family members more often. And we would probably be allowed to invite more than one guest at a time. But honestly, it's a pain to bring family. Most of them think we work Street Crime, and everyone has to play a role to make sure that stays the correct story throughout the evening. It's stressful. But we will absolutely do it for the guest of honor if they choose to have a family member present."

His face brightened. "Oh. That's good, then. Do you think Harmony will mind if I ask her?"

"No. I think asking Harmony is a great idea. She'll be thrilled." Mina was almost positive. Harmony was new to the agency and certainly a hydro-cracker, but she and Lee had a shared past because they were both hackers and had been on the boards together for years. "She probably wouldn't have been extended an invitation since she's still in a trial phase, so she'll likely be happy she can attend."

Harmony was spending quality time with Kaylee to see if she'd be a good fit for the agency. Harmony desperately wanted a job, but that didn't mean she was cut out for work in the field. There were lots of roles for a superhacker interdepartmentally.

"I'm sure she's already signed all the confidentiality waivers that go along with this job, so that's a bonus credit."

There were a lot of rules to follow. And if agents broke them, things got messy.

"Who are you going to ask?" Lee asked as they began to walk toward the drones.

"Nobody. It's more fun that way." Her plus-one was usually Kaylee, but Kaylee would have her own invitation to this.

"I think you should invite Vincent Kramer." Lee's eyes skittered toward his craft. "I mean, he's already worked two cases with us. He knows how to be secretive. I'm sure McAllister would give him clearance."

Interesting thought.

Mina banged around in her brain for two seconds. "Nope," she concluded.

"Suit yourself." Lee gave her a salute as he jogged to his drone.

Mina stood rooted in place. Did the rookie just dismiss her?

She shook her head. She wasn't going to be able to refer to Lee as a *rookie* after tonight's ceremony. He had officially earned the title of agent. Weird. She smiled as she climbed into a craft. It didn't matter which one they boarded. As soon as their DNA was scanned, their designated operating orders would be enacted, which McAllister or someone at headquarters had already set up.

Once inside, Mina stuck her finger in the appropriate slot.

The sim intoned, "Destination Bellatone Tower. Travel time one minute, seven seconds. Do you wish to make any changes?"

"No." Mina sat back and thought about what Lee had said about asking Vince to this thing tonight.

Maybe it wasn't a bad idea. But maybe it was? Hard to know.

Her mind drifted to the apology vid Vince had dropped off yesterday, and Mina had subsequently watched multiple times last night and again this morning.

It was a clip from when they'd been kids together and unleashed a room full of holo butterflies. Mina's mother had recorded the event and had sent the vid to Vince's mom, as she often did. She and Vince had been young, happy, and free. Mina could hear their tinkling laughter in her mind. The years of her life that she'd shared with Vince had been special, in part because he'd been such a great companion. They'd had a lot of fun together.

Now she wondered why they'd lost touch over the last seven years.

She didn't have a good reason. But then again, Mina didn't hang around with anyone from her past. After she'd joined the CIU, and her life had become secretive, she'd adapted to that way of life and never looked back.

All too soon, the sim announced, "Landing in thirty seconds."

The door opened, and Mina hustled out.

The executive hub of The Bella was enormous, catering mostly to private transpo in and out. The entire building was the epitome of lux, and people who lived here had currency to burn.

Mina moved toward the doors, trying to ignore the whipping wind as best she could.

Inside, she glanced around. Yolanda had been waiting for them last time. No one was here now.

Mina's director, or another agent at headquarters, had the job of contacting the appropriate people on her behalf to allow her access up to Petra's residence. All the preplanning was done from headquarters, just like the drone instructions, as to not waste the agent's time in

the field.

She moved toward the transpo attendant, since she was the closest. The air breather, who sat inside a plexan box so she could be easily seen by everyone, had canal phones in both ears and was busy typing on a huge, built-in crystalline board. Her jet-black hair was pulled back in a severe tail, her eyelashes nearly three centimeters long.

They put Mina's enhanced ones to shame.

"How may I help you?" she asked as Mina positioned herself in front of the communication link.

"I need entrance to a residence, and there's no one here to meet me."

"The concierge office is straight through there." She gestured toward an opening in the otherwise seamless white marble wall. "They'll be happy to help." Her head bent at an angle, she intoned into a mic, "Approved. Craft landing on pad seven in one minute." Then she tapped something on the megaboard in front of her. Her eyes flicked up, and the woman was surprised to see Mina still standing there. "Is there anything else?"

"I guess not." Mina turned and walked toward the opening.

She'd been hoping for easy, but it seemed this was going to take a few minutes to figure out.

The concierge area was spacious. A long counter took up most of the back wall, privacy shields up every three meters. Air breathers were positioned in the middle of each partition. She went to the nearest one.

"How may I help you?" a young man with hair the color of a meadow and eyes diffracted the color of celery asked.

"I'm here to see Petra Pebbles. No one's here to meet me."

He tapped a few things into a board Mina couldn't see. He had a single lens over one eye and squeezed the other eye shut so he could focus on the data.

Mina detested lenses. Everything was much too close.

"Ms. Pebbles is not accepting visitors at this time. She has enacted full and complete privacy, no alerts," he announced by way of dismissal.

Leave it to Petra to put a full block on her calls when someone had tried to murder her last night.

Mina popped her badge up on holo. "Scan this. Orders should be in your system. Please send someone to escort me up, or better yet, approve my DNA, and I'll go up myself."

His face registered shock. Federal agents must not visit often.

"Yes, ma'am." He glanced around. "Just give me a second. I have to find something to scan it with."

Mina kept her face neutral, even though it was itching toward a scowl.

He finally came back with a portable scanner the size of a cube of cheese. She held her wrist up, and he ran it over the badge.

He shook his head slowly. "I'm sorry. I don't see anything here."

"There's no readout to go along with my badge?" Mina inquired skeptically. It could be that McAllister hadn't gotten the order together yet, but that was unlikely, since her craft had had the right instructions. An order by the federal government had to be followed. "Contact your guard captain." The Bella had its own security detail. That's why Vincent Kramer was approved to stay here. "They can use their scanner, or choose to contact my director personally."

"I'm sorry." His voice wavered. "They're on a very important call right now. There's been some kind of emergency."

Mina could report to McAllister and wait to let him fix it, but why waste his time when she could fix this on her own?

"Supersede Petra's call for privacy and ping her residence. I'm certain she'll see me."

His expression switched from worried to downright scared. "I... I...can't do that. It's against all of the rules. I could get fired."

She didn't want this kid to get fired. It wasn't his fault.

Mina thought for a split second. "Then contact Vincent Kramer. Tell him Agent Kane is at the transpo hub, and I need an escort up. Petra approved him for entrance last evening. I'm sure she doesn't have him on her censor list."

If he'd looked scared before, he appeared *appalled* now. "I can't just call the colonel-in-arms of the French

Protectorate!" His voice was rising toward atmospheric panic.

Mina suppressed an eye roll. "Then I'll do it myself." She took a few steps back and held up her cuff. "Contact Vincent Kramer. Holo chat. Mark as urgent."

It didn't take long for Vince to answer. "Hello, Agent Kane."

How could he look that good in tiny holo form floating above her wrist?

Not fair.

Before he could say anything more, she said, "I'm at The Bella, executive transpo hub. I'm here to talk to Petra. My orders didn't come through, the guards are busy, and I need an escort up. Petra will probably take a call from you. Are you busy?"

"Not at all," he concluded. "I'll be down in a moment."

Mina glanced up to see the concierge kid looking at her incredulously, his mouth hanging open.

Vince disappeared off her cuff, and Mina shrugged. "I told you I'd handle it myself. In the future, if any federal agent or PPF officer comes in with a badge, it will be in your best interest to help them in any way possible. We're never here for fun. If my orders are actually in your system, and you got it wrong, you could be fired. Got it?"

He nodded quickly. "Of course."

Mina turned and walked out.

She made her way toward the enormous tube station just past the hub, twenty to a side. Most likely, Vince would arrive via one of these.

Not two minutes later, the colonel-in-arms himself stepped out.

Because Mina didn't want him to catch anyone's notice, she gave a subtle nod. He immediately took a step backward into the tube, shielding himself from view, one hand blocking the door from closing.

She entered, and the door whooshed shut.

He wore a silly grin. "Where to, Agent Kane?"

"Do you still have access to Petra's tube?"

"She granted me access last night, but it's likely expired by now."

Mina nodded. "Give her a call, then. I'm sure she'll accept if it comes from you."

"I can't do that. We didn't exchange information."

That was unexpected, since Vince had been her date last night. "Okay." Mina thought for a second. "How about we pay a visit to Daniel Haroldson, the bot coordinator? He can probably get me through. I've got some sensitive news to share with Petra, and it can't wait."

"We can do that." Vincent was used to covert operations and didn't question Mina's request. He inserted his finger into the shallow groove and commanded, "Concierge floor three hundred and seventy-five."

There were certainly a lot of concierges in this place.

The tube shot upward. She barely felt it.

"Thank you," Mina said, meaning it.

Vince crossed his arms, smiling. "It's good to see you. Did you solve the extortion piece?"

"We did. Lee really came through." Even though Vince

had helped them last night, she wasn't inclined to share the details of the case with him.

Vince bowed his head, seeming impressed. He made a show of looking at his cuff. "It's not even quite nine a.m. You've been busy."

Luckily, the tube door opened, ending their conversation.

An air breather sat behind a lavish desk with a large chandelier dangling over it. The marble was expansive, just like the hub. The lux was extravagant and a little discombobulating. When the woman, somewhere in her late fifties with a platinum updo, saw who was coming toward them, she stumbled up out of her seat.

Mina understood. She'd been there herself.

"Colonel Kramer," she gushed. "How can I help you?" Implied was, *Anything you want, you get. Just let me know, and I'll make it happen.*

Mina stepped forward, her badge up again. "We'd like to see Daniel Haroldson, please. If you could direct us to his office, that would be fantastic."

The woman's face fell, but she regrouped quickly. "Of course. Head straight down that hallway and take the first right. I'll alert him that you're on the way. If there's anything else you need, please let me know."

"Thank you, Helen," Vince said graciously. "I may need to book a dinner reservation shortly. I will come to you personally."

The woman nodded like gears had been loosened in her neck. "Of course! I'll be here." Then she giggled like she was in middle school programming.

Mina was already on her way toward Daniel's office. Vince caught up with her.

She gave him a look out of the corner of her eye. "Doesn't all the attention get tiring?"

"Yes." He shrugged. "But it's not like I'm going to outrun it. At least not for a while."

That was cryptic.

The only way he would outrun it was if he stopped being who he was and took a total break from the public for, like, ten years. Even after all that, people might not forget. Humanity had a pretty good memory.

"I find it's better to embrace it," he said, "and make sure whoever I'm dealing with feels seen. It's just easier that way."

Mina nodded. "I can understand that. I'm sorry you have to deal with it all the time. It seems like a huge burden to have to constantly fulfill or disappoint people's expectations."

She stopped in front of a door labeled Bot Protocol and pressed the green button next to it.

"That's why hanging out with you is so enjoyable," he said. "You don't have any expectations."

Hm. She might have a few.

Chapter 5

A BOT DRESSED in a black uni, auburn hair falling around slim shoulders, opened the door. "Hello. How may I help you?" Her inflection was excellent. Very human. Whoever was in charge of designing bots was getting closer to blurring the lines each and every day. "If you're in need of a service, and we have a wide array to choose from, please head down the hallway. The concierge will be happy to fulfill your every need."

"We'd like to speak with Daniel Haroldson," Mina ordered. "Locate him and let him know Agent Kane is waiting. Thank you."

"It will be just a moment." She disappeared from the doorway, leaving it open.

Mina peered in. Several boxes were stacked against a wall, freshly pressed uniforms hung on a rack, and chairs were lined up in a row, each next to its own power source.

Looked like a place where you would keep a bunch of bots.

A few moments later, Daniel Haroldson, the air breather in charge of the twenty-one upper-tier bots for The Bella, came to the door. "Oh, hello," he said, bowing his head, indicating he remembered his meeting with Mina yesterday in Ms. Pebbles' residence. "Can I help you with something, Agent Kane? Thank you for bringing Betty Three back so quickly, along with the compensation." A blush crept along his cheekbones. "It was greatly appreciated."

Mina was certain it was. That compensation had most assuredly landed in his borrow account.

"Sorry to bother you like this, but I need to get a hold of Petra, and she's enacted strict privacy today. The concierges won't break protocol to contact her. Usually, my badge will get me where I need to be, but for some reason, my orders aren't showing up in The Bella's system. I'm hoping she has a bot appointment on the schedule shortly, and you could contact her and let her know I will be accompanying the bot."

The man recognized Vincent Kramer and was trying not to stare. He took a mini handheld out of his pocket and tapped a few things into the screen. Mina appreciated his professionalism and the fact that he hadn't gone on about seeing her badge and demanding credentials and such.

"Unfortunately, she has canceled her bot appointments for the day." He looked up, frowning. "I realize that you're a government agent and have orders straight from the top. But if I personally try to contact her or take you into her residence, and she's upset with my actions,

I would lose my job. The residents of The Bella are... particular."

Rich, bratty, spoiled, entitled. Mina could go on and on.

But she wasn't about to get this man fired any more than the kid downstairs. Jobs were hard to come by, and he seemed well equipped for his. Mina turned to Vince, who cleared his throat.

"How about you contact Ms. Pebbles directly to let her know I'm looking for her?" the colonel-in-arms suggested politely.

"I'm sorry. I can't do that, even for you," Daniel said. "I cannot afford to lose this job."

Mina sighed. Her only choice now was to contact headquarters. Then she'd double-check that the new orders came through, track down another concierge, convince them to override Petra's privacy orders to follow direct orders from the government, which should supersede Petra's, but wouldn't necessarily in this place. It would all take time.

She shot Vince a wry look. "You were right about The Bella being secure. It makes my job much harder than it has to be."

Vince raised an eyebrow, then flashed a dazzling smile at Daniel. "What if you give us Petra's call address, the one you use to contact her about the bots?" He nodded toward the handheld in Daniel's grasp. "That way, *I'm* the one contacting her, not you. In exchange, I will do something for you. A digigraph or a message to a loved one or an image capture of the two of us?"

Mina appreciated Vince's angle. He didn't have to do anything.

"Um…um…that would be breaking protocol," Daniel hedged.

Vince leaned in, whispering, "Would it help if I told you that Ms. Pebbles offered me her address, and I politely refused?" If one person offered their address, it was custom to offer yours in return. A mutual sharing of addresses. "I can promise you that she'll be thrilled to hear from me and very disappointed if she finds out that you could've given it to me and didn't." Vince was right about that. Just about anyone in The Bella at this moment would love to hear from international celebrity heart-throb Vince. "I can credit you with being the generous soul who made it possible, if you'd like."

"No. No, that's okay. I would rather her not know it was me."

"Of course," Vince replied, like silky, smooth water cascading over slippery rocks. Mina was impressed with his technique. He'd done it all in a friendly, non-intimidating way. "She'll never know. I guarantee it."

Daniel tapped his board again. "Place your cuff directly above, and I'll airmeld it to you."

Once they were finished, and Daniel slipped back into his fortress, Mina and Vince made their way to the tubes.

Helen jubilantly waved at them from her desk.

"The best place to make this call will be in my residence," Vince said, his voice low. "I may have to cajole Petra into seeing us."

"Us?"

Vince didn't need to swipe for the tube. Helen had already taken care of summoning it for them.

The door opened, and they walked in.

Vince grinned. "I'm in this now, and I plan to see it through." Then he helpfully pointed out, "You didn't have to call me. You could've dealt with headquarters and eventually gotten one of the guards to take you up." He was smug, enjoying this. Immensely.

"That's true," Mina answered. "But I chose you because I was looking for the most hassle-free way to get to Petra quickly. You're upping the hassle factor. By the time we're done with this, I could've gotten orders from headquarters and found my own way up."

Vince shook his head. "I beg to differ. Even with your orders, you'd hit trouble. No one in this building wants to go against their top-currency residents. You're a temporary nuisance, but the resident is a permanent one. Every concierge and guard in this place is trained to make the residents happy at all costs. You'd definitely have to get the captain of the guard to escort you up, which could have taken all afternoon, as they've been dealing with an emergency. You chose right. I *am* your most hassle-free option."

"You're getting updates from the guards on emergencies in The Bella?"

"Of course."

Mina snorted. "Honestly, people around here have their priorities seriously screwed up. Currency over reason. However, not even a fiber of a cell of an atom in my body is surprised. But we have Daniel, who is living proof that not everyone has coins clinking around in place of their brains."

Because Daniel was a standup guy, he hadn't asked Vince for anything in return.

So at least there were a few smart, decent people floating around the universe.

The tube door opened, and they stepped out into a very lux hallway covered in shiny gray and white marble, lush greenery flowing out of multiple planters, and several pieces of artwork in gilded frames.

This tube hadn't opened directly into Vincent's lavish accommodations, like Petra's did. Vince veered to the left, and Mina followed.

There were only two doors, one left, one right.

The one on the right popped opened, and a man dressed in the French Protectorate uniform leaned his head out.

"It's okay, Sergeant Bissett," Vince said. "This is Agent Kane. I'm helping her with an internal issue. I'll be inside for a short time, but will be leaving soon. I won't be exiting the building."

The man saluted Vince, nodded to Mina, then shut his door.

Once they were inside Vince's rooms, Mina asked, "Was that Ambrose's watchdog? Are you being monitored?"

Vince placed a finger to his lips.

"Welcome back, Colonel Kramer," a male sim intoned. "Would you like me to order a meal or perhaps a spa treatment?"

"No. Remain on standby until summoned," Vince answered.

"Standby enacted," the sim confirmed.

Mina's eyebrows rose as she glanced around. The room was modest in size, but it was beautifully decorated. Plush furnishings in rich browns and golds were accented by copper and bronze, with hints of cream to break it all up. Masculine, but not over the top. Mina headed toward the large solar-catch windows. They weren't as impressive as Petra's, as there were only three, and they weren't curved, but the view was incredible.

Instead of sticking around to linger over the city and the sea spread out in all its brilliance before them, Mina paced through the living area silently, searching for cams and mics, which could be as tiny as grains of rice.

Nothing was visible, but that didn't mean they weren't there.

In the corner sat a meal-prep area with a generous table and four chairs. Any meal printers or grinders were masked behind large doors stretching up to the high ceiling, sleek with a rich brown finish accented by shiny handles. The handles were probably for looks, because Mina guessed everything here was voice-activated. Spa treatments included.

A set of regular doors were inset against another wall, which likely led to Vince's sleep room. She wasn't about to go in there. Though her brain was urging her to take a gander. She refused that unsmart logic and walked back into the living area, where Vince stood next to the lounger.

News that Ambrose Bernard, head of the French Protectorate, was spying on his third-in-command was telling. Vince had broken his oath and alliance to the Protectorate by coming to the US, without direct orders, to take down Veritus.

If spying on Vince was where the French government was at, Mina wasn't sure Vince would ever be accepted back into France.

She didn't voice any of her theories, however.

"Hi, Petra, it's Vincent Kramer," Vince said into his cuff. "I'm hoping to get a hold of you. If you could contact me at this address, I would be grateful—"

"Hello, Vincent." Petra's sleepy, slightly slurred voice issued out of his cuff. No holo. Vince hadn't enacted that option. "How *nishe* of you to get *ahh* hold of *mehh*. I'm doing *fiiine*. Things are *preeety* good over *heeere*."

Mina moved closer, and Vince flashed her an uncertain look. "I'm here with Agent Kane. She would like to discuss the case with you—"

"I'm *shorry*. I'm not up for *vistooorsh* right *nooow*." Petra was definitely not all right. "Unless *youuu* want to come *uuup*, because you're *shooo* handsome—"

"Petra, this is Agent Kane," Mina interrupted. The vid star was obviously on something. "Are you okay?"

"*Yesss*. Just *tiiired*."

Okay, sure. "I'm here to let you know your case has been resolved. We have a full confession from your assistant. I also have news to share with you about your aunt, which I'd prefer to do in person. If you refuse, that's your right. I can tell you over the cuff now. In my opinion, it would be much easier and quicker if we do it in person. Then you can put this all behind you."

They waited a moment.

"*Fiiine.* Come *uuup.* I don't *caaare.*"

"You're going to have to approve me within your system and tell me which tube number is yours."

"Just have *Kramerrr* do it. I *neverrr* took him off my approved *liiist.* He likes *meee.*"

Mina raised her eyebrows. "Okay. We'll be up in two minutes."

Vince dropped his arm. "See? You needed me. I'm still your most hassle-free option."

"Let's go, Hassle-Free. I want to make sure she's all right. She sounded pretty out of it." Mina headed for the door.

"She had a rough night. She probably took something to take the edge off."

The colonel-in-arms followed her out into the hallway. This time, the door on the right stayed firmly shut.

"Just get us up there," Mina said.

"We have to take this tube down to the transpo hub and shift to the other side to get to Petra's private tube."

Mina nodded. She'd been on it yesterday with Yolanda.

Vince stuck his finger in the slot. The tube opened immediately.

Once inside and on their way down, Vince casually asked, "Did you get a chance to watch the vid I left yesterday?"

Mina couldn't look directly at him.

She didn't know why. Possibly because she didn't want to get sucked into his smile vortex. That made sense, right?

"I did," she confirmed. "I watched it when I got home last night." She wasn't about to divulge how many times she had partaken in the sweet nostalgia. Why was it so hard to talk about this stuff? "It was fun seeing us together as children. We knew how to have a good time, didn't we?"

"Yes," he said wistfully. "We certainly did."

"That's actually one of my favorite memories. Thank you for delivering it. So many adventures, so many experiences. It's hard to remember them all, but that one was special. How many hours did we try to catch those butterflies? They were so lifelike. Amazing."

"It's special for me, too," Vince said. "I remember it like it was yesterday. Watching the happiness on your face is lasered into my brain." *Okay.* "That holo box was cutting-edge back then." He chuckled. "It only held a few elements, but the butterflies were the best. Remember the fish? Not exactly spectacular."

"I do remember the fish. They weren't lifelike at all. Their tails were robotic, and the lack of simulated water made it feel weird. And the ladybugs were just creepy. My room felt like it was infested with bugs. I had a hard time sleeping after that one."

The tube door opened. Mina gestured for Vince to go first.

She trailed behind, glancing left and right, making sure nobody noticed them together. The Bella was a good place as any to be seen with Vince, as most people went out of their way *not* to look at one another. A number of vid stars lived here, as well as several other high-profile individuals. Averting gazes was the norm.

Even Helen upstairs, who'd shown her exuberance in seeing Vince, would rather eat her printed shoes than gossip about a single guest who lived here.

Vince summoned Petra's tube and stepped inside, his hand casually keeping the automated door from closing.

Mina entered after him, and the door whooshed shut.

"My director will probably make you sign another confidentiality agreement after this visit, just so you're aware."

"I'll sign anything he puts in front of me."

She bit her lip. Should she ask him? "Hey, I have this thing tonight, and I was wondering if—"

The tube door slid open.

Petra Pebbles, a pink sleep wrap splayed around her, was out cold on the floor in front of her remarkable windows.

Chapter 6

"SHE'S BEEN TAKEN to the Medi Center as a precaution," Mina told her director through the aural system of her craft. "I'm on my way back to headquarters to pick up my order from Tech and the coin for the safe house payment, then heading to Pormal."

"Were you able to make your report to Ms. Pebbles?" McAllister asked.

"Kind of?" Mina sighed. "The in-house medi-unit at The Bella was able to give her something to offset the effects of the pharma she'd ingested. They didn't disclose what the drug was, but she was fairly coherent before they took her away. I was able to give her a short report." If Petra had consumed illegal substances, there would be a report filed. The drug had probably been legal, just taken in quantities that were intolerable. Petra Pebbles was tiny in stature. "I don't think she was trying to end her life or anything. I believe she was just trying to escape reality for a while. She had a rough night, and this morning, the newscasters were spewing harsh commentaries about her premiere and mocking her exit through the stage floor. They called her vid the worst in the last century. However, she seemed genuinely sad that her aunt was gone, but bolstered by her resulting status as the new owner of a business. I think she's going to be fine. Kramer offered to accompany her to the Medi Center, which was nice of him. She accepted. Experiencing a little media exposure with the colonel will probably be enough to cure her."

Mina had already reported that Vincent Kramer had assisted in getting her into Petra's residence. If they hadn't found Petra, there was a chance she could have died of an overdose. So there had been relief all around.

Petra, even in her altered state, had been genuinely thankful they'd shown up.

"I'm happy to hear she's going to be all right," McAllister said. "Just to be overly cautious, I'm going to have the report printed and delivered to her personally, with written verification required. Then we can officially check her case off our list as closed."

Having nothing more to do with Petra Pebbles was fine with Mina. "Has our new op designation come in yet?"

"It has not." Mina heard the frown in his voice, even though she couldn't see him.

"Is something wrong?"

"Not exactly."

Mina sat up. The craft was about to land at Government One. "What do you mean 'not exactly'?"

"There appears to be an interest in your last two cases from the top. An audit has been ordered. It's just come across my board within the last five minutes."

"An audit?" Mina had never heard of an agent being audited before.

"During my long career, audits have been common." Before becoming director of the CIU, Duncan McAllister had been an agent with the FBI-CA, or the Federal Bureau of Investigative Crime Abroad, living mostly overseas investigating cases against the US on foreign soil. "They have become less frequent over the years, and I've never had a request taken up for a CIU agent before, but this should be nothing to worry about." Even so, it didn't sound good. "You had back-to-back high-profile cases, and it's caught the attention of upper management. They've requested a thorough investigation of both cases and your part in them."

The CIU had been formed roughly ten years ago as a secret agency within the government to investigate high crimes that affected the government. Mina wasn't sure if McAllister knew who he reported to, but that person operated within the legislative branch of the government.

"Does this extend to the rookie?" she asked, trying to mentally prepare herself.

"Yes. The order specifies both agents involved."

"So just the two of us?"

Other agents had assisted on both cases. Mina hoped they would be spared.

"Agent Kane, I can't stress this enough—there is nothing to worry about. Everything you did was cleared by me. If they find issue with your actions, or the rookie's, then they find issue with my leadership. They will not do so lightly."

Mina wanted to speak to everything that was tumbling around in her brain right now, but doing that over the drone's comm system would be a mistake. She focused on Lee going rogue with the pixel mirror when they'd dealt with Veritus and his involvement in that case when he had a very personal tie, which went against every policy they had.

Lee had worried he would be fired over that. Now here they were.

Then there was Vincent Kramer's involvement, which could get messy, since he was a foreign agent.

"I know what you're thinking," McAllister said. He was smart like that. "And Agent Adams is not in danger of being dismissed either. All the facts of both cases will come to light, and they will all be explained to the satisfaction of everyone. Agent Adams followed my direct orders on every case." That viewpoint might not be shared, depending on how many agents an auditor decided to interview who had been in the room with Mina and McAllister when Lee was with Tedesco. Several higher-ups from varying departments might have concerns about Lee's actions.

Mina rubbed her temples as the sim announced they were landing.

"Both of us will be interviewed?" she said.

"That's correct."

Mina stifled a groan. Lee could barely hold his emotions

in check on a regular day. She had her work cut out for her. "Can I be the one to tell Agent Adams about the audit?" She could already see his face and the mounting panic that would accumulate.

The craft landed, and the door rose.

Mina stayed inside. She could switch the call to her cuff easily, but this was fine. Less of a chance for someone to overhear.

"Telling the rookie yourself is fine by me. When more information comes my way, I will share it immediately."

"Does that mean we're grounded?"

"Not officially. During the time that you're under audit, you will not receive a formal op designation. But my plan, once you're finished with your agenda today, is to assign you both fieldwork as the need arises."

"Like tracking down a kiosk thief?"

McAllister chuckled. "Possibly. Report back when you're finished in Pormal. Oh, and Agent Poston is in the building. She's not receiving a designation today either, as she's working with Ms. Biggins. If you'd like her to accompany you to Pormal, as your partner is indisposed and Ms. Biggins is taking some exams, that is an option."

"I'll definitely check in with her, thanks," Mina said.

Having Kaylee around was always a bonus credit.

"I've approved your guest for tonight's ceremony, as well."

Mina tried not to blush. It wasn't working.

While the Petra ordeal was being sorted out, Mina had completely forgotten that she'd started to ask Vince to the ceremony tonight. That was, until he'd refused to leave with Petra until she told him what she'd been ready to ask in the tube before they'd discovered Petra on the floor.

Mina had almost lost her nerve, but she'd gone through with it, and he'd accepted eagerly. She'd sent the request via cuff to her director before she'd boarded the craft.

She'd half expected McAllister to say no and would've been fine with that. Vince's presence could be problematic. Maybe she'd temporarily lost her mind? That was probably what happened.

Mina was about to respond, to thank her boss, but the sim interrupted. "Thank you for flying with us today, Agent Kane." That signaled that McAllister had disconnected, and the drone wanted her out so it could fly on to its next assignment.

How did a drone have an assignment, and she didn't? *Ugh.*

She climbed out. Agent Darian wasn't waiting for her, as Mina didn't need to go through a labyrinth of ten security stops to get to the underground interrogation rooms. She was simply heading to Tech and Payables.

Once she was in a tube, she tapped her wrist.

Her new, snazzy cuff could hear her just fine from a good distance, even if her wrist was covered by a jacket, but it was habit to bring it closer to her mouth where it felt comfortable. "Call Kaylee Poston. Audio only."

A second later, her pal answered. "Hiya."

"I heard you're in the building," Mina said. "I'm on my way to Tech."

"You don't say. I *am* in the building. Harmony is taking a bunch of competency tests today, which she will absolutely comet-sail through, so I'm hanging out like a big dumb mentor with nothing to do. I was hoping to get a teensy op, something to keep me fresh-faced and energized, but McAllister said no. The kidlet will be out in a few hours."

"Kidlet?"

"I'm trying out new, punchy nicknames. Judging by your tone, that one is a no. I had to throw it out there and give it a nice, solid try."

"Want to accompany me to Pormal? A mini op designed just for you. Well, not exactly an op. More like shoring up some loose ends and delivering payment."

"Oh, goody gel-sweets! Does that mean I get to have a little monster encounter?"

"That's a very strong possibility."

"Sounds much better than lurking in the halls. I'll meet you at Tech."

The tube door whooshed open, and Mina stepped out.

Tech took up the entire floor.

Providing cutting-edge technology for all the agencies in the federal government was an enormous endeavor. Agents were allowed use of one entryway, so Mina headed toward it.

"I'm here to pick up a bot," Mina announced into an intercom after DNA approval.

"Somebody will be with you in a moment," a female replied. Mina couldn't tell if she was an air breather or a bot.

A few seconds later, a piece of the wall slid back, revealing a Tech agent. The man was dressed in a pale gray uni, goggles, and a slightly harried expression. "Are you the one who requested the NannyBot?"

"I am."

He glanced down at the crystalline board in his hand. "It says here you wanted standard teaching software installed, and preferably you wanted the oldest bot we had. In your words, 'Dinged up and filthy is fine. Even better if she has circuitry hanging out.'" The Tech agent glanced up. His expression mirrored his dismay. "Um. We've never had an order like that before. Pretty much ever."

"This bot is going to the outskirts." That was close enough to the truth. Mina hoped it was enough of an explanation to make this Tech agent understand what was happening here.

His whole demeanor relaxed as relief poured out. "Oh. Why didn't you say so? We were worried this would reflect somehow back onto the federal government."

"Is it ready?"

"Yes. Wait here, and I'll bring her out." The window shut just as Kaylee stepped off the tube.

Mina's best pal wore what they both referred to as "pro-field," short for *professional in the field*. It pretty much consisted of a pair of tuck pants—in this case, Kaylee wore black. A pair of euroboots—these were chocolaty brown with a curved heel, which was actually more Eurasian than European, so euraboots? A cropped flow shirt, snug on top, wider for ease of movement at the waist, this one in deep burgundy. It was normal clothing, like that worn by most humans, but Kaylee still managed to look extremely professional and much like she could sit you down on your backside in an instant if she felt like it.

Mina glanced down the front of her own uncropped navy flow shirt, deep violet tuck pants, and basic euroboots with a cubed heel.

It just wasn't the same.

"Whatcha picking up?" Kaylee came to a stop in front of the sealed window.

"You'll see."

"*Oooh*. Secrets! Give me a hint."

"And miss seeing the look on your face? Not a chance. You give good face."

Kaylee patted her cheeks, grinning. "I do, don't I?" Since her wrist was there, she checked her cuff. "How long are we talking?"

Before Mina could give a guesstimate, the door behind them buzzed, then powered open. The same guy Mina had just seen through the window led a bot out.

"*Hoooly* shite on a thin-printed cracker!" Kaylee hooted. "She's a *looker*."

The man hesitated for a moment at the outburst, but Mina beckoned him forward.

"She's perfect. Just what I was looking for."

The bot had hair, but not too much of it. The patchy places had been colored over in the same brown tone as the locks, so it kind of blended if you squinted hard enough. One side of her face had what looked to be claw marks running from temple to chin. She had a few puncture holes in her neck. Both eyeballs seemed to be intact and working, which was a bonus.

At least her uni was clean.

"Was she attacked by a wild animal?" Kaylee asked.

The tech's face went red. "Yes, actually, she was. She was a vet bot, installed at the largest federal animal rehab in the city. A panther took issue with her. Her torso and legs have been patched together with skin cement, which should hold, but she looks a little...rough." He cleared his throat. "She was scheduled for a complete overhaul before Agent Kane's request came in." He shrugged. "So we figured she would fit the order fine."

Kaylee shot Mina a look, coupled with playfulness and a bit of incredulousness. "You asked for a bot torn apart by a panther?"

"Not exactly." Mina chuckled.

The tech offered, "She requested a dinged-up, filthy bot with circuitry hanging out. The circuitry is all inside, but she's certainly dinged up." He gave them a bright smile, but since he still wore goggles, he looked manic.

"Welp, looks like you got what you ordered," Kaylee said.

"Here, let me turn her on," the tech said. "She can move, but she hasn't been enacted. You said her primary would be assigned later?"

"That's correct," Mina said. "Her primary can be a child, right?"

The primary got to make all the rules, and the bot followed that person's commands above all others.

"Of course. There are no age limits. She is severely restricted, as all federal menial bots are, with several layers of safeguards installed. She won't harm anyone. She won't take up a weapon, even if pressed or threatened. If she does, her circuitry will literally melt and leak out. And she, um, has a lot of places for that to happen, so it would be a mess. She has pinhole cameras monitoring all her movements. Those cams supersede her database." He pointed to various positions on her body, then reached around to the base of her skull, flicking a switch.

Her eyes came to life, brightening up a pair of brown irises.

The bot reached out her hand. "Hello, my name is Beverly. I'm well versed in teaching and childcare, and I'm happy to serve you."

"Hold that thought," Mina told her.

CHAPTER 7

"THE LITTLE MONSTER'S going to lose her moon rocks when she sees this thing." Kaylee jacked a thumb at Beverly, who sat beside them in the craft, silently looking out the window. Was she really looking at anything? Who knew with bots? "You have a truly brilliant mind. I bow down. Can't give them anything shiny and new, or there would be distrust that you're spying on them or something. Even more of an issue, there would be looting. But dress her up in some rags, and you've got a winner."

Mina chuckled, glancing at the case of currency on the seat next to her. She'd had been happy to find that McAllister had gotten the military-grade pay approved for the safe house. The box was heavy. She knew what was inside would serve the people of Pormal well.

"I'm hoping Quaz will put together some sort of school programming situation." Mina had no idea how many children lived in Pormal. "But who knows? They might rip her apart for parts. It's their call. I'm just making my payment to Suli, as promised."

"You did threaten to bring her a NannyBot, and here she is. The kid will absolutely adore it, even though she'll never admit it in a trillion million light-years."

Mina *had* threatened Suli with a NannyBot, which had given her the idea that an actual teaching bot would be of some benefit to her and the community.

"Do they know we're coming?"

Mina shook her head. "Nope. I gave Quaz my address, but he never offered his." She wasn't sure if he had one to give. "The only way to contact him is through Norm, and he's not picking up, which is strange." And a bit alarming. "He always answers or sends me something explaining." Mina had tried the spider right after she'd left The Bella, then again right before she and Kaylee and the bot had gotten into the craft. "I'm thinking Vince might be right, and Norm had us come to Pormal for a reason, and something might've happened."

"Not cool for agents to keep things from other agents, even if they're ex-agents. If he had an agenda, he should've come clean." Kaylee glided her hand through the air in a slashing motion. "No exceptions."

"Agreed."

The sim announced, "Landing in thirty seconds."

Mina had programmed the craft to land right behind Biters, Quaz's restaurant in Pormal. *Restaurant* was a loose term. It served barely passable food, and Quaz and his people used the building as office space.

She figured she'd come in with a splash, announcing her arrival. No need to sneak around.

"Before we land, I should tell you that Lee and I are being audited."

Kaylee's gaze whipped to hers. "What you mean 'audited'?"

"Apparently, because our last two cases were high profile and fairly dirty, involving people in the government and bankers, the higher-ups want to look into them."

"Why would they want to do that? You brought in the bad guys. Cases closed."

Mina shrugged. "To make sure we followed the law? Honestly, I have no idea." The craft set down ten meters away from the back of the building, and they climbed out, Mina beckoning for Beverly to join them. Once they were outside, she addressed the bot. "Your new primary's name is Suli. She's a young girl. I want to ask you a few questions before we go inside and I introduce you to her."

"Of course," Beverly answered.

"Because you're a federal bot, you have protection protocols embedded."

It wasn't really a question, more like confirmation.

"I do. I am equipped with Bot Protection Protocol 18745. In case of grave danger or serious threat, I will protect those around me even if doing so results in grievous injury to me."

"Like if a panther decides to eat you for breakfast?" Kaylee joked.

"I do not understand your question," Beverly replied.

"Large predators do not require protection."

"Never mind. I'm sure it was a horrific experience, even for a bot." Kaylee sighed as she glanced at Mina. "They probably scrubbed the memory so she doesn't short-circuit thinking about it."

Mina wasn't well versed in the specific bot protocol Beverly had cited. "Is there a way to increase your vigilance for protection of your primary? A switch in your database that we can activate that specifies you are inhabiting a high-risk environment? Extra alertness, particularly at night, for example. Does that exist?"

"Ah, I see where you're going here," Kaylee said. "Smart woman. Once again, I bow down." She placed her hands on her hips. "What she wants to do, Beverly, is enact War Zone Protocol."

"War Zone Protocol?" Beverly glanced around, apparently looking for evidence of a war. "Unless there are visible cues and repeated auditory alerts of weapons fire, War Zone Protocol cannot be enacted."

Mina wished she'd the foresight to ask the technician about this before they'd left. She was only considering now that this NannyBot could also be used as heightened security for Suli and the people around her. "Is there a way your database can remain on constant standby, like you're anticipating that there could be a war at any moment? Like War Zone Protocol Light. Is there a setting for that?"

"Bot Security Protocol 56723 allows my internal system to remain active, even in rest, and to assess for potential danger every thirty seconds."

Mina nodded. "Yes. That's what we want."

"This can only be enacted by a federal technician or agent."

"You're in luck," Kaylee said. "You got two of them standing right in front of you."

"Scan my badge for approval," Mina ordered, popping her wrist up.

Beverly took in the information. "Bot Security Protocol 56723 enacted."

"Make sure it can't be shut off," Kaylee cautioned.

"Security protocols can only be turned off by a federal technician or agent," Beverly replied.

The back door to Biters whipped open.

A slightly aggravated eleven-year-old child stood in the doorway. Her long, dark hair was bunched around her shoulders. Her clothes were a little frayed and a little too big, but they were clean.

"Why are you loll-a-gagg-ing out here? Come in, already." She disappeared back into the bowels of the stumpy cinder block building. Before Mina and Kaylee could get to the back door, she reappeared. "Who's that? She can't come in here. She hasn't been approved." She crossed her arms.

"This is your new bot," Mina announced, leaving off the *nanny* part. She didn't want to aggravate the kid more than she already was. Mina also left off the *teaching* part. No need for things to turn sour right from the get-go. "Ever seen a bot before?"

"Yes." She stuck out her chin.

"It's not advisable to lie to federal agents." Packard came up behind Suli.

"I'm not *lying*," Suli insisted. "One time, when I was on the wall, somebody walked by with one in the outskirts. I saw it. I know it was a bot. I *know*. It talked weird and was too clean and, like, shiny."

Packard, ex-military and one of Quaz's right hands, gestured for them to come inside. Suli stepped back, her eyes widening with each step they took. She was beyond curious about the bot, and if she didn't watch herself, she might even let some excitement leak out.

Once they entered, Quaz got up from a desk. His long, dark hair fell around his shoulders, mirroring his daughter's. "I didn't expect you back so soon." Mina had told him that she'd be back with a full report once the investigation into the Nesbits had been completed.

"Things fell together quickly." Mina handed him the case of coin. "Safe house payment is inside, as well as coin for the meal we had yesterday morning."

He took the proffered package from Mina and set it on his desk. He flipped it open and tried not to gape.

Silver disks the size of small cookies came right up to the top.

The standard currency exchange was one coin to ten borrows.

Technically, if someone amassed enough coin, they could take it to a bank and trade it in for borrows. But once people lived in a place like this, their trust of banks was pretty much somewhere in the bowels of a grinder.

Quaz cleared his throat. "I... I...wasn't expecting so much." His expression was thankful, coupled with wariness. If he accepted this much coin, he feared that Mina would want more from him.

"My director secured a military pay rate. That's what we pay for a fortified bunker. It's free and clear. It's up to you if you want to allow us access again, but it's not necessary. The pay rate will continue to be the same."

"You weren't even there for twenty-four hours," Quaz said with some puzzlement.

"True, but it's the same rate for one hour or twenty-four."

Suli had waited long enough. She pointed at the bot. "What's she for? Huh? Why'd you bring her? Why is her hair missing? You can see stuff behind those scratches. What is that stuff? Is it elec-trod-ers?"

Mina took a step back, smiling. Now for the best part. "Beverly, I'd like to introduce you to your primary. This is Suli." The bot moved forward as Mina addressed the young girl. "Remember how I told you we were in business together and that if you brought us to Biters, you'd get a reward? Well, here she is. Your very own bot."

Suli's mouth tumbled open before she could stop it. "It's mine? No way." Her gaze shot to her dad. "She's pulling a prank on me, isn't she?"

Quaz shook his head, smiling. "I don't think so."

The look of distrust the girl shot Mina made her heart clench. It was clear people here didn't receive gifts very often and certainly not one as big as this. "I'm not lying to you. This bot is yours. Once you enact the primary protocol, she'll follow all your directions above anyone else's. She won't do anything harmful to anyone, though, no matter how much you ask her to."

"Why is she all banged up?" Suli asked cautiously.

"She has to fit in around here," Kaylee answered. "If she looked all pretty, everyone would want her. My advice? Hack off the rest of her hair, dress her up in some banged-up clothing, and peel off more skin. Make her look like a monster. Seems kind of appropriate for a little monster to have a bot monster. Dontcha think?"

Suli's eyes were as big as a couple of currency coins. "I can do that? And nobody's gonna stop me?"

Kaylee settled her hands on her hips. "She's yours, but that means you have to take care of her. Bots need to be charged, and their circuitry needs to stay clean, so no leaving her out in the rain. You also have to make sure she doesn't get into trouble and that nobody steals her. Do you think you can handle all that?"

The child nodded vigorously. "I can. And more." Her eyes glazed over. "I can't believe I have a bot."

"Come here," Mina said. "I'll show you how to activate her." Suli moved closer. "Just because you're her primary doesn't mean your dad or someone else can't give her directions to follow. It just means she listens to you more carefully. But if you tell her to do things that go against what's programmed inside her, she won't do them. In fact, if you keep it up, her circuitry will start to fail, and then you won't have a bot anymore."

"She will melt from the inside out." Kaylee made a face. "It's pretty gruesome, so treat her right, and she'll help you out. If not, no more fun. I heard she knows a few languages. She can also shoot stuff out of her chest in holo. You can ask her anything, and she'll know the answer."

"No way," Suli scoffed. "She can't know everything."

"Place your finger right here," Mina said, lifting Beverly's shirtsleeve, exposing her wrist. A small patch of Beverly's humanlike skin was extra smooth right above the palm.

The girl placed her finger on the bot's wrist.

"Now watch her eyes," Mina instructed.

Suli studied the bot's face. After a second, Beverly's brown eyes flashed twice, and the bot said, "Hello, what is your name?"

When the young girl didn't answer, Kaylee came to stand by her, placing her hand on Suli's shoulder, giving it a squeeze. Mina and Kaylee had the wherewithal to understand she was overwhelmed. They would give her time and encouragement.

Everyone waited.

Finally, she said, "Suli Barker."

"Suli Barker, my name is Beverly. I'm happy to make your acquaintance. Is there anything you'd like me to do?"

"Yeah. Go clean the waste room."

Chapter 8

"WHAT'S GOING TO happen to Nesbit's lab?" Quaz asked after Mina had finished briefing him on the confessions and what would likely happen to all parties involved.

He'd requested he speak with Mina alone.

They sat in a booth in the restaurant part of Biters. They were the only ones occupying the entire space, at a table surrounded by a short polycarb wall.

"Nesbit's laboratory is in the outskirts, so I'm not sure." Mina hadn't extrapolated that far. "The government might decide to seize some of the assets, but because the operation didn't get off the ground, and no currency was lost to the banks, they might decide they don't have a good reason."

That didn't mean they couldn't find one eventually.

"When is this going to be made public?" Quaz asked.

"As in media breaks? Probably soon. Banking, Borrows & Credits has taken over the case, and they're going to want to expose this to the fullest and follow up with any leads they can." Many times during a big investigation, the lead agency would post rewards for information. Since people, for the most part, lived in perpetual debt, those rewards meant something.

BB&C would likely be inundated with tips, as bankers liked to brag to anyone who would listen.

Mina continued, "They're pretty unhappy that an operation of this magnitude was gearing up right under their noses. BB&C watches over any corporation that handles currency and borrows. Their job is to make sure things like this don't happen and that corruption stays out of the banks and, ultimately, that bankers don't break the law." Mina could barely relay the information with a straight face.

Quaz looked amused, too. "So you're saying if they decide to seize the lab's assets, it will happen fast, but we still have time?"

Mina held up a hand. "I don't want to know what you're planning, so don't tell me anything. The outskirts is not my jurisdiction." Or really, anyone's jurisdiction. "The government didn't leave any agents behind to keep an eye on the lab, and that's saying something." Mina leaned forward. "How do you know it hasn't already been looted?" One sniff that Dominic Nesbit had left his space unoccupied, and Mina would think that people in the outskirts would have descended on it like flies on a decomposing corpse. Mina didn't know how extensive Dominic's rule had been over the people who lived there, or how many cronies he had. There had to be some loyalists lurking around.

"I know, because—"

Mina shook her head. "Sorry I asked. I'm not condoning or encouraging. This is your area of expertise. I just came to deliver payment to both you and your daughter and let you know that you will be Nesbit-free for the foreseeable future."

It was pretty good news to deliver. Mina didn't have these opportunities quite as often as she would've liked.

Quaz was pensive for a moment, rubbing his chin, finally settling his gaze on Mina and nodding. "You came through."

"Looks that way." Honestly, that surprised them both. It shouldn't have happened the way it had. Which made Mina remember why it might not have been that surprising that she'd found herself in Pormal in the first place. "Do you know where Webb is? He's not picking up my calls, which is...odd." The ex-marshal was reliable to a fault.

Quaz glanced away.

Mina narrowed her eyes. "What?"

The man across from her fidgeted, not meeting her gaze. "He told me not to say."

"Not to say *what?*"

"I don't want to break his trust."

"You two know each other." It wasn't a question.

When Mina had asked Norm yesterday how he'd known to come to Biters to seek safety for Harri, the spider had cited Packard as his connection. When Mina had brought up Quaz, Norm had feigned that he had no knowledge of someone by that name.

Clearly, that wasn't true.

Norm knew Mina wasn't stupid.

He knew if she went searching, she'd find out that he'd lied. Why risk it? Lying meant that word would get out. As Kaylee had already stated, nobody wanted to deal with someone who would purposely withhold information.

Betrayers were not tolerated.

Mina laced her hands together on the table, settling a genial smile on her lips. She needed information, and she wasn't leaving without it. "Tell me what you know. If not, summon Packard." Being ex-military meant he'd been closely linked with government agencies. He would know the need to have each other's back. "He'll understand. Webb's obviously in trouble. He picked Biters for a reason when he was on the run with Harri. I want to know what that reason is. And finding him, even if it's just to check in, has just become my number one priority." Quaz looked as though he was going to deny her request again. She kept going. "In the short time we've known each other, I've been honest and upfront with you. Do I look like someone who's just going to back off? I'm not leaving here without information I need. If I have to resort to it"—Mina lowered her voice to a whisper and pointed toward the kitchen door—"I can march that bot right out the back door and leave you with your daughter's heartbreak. Just because I'm nice doesn't mean I can't be ruthless. I care about Webb. He matters to me more than your daughter's happiness."

Did he? *Yes.* Mina had a long history with the ex-marshal, starting with when he was still a marshal. He was family.

Though, if Mina was forced to play the ruthless card, she'd likely bring the bot back after she figured out where Norm was and made sure he was safe. Being ruthless and being an *actual* monster were two separate things.

But Quaz didn't have to know that.

"What's it going to be?" she asked.

The man across from her shifted in his seat, obviously wishing he were anywhere but here. "You've been honest with me," he agreed. "I have a lot to be thankful for because of it. Even though I didn't think it was possible, you actually stopped the outskirts from overtaking us. That was a big feat—bigger than I thought anyone could handle." He shook his head. "It's something that's going to take time for me to wrap my brain around." He was hedging.

Mina waited.

Quaz was quiet.

She shot him a look that conveyed, *After everything I've done, I deserve this. I just want to help my friend.*

Quaz nodded.

Mina wasn't sure if she communicated this well with anyone else without words, other than Vince.

The man sitting across from her was very introspective. He almost didn't need actual conversation. But she did. She motioned for him to talk, curling her fingers in front of her.

He blew out a long breath. "Okay. Here's what I know.

Webb came by about a month back and alluded to being caught up in some trouble. Pack may know more about the specifics, but Webb asked if he could stay at the pay-a-day for a few, and I agreed. Normally, we don't let city dwellers in, but he and Pack have a history, and I trusted that." Norm had taken Harri to the same pay-a-day, which was literally a room for an overnight sleep, paid for with physical currency. "He stayed. He left. Then I got a call the night before last. He said he had an emergency and wanted to bring the kid in. I agreed again." He stopped.

It seemed he was done telling the tale.

Mina shook her head. "You're expecting me to buy that's all you've got? I need more. He alluded to trouble. That means he's *in* trouble. I helped you get out of a big reeking pile of it. He's family. Most likely, Webb, being Webb, didn't want to get me involved. Now that I am, it's not going to change anytime soon."

Quaz shrugged. "He didn't go into it with me. Like I said, maybe he said more to Pack, but that's all I've got."

"Then bring Pack out." Mina huffed, leaning back, crossing her arms. "When Webb mentioned the word 'trouble' specifically, what did he say? What was his tone?"

"He didn't seem worried. More like perturbed. No panic, just quiet contemplation and a few grunts."

Sounded like Norm.

"In the beginning of this conversation, you said he told you not to say anything. How did he specify that?" Mina knew there was more. Quaz probably felt like the small details weren't necessary, but they were. "Every time I've seen you since yesterday morning, I've been with Webb. So unless you visited the safe house while he was guarding Harri, you haven't been alone with him. So when did he tell you to keep quiet?"

The man across from her rubbed the back of his neck. "He told me the first time he came to stay at the pay-a-day. Just said keep it on the down-low."

"Did you ask Webb, like you asked me, for help with the Dominic Nesbit issue and what was going on here in Pormal?"

"I might've mentioned it," he hedged.

"Just answer the questions as clearly and concisely as you can. Let me surmise for a moment—maybe that will help jog your memory. In exchange for allowing him to stay at your pay-a-day, you asked him for help. He told you he had no federal authority but he might know somebody who could help?"

Quaz frowned. Then he looked resigned, sighing. "He wasn't specific like that. He said he couldn't do anything, that he was only a civilian now, but he'd check into it. Sniff around. Try to see what he could do." Also sounded like Norm.

"Yesterday in the early hours of the morning when he came in with Harri, and you agreed to let them stay, did you ask him about the sniffing around he agreed to do for you?"

"I did." Quaz looked pained. He really felt bad about going against what Norm had asked him to do.

Mina didn't blame him, but she also didn't care.

"Did he mention my name specifically?"

"No. He just said the good guys were coming in and that I could trust them."

"You decided he was right, because when I entered your shop, you recognized me from before." Quaz had retold the story from when Mina had been involved in an op in the outskirts early in her career. She'd helped a child who'd been hurt while she was trying to take down Quaz's brother. She'd called in a medi-unit and made them help the boy.

"Yeah. It pretty much went down like that."

It wasn't in Norm's nature to lie right to her face, yet when Mina had asked him if he'd known Quaz, Norm hadn't verbally said no, but he'd acted like he hadn't.

That was the same thing as lying.

If Norm had known these people were in trouble, there was no reason why he couldn't have just told Mina what was happening, unless he felt he couldn't tell her because of whatever trouble he might be in himself.

"When Webb first reported to me that he was here," Mina told Quaz, "he used the outdated term 'code teal.' Does that phrase mean anything to you? Does it have a meaning here or in the outskirts?" McAllister had recognized the term. Back in the day, it'd meant there was an emergency with bodily harm expected.

Mina had told Norm that she hadn't understood his reference. He hadn't clarified. Now that she thought back on it, she remembered how he'd just glazed over it.

Maybe *code teal* meant something different here.

Quaz shook his head. "No. Never heard it. Let me get Pack out here. He might be able to clear some things up."

He slid out of the booth.

"Don't get too comfortable back there," Mina cautioned him. He walked around the counter toward the kitchen. "I'll stick around as long as necessary to gather the information I need. And you definitely want your daughter to be able to keep that bot."

Mina did, too. She knew the bot would bring a lot of value to the community. She didn't want to strip anyone of that opportunity.

But she would if she had to. Temporarily.

"I get it. Hang tight." He disappeared through the kitchen doors.

Not three minutes later, Packard came out.

The man was enormous, not a stitch of hair on the top of his head, his outfit military, but not official. The insignia was gone, and all that was left was a well-worn, standard two-piece. He wore a pair of striker boots that made an intimidating sound as he moved forward. Less of a *clack*, more of a *stomp*.

He slipped into the seating area, which was hard to do cleanly because of his size. Once he was settled, he placed his hands on top of the table and gazed at Mina pointedly. His eyes were an unusual dark amber, but she didn't think they were diffracted. The people around here wouldn't do anything that frivolous.

"Are you ready to talk?" she asked.

"That depends." The underlying growl in his voice might be the way his larynx was built, but it still went a long way, coupled with his looks, toward doing a solid job of intimidation.

Mina wasn't intimidated.

"When Webb called me yesterday morning," Mina informed him, "first thing he said was 'code teal.' Mean anything to you?"

"Yeah."

"CARE TO ELABORATE?" Mina asked after several moments.

The massive man reclined back in his seat, crossing his burly arms. There was barely enough room to do such a thing, but he managed. The polycarb wall rocked under his weight, but held. "When I swear an oath, I keep it."

"He made you swear an oath? Like, actually recite something out loud?"

Oaths were usually just for vids and pretend stuff. Nobody used them. Honesty and trust were things that were earned, not orated for show. If you didn't trust someone, you didn't tell them something that you wanted to stay a secret.

"Not exactly."

Mina shot him a pointed look. "Why are you wasting my time? You know what a code teal is. You now know Webb said those words to me. He knew I'd end up here one way or another. If he's in trouble, I can help him.

I might be the only one. You know all this already. Why the runaround?"

He leaned forward suddenly, the wall shaking behind him at the sudden loss of his weight. "Because I don't *know* you."

Ah, the heart of the matter.

She hadn't earned his trust.

Mina bobbed her head toward the man, acknowledging his issue. "I get it. All you have to go on is what's happened in the last few days. But, you know, what went down isn't exactly minimal." Quaz had asked her to help defeat Nesbit, which she had done in less than twenty-four hours. "And as you can see, I'm back here within a single day to deliver on the promise of payment to your boss and his kid. I'm sorry we don't have more time to get to know each other. I get that mili deals in trust. I take that very seriously." She met him across the table halfway. "When I sat in this booth yesterday and asked Webb what his trust factor was for you, he answered 'ten plus' with no hesitation. He thinks very highly of you." She pinpointed her gaze on him. "If you asked him what his trust factor for me was, what do you think he'd say?"

Pack stared at her, unblinking.

Mina kept her frustration in check. She needed to move this along. "You and I both know he'd say ten. So he trusts you ten, and he trusts me ten. I think it's safe to say we can trust each other." Mina brought her cuff up, pretending to check some data. "I'm running out of time. If you can't give me what I need, I'll have to start from scratch. That'll delay helping Webb, wherever he is. If the trouble's bad enough, will I be too late? I have no idea." She paused for a few seconds, staring right into Pack's hooded eyes. "But you do."

"No need to make this into a vid production," Packard retorted, arching back. Mina hadn't realized she was being overly dramatic. Maybe a little Petra had worn off on her? She'd have to work on scrubbing that off. "He didn't make me swear an oath, but the intent was there. I take that serious. You're right about the ten. I know he trusts you. But he wanted this to stay on the down-low. The way, way down-low. The basics of it are some guy he boxed is out and has a vendetta. Didn't tell me who. Told me he had it covered. That's all I know."

"Did he give a time frame of when the perp was released? Or say anything more specific?" Mina asked. "Quaz said he was here a month ago. If I can time it, I can look into his arrests. See who got sprung recently."

Pack shook his head. "No time given. Webb bragged that he could handle it. But I saw the worry. Right behind the eyes." The man brought his large fingers up and waggled them in front of his own eyes. "He didn't want anyone worrying about it. Not sure if he thought it made him look weak, or if he didn't want to involve anybody else. Probably the latter."

"What's a code teal? Is it a marshal term or a military term?"

The big man shifted, frowning. Now that he was talking, he wasn't sure if he should be, but Mina was relieved when he kept going. "'Teal' means physical. Lots of departments used it unofficially during the Global

Climate War. A teal is a kind of duck, and right before the war, their water sources were polluted with chemis, and it made them go crazy. They fought each other to the death. The term died out once the good guys won and cleaned up the messes. When teals stopped pecking each other to death, the term was aged."

Eighty-five years ago, the world had been heading in the right direction, taking precautions with clean energy. For more than twenty years, they'd succeeded in reversing many of the climate issues, inventing much of the clean tech they used today, like solar-catch windows and recycling at an atomic level.

Then, in 2042, industry and greed took a solid, damaging foothold, changing society as our ancestors knew it. All the progress that had been made deteriorated at a rapid rate. Leaders abolished regulations and paved the way for massive corporations to pollute the earth once again. And they did so with reckless abandon.

Sixty-five years ago, the Global Climate War was militarized across countries to try to mend the environment before it was too late. The war lasted eight years.

Then it took twenty more to get things back on track.

Policies put in place during that time mostly held, but Mina, along with everyone else, knew they were weakening once again. Greed had made a resurgence in the last fifteen years, and Mina had taken a dunk in the chemi-filled waters of the harbor to prove it. In order to stop another war from happening, climate and environmental groups were rallying to mandate big changes. Mina hoped that would work and that their greedy government and corporations would see reason.

Mina was thoughtful for a moment. "So Webb used an outdated term meaning he expected violence. When he said it, I thought he was talking about what was going on with Harri. That made sense at the time. Now I think it was a blanket warning. When I told him I didn't know what it meant, he chose not to clarify."

She pushed out of the booth.

"Where are you going?"

"I need to check out the pay-a-day. Then I'm heading back to headquarters to figure out who was recently sprung from a box. Since Webb didn't give you any other specifics, that's where I start."

Pack followed her into the kitchen.

Kaylee stood as she came in, hands on her hips. "Well?"

"You and I are going to check out the pay-a-day, then we fly out," Mina told her friend.

Quaz moved forward. "Nobody's there at the moment."

"Good," Mina said. "That makes things less compli-cated. Did Webb stay in the same room with Harri that he occupied a month ago?"

"He did," Quaz confirmed. "He requested it. Since I have very few customers, it wasn't hard to accommodate his request."

"I figured," Mina said. "Anyone been in there since?"

"No," Quaz answered. "We don't get a lot of *guests* in these parts."

Mina glanced around the room. "I had no idea this was going to turn into a Norm Webb investigation. Do you have a lidar wand around here?"

The man in charge of Pormal raised his eyebrows. "You think he patched something into one of my walls?"

Mina shrugged. "Won't know until we get there, but my guess is he left something. Not necessarily for me to find, but something he'll need. It might already be gone. Either way, there might be a clue to what it was."

Quaz made a move toward the door. "Not sure if I have a working wand. I'll have to check. Pay-a-day's not too far from here."

"Me and my partner go in alone," Mina said.

Pack crossed his arms. "You think we got something to do with this?"

"An investigation means we *investigate*. Everything's up for grabs." Mina wasn't overlooking anything. Yolanda had been a talented actress. Either of these men could be, too. "I need full access to make a determination of my own. An ex-marshal's life could be in danger, and I want every clue in that place that's available to me. The more people go in, the more messed up the scene gets. If Webb stays missing for another full day, this case gets elevated to a full-blown op. That means you're going to have marshals descending into your zone to search for him. He's a fan favorite, like family to many. Let me do my job, and there's a chance I can keep that from happening."

After a moment, Quaz gave her a nod. "Suli will lead you there and get you in."

Suli stood, commanding, "Come on, Beastly. Let's get

going." The bot stood immediately, recognizing her new name. Mina noticed that the bot was missing more hair. Since the bot's scalp hadn't been colored in to mask those places, the bald spots stuck out more.

Mina fell into step beside Kaylee, leaning in. "The kid's been busy."

"Oh, yeah. She's taken to that thing like bees used to suck up pollen. She's going to get it to do things we can't imagine."

They walked out the back door.

"Should I be worried?" Mina asked.

"Nah. After testing some boundaries, they'll figure out some kind of symbiotic relationship."

"Think she knows it's a teacher bot?"

Kaylee shook her head. "Also, no. Beastly's tricky, though. She's already offered clarification on some of the kid's word choices and offered a full vid introduction on the continent of Asia." She snarked out a laugh. "Pretty soon, the little monster will be educated, and she won't know how it happened." She glanced around at the empty buildings they passed. "Maybe she'll actually get out of here."

"That's the hope," Mina said. "Plus anyone else she decides to let that bot educate. My hope is her dad will figure out it's worth it and set something up. But I'm not going to tell them to do anything, because you know what happens then."

"People love to be contrary. A deficit of our nature."

Suli was ahead of them with Beastly, an apt name considering, chattering away. The kid couldn't care less if

Mina and Kaylee followed. She was officially done with them. They no longer held any allure, even Kaylee, who'd become a real-life superwoman to her.

"So what happened with your meets?" Kaylee asked. "What are we looking for here?"

"Pretty sure Norm is in trouble. Quaz and Pack gave me some details. Seems a former perp, recently unboxed, might be in pursuit of some revenge. Norm didn't give any other solid info. Gave Pack a happy version, but the ex-mili saw through his tough facade. Detected the worry. That's the only reason Pack came clean. Like the rest of us, he doesn't want to see Norm in any real danger. He likely knows more, but this will do for now." They turned down a skinny alleyway to find Suli stopped in front of a door. "This is the pay-a-day Norm stayed at."

The structure was skinny, four stories, and not much to look at.

"If it were me," Kaylee said, "and I knew I was in for some trouble, I'd stash stuff for later. Things must've been heating up for him when he agreed to watch Harri."

Mina nodded. "Norm was very careful about telling me to watch for a tail. Now I'm thinking the tail wasn't only for Pormal, but possibly someone who might be following him."

"Kind of goes against what we're all about," Kaylee muttered. "I don't know Norm as well as you do. I've only consulted him a few times over the years. But this rings one of two ways. One, he felt like he had it solidly in hand and wasn't too worried, just being a little cautious. Two, he's concerned that whoever this freak is doesn't care if there are other casualties. Wanted to try and keep you clean. That being said, omitting a possible vendetta against him while accepting a job isn't cool. He should've been upfront."

"Agreed," Mina said. "My hope is he has a good answer."

Suli opened the door, ordering Beastly to go in and do a "sweep" before they were allowed inside.

"Using the bot for protection already?" Mina grinned. "You're catching on fast."

"Don't be dumb," Suli replied. "There's nobody hiding in there. No one from Pormal is allowed to come inside. And if someone slipped in from the skirts, we'd know before they even got here. But that bot records everything with the cams in her eyes." Suli stuck two fingers right up to her own eyeballs, almost touching them. "So I'm going to take the feed and make it into a vid production and charge people to watch it. Then they'll know what's inside."

Mina glanced at Kaylee, who shrugged. "I mean, it makes sense to me," Kaylee said. "Why not have a little enterprise on the side?"

"No comment. I'm going in," Mina said as she crossed the threshold, glancing over her shoulder at the kid as she thought of something. "You know, bots have megatera memory capacity. My guess is Beastly has more than enough vids to project a show every day for the next ten years. And whatever she has preloaded would be much more scintillating than the mundane insides of a pay-a-day." Mina chuckled as the kid's face went slack.

Mina wasn't about to tell her that most of the vids would be educational. Why ruin the surprise? Mina glanced at Kaylee. "In and out in thirty."

"Or less," Kaylee said, following her through the doorway.

CHAPTER 10

"THE ROOM WAS clean," Mina reported to her boss. They were in a drone on their way back to headquarters.

"Emptier than a fric-free vac," Kaylee added.

They hadn't found any evidence that Norm had stashed anything. He'd left no clues behind whatsoever. Which wasn't that unusual, since he was a talented agent. The furnishings had been the definition of minimal. The walls were solid. No loose flooring. Nothing showed up on lidar, which luckily Beastly had the capability for through her cams. The bot was going to be incredibly useful, even if she looked like a horror.

"You swept the entire building?" McAllister asked.

"We did," Mina confirmed. "We even investigated below pedestrian level."

The basement hadn't gone as deep underground as the safe house, but there'd been a couple of stories to go through. The entire search had taken over an hour.

So much for in and out in thirty. But they'd wanted to be thorough, and that's what it'd taken.

"Having Webb go missing is troublesome," McAllister said. "But this isn't our jurisdiction. Even if a case opens up into his whereabouts, the marshals would take lead to find one of their own."

That was true.

Mina kept the *please* out of her voice. It was tough, but she managed. "Waiting the full forty-eight to put in the request for a missing-persons case to be opened could prove detrimental. We could miss our opportunity to help him. I'm not exactly being assigned anything else at the moment. I could use that time to search for him."

"There's no actual confirmation he's missing," their director pointed out. "Other than he's not answered your calls this morning. But since you're on your way back to headquarters, I'll allow you to use the next few hours to look into what you can about any recently released perpetrator. After that, we'll discuss it. If I feel that Norman Webb's life is in real danger, you may peruse."

Mina understood.

"Anything to do with the audit takes precedent," he added, his voice firm.

Mina made a face for Kaylee's benefit. The word *audit* was a terrible word all around. "Got it. I'll contact Lee after this call."

"Agent Poston," McAllister said, "Harmony Biggins will be finished with her exams in the next ten. Pick her up and come to my office."

"Are we going to be assigned our first op together?" Kaylee asked.

"Not quite, but close," he said. "Signing off."

Mina slumped back in her seat. "What if this audit finds that either Lee or I broke the rules in some way? What if they're able to get us fired?"

"I mean, it might be a possibility. A very small one. Infinitesimal." Kaylee made a face. "But if they did that, then they'd have to deal with the wrath of McAllister. He's not going to let you go that easily. You're a superstar agent. Losing you would be a colossal blow to the agency, and it would set a precedent that agents who bring down high-profile criminals will face retaliation. You fulfilled your duties. You captured the bad guys. I think this is about the higher-ups who are getting caught red-handed in their criminal endeavors. If I had to speculate, I'd say somebody's nervous. I mean, seven or eight people who worked for the government were involved with Veritus." Her voice held the same disgust Mina felt. "It's unacceptable. How many more are dirty, and we just haven't found them yet? At the rate you're going, you're going to round them up soon. If I was a sneaky, suck-it criminal, I'd be nervous."

Mina rubbed her face with both hands. "You're probably right. That makes the most sense, but we won't know until we get in there. By the way, I'm not a star, super or otherwise. I'm just glad the rest of you aren't being dragged in along with us. I haven't told the rookie yet. I'm dreading it. He's going to be ridiculously worried.

Speaking of which, I have to contact him. He's expecting to hear from me."

Kaylee grimaced. "You're not going to tell him over a call, are you?"

"No. I'll tell him at headquarters. Then I can look right into his innocent, baby-owl eyes and tell him that the higher-ups are going to dip his feet into some hot lava, hoping to lessen the chance that more of their own will be caught in future criminal activities." Mina addressed the craft sim. "Call Agent Adams."

Lee answered, sounding a little haggard. "Are you back at headquarters?"

"On my way," Mina answered. "How did it go with you? Did you get the landlord stuff figured out?"

"Kind of?" He'd formulated his response as a question.

"It's either solved, or it's not," Mina countered.

"I have an appointment with my bank this afternoon." Mina heard the worry. She was going to add to that exponentially in a few minutes. Big sigh. "I hope I have time to fit it in." She did, too. "Or I won't be able to move in the morning."

Technically, that wasn't true, but Mina would set him straight later.

"Meet me at headquarters as soon as you can, research level," Mina instructed. "Norm's missing, and we've been given a few hours' head start to find him."

"He's missing? Like, he was kidnapped?" Lee lost the worry about himself, concern for the ex-marshal taking its place.

"That's the probability I'm working with right now. He

always picks up my calls. If he's on another call, he sends an audio in the next two to let me know when he'll get back to me. I've tried him three times so far and received nothing back. At headquarters, I'm going to investigate a lead I received from Pormal. Then you and I are going to swing by and talk to Harri." With McAllister's blessing. "Norm may have mentioned something to him, or Harri might've overheard something. I'm fairly certain McAllister will give us the next twenty-four on this if we uncover anything suspicious. That's if nothing else gets in the way."

Nothing the rookie knew about yet.

"I'll be there in the next ten."

"Sounds good. See you then." To the sim, Mina said, "End call."

"Call ended. Landing at Government One in thirty seconds."

"You've got your work cut out for you," Kaylee said. "I hope you can track Webb down soon. If something happens to that old spider, a lot of people will be very unhappy, including me. I wish I could help. But you heard McAllister. I hope he gives Harmony and me something easy. I want her to cut her teeth on petty thievery. I can already see her now in a full sprint after some unlucky perp, shouting indecent things at him, then tackling him to the ground like a quarterback on some old sports arena team."

"Quarterbacks don't exist anymore." Mina chuckled. "And if they did, they wouldn't be the ones doing the tackling."

"You couldn't let me have this one awesome visual, could you?" Kaylee snarked as she shook her head. "You are anti-sportsmen to the bottom of your cold toes. Plus, I heard football was making a comeback. It's been over sixty years without that wobbly ball-throwing game. People are crying about it. Some elderly men openly weep when they talk about it. It's sad to watch, but I can never look away. I mean, it's an old man weeping about someone else throwing a ball that looks like a swaddled newborn."

"The only way that game is making a comeback is if they strap players in mini jetties. Running is too slow. Everything nowadays has got flight in it or some other interesting tech. And if they tackle each other in the air and then crash onto the field, the concussions that shut down that sport in the first place would be even worse."

"Welcome to your destination." The drone set down, and the door opened. "Have a nice day."

As they got out, Kaylee said, "Jetty tackles might be dangerous, but our medical prowess has come a long way in the last fifty years. I can see old sports coming back into vogue." They walked to the sky screen, where they each swabbed in twice. "As a culture, it would do us good to learn to be a little more patient, then we could have old nice things again."

A tube door opened, and they boarded.

"That may be true. We'll just have to wait and see."

At her destination, Kaylee stepped out, giving Mina a three-finger salute. "Good luck and keep me posted. If anyone can find that grouchy old spider, you can."

"That's the plan."

The door slicked shut.

Mina stuck her finger in the helix receptacle and announced, "Research level."

The tube shot down one hundred floors.

The rookie—Mina was going to be sad not to be able to refer to him as such much longer—glanced around the main research room like he was seeing it for the first time, and maybe he was. Mina herself still hadn't seen much of all four government buildings.

She'd found a chair for her partner. The semi was open. The entire setup reminded Mina of their op at Cullen, but these semis were higher tech and bigger, with crystalline surrounding them, making it one big screen.

The research room held over one hundred cubicles, but only a few were taken.

"Find anything interesting?" Lee asked.

The crystalline was up close and personal, so Mina used her fingers to manipulate the data instead of her voice. "I have. I've narrowed it down to two suspects. Both were released within the last month, and both are connected to Marshal Webb. Each are unusual in their own way."

Marshals spent the majority of their time apprehending federal fugitives. They also transported criminals for the federal government, as well as operated the Witness Protection Program, which had been in continuous use for hundreds of years.

"In this case, however"—Mina dragged a data box from the right and slid it in front of them, expanding it—"there was an overlap. Meaning Norm went after a single perpetrator, but ended up apprehending two. It says here he was assigned to pick up one Roy W. Fox, but he also picked up Lance S. Fortune." The image accompanying the report showed Lance Fortune as a man in his late fifties with light brown hair cut so short it stood straight up on top. "Lance was released last month. A marshal can't arrest someone on the spot without witnessing a crime firsthand or having ironclad evidence of a crime, but Norm obviously had that evidence. After breaking down a door, Norm found Roy and Lance covered in blood and standing over the beat-up body of one Joshua T. Mackey. A very bad day for all three men. Roy was going to be taken into custody regardless, and Lance was caught red-handed. Literally."

Mina moved that box out of the way and slid another one forward. "This one has my full attention, though. Wilbert Weston Waterbury." That was quite a moniker. "That's his recorded birth name. No identity chip was ever activated." Indicating that he'd kept his given name, which wasn't as common, especially when you were blessed with one like that. Teenagers loved to rename themselves. It was almost a rite of passage. Dark, shaggy hair fell around his face. No enhancements that she could see. He looked younger than his forty-three years, but this image could've been taken a while ago. "It says he was a friend of Norm's. When Norm discovered Wilbert was defrauding the government by claiming his mother was still alive so he could collect her security borrows, he turned him in. He was rounded up and brought in by someone else, but after a lengthy investigation, it was discovered that Wilbert also enjoyed torturing animals. Big and small. Some of their remains were found in his cooling unit. After that discovery, there was a battle in court over whether to give him Babble. The suspicion was that since he'd killed animals, he might've also murdered humans." Sound reasoning, in Mina's estimation. "But this happened right when the government was beginning to severely restrict Babble."

The Babble fight had been highly publicized at the time, hitting major media outlets daily. Not to mention, people were committing suicide in large numbers, some before they were scheduled to receive it. Under the influence of the extremely powerful truth serum, the recipient pretty much confessed everything they'd ever done wrong in their entire life. Many crimes didn't have a statute of limitations, so charges could pile up, even if some were petty.

"A judge ordered Wilbert would not be subjected to Babble. Waterbury must've had good lawyers. It helped that no unidentified human DNA was found where he tortured and killed the animals."

"How much time did Wilbert do?"

"Seven years." Mina contemplated. "That's a pretty long sentence for killing animals, even when you throw in misdemeanor defrauding." Animals were, of course, protected, but if someone was cruel to an animal or killed one, the sentence usually was a year or two, max.

Defrauding a pension carried about the same. Seven years would be enough to make this man angry, particularly at the person he would blame for turning him in.

His former friend Norman Webb.

"This rings as grounds for a possible revenge scenario," Mina said. "Now we have to convince McAllister of same. Time is critical, because we might be called back here at any moment." Mina shifted in her seat to face Lee, dreading this next part. "I've got something to tell you. I've been putting it off since I found out this morning, but it's just because I don't want you to worry about it."

If only that could be true.

Lee sensed Mina's change of tone and immediately pulled his worry face. "What? What is it? Am I getting fired?"

Mina tossed her hands up. "Why would you go right to that?"

"I don't know. You've got your serious face on. When you're serious, it's never good news."

"What does my serious face look like?"

Lee furrowed his brows and frowned, then sucked in his cheeks.

"I do *not* look like that," Mina protested, checking her expression in the gleam of the crystalline, but the reflection wasn't clear.

She could very well look like that.

"Just tell me," Lee pleaded. "Did I lose my high-rise? I knew it was too good to be true. It's okay. I can stay where I am. I've been living there for a long time. I can stay longer."

Better just to be done with it.

"It's not your high-rise. We're being audited. You and me. Our last two cases were very high profile, and the higher-ups want to make sure everything was done by the book. That's it. It's nothing to worry about. McAllister said this was normal back in his time. Agents got audited all the time." Teensy truth stretch. Mina wasn't ready to go into all the aspects she and Kaylee had talked about. She just needed to get through this first bit with him. "They're going to ask us some questions about our cases, and we're going to answer them truthfully. It will be quick and easy."

Lee jumped out of his chair, startling Mina.

He began to pace inside the small semi like a caged lynx. "If I answer truthfully, they'll fire me. I know they will. I could even do time in a box. When I was in Tedesco's office, my job was to airmeld incriminating files to a government satellite. Instead, I created a pixel mirror and sent everything to the media." He raked both his hands through his hair. Managing to do it the opposite way Vince did, so when he was done, his head resembled a rumpled pile of bedsheets. He didn't even notice. He stopped midpace, turning to face Mina. "I love this job. Truly. It's the only thing, other than hacking, that I've ever been good at. It's given my life purpose. I don't want to lose it. I *can't* lose it."

Mina stood, settling her hands on the rookie's shoulders, steadying him. "Take a deep breath. I mean it." They didn't have time for him to hyperventilate. She watched as the rookie breathed in, then out. He did it again. "Good. Now, I want you to remember that you're receiving a commendation tonight for your work on the Tedesco case." When he tried to glance away, Mina gave him a small shake. "This is important." His head came back, but reluctantly. "You did create the pixel mirror on your own, but McAllister okayed it. If he'd ordered you to stop, you would've." The rookie made a face. Mina chose to ignore it. "Everything you did in that residence had approval from the top. You shut down Tedesco's lethal gas that night so no one got hurt. You're incredibly brilliant, your instincts true. You did work that night that no other agent could have done, because of your skill and your brain. You *deserve* this commendation." Mina let go of him. Now *she* wanted to pace. She remained stationary. "The Nesbit case is all mine. I decided to help the people of Pormal. I decided to take Petra there. I pushed to get the warrants. We had no idea going in that Nesbit would be so well connected to bankers. I can assure you that the banks caught up in this mess, which will become very public and newsworthy shortly, would love to prove that the Nesbit case was unfounded. Or that we went in illegally. Anything to discredit us or make us look bad and make them look better. It's probably what triggered this audit. Someone at the top is worried we're getting too good. We have no choice but to participate, but McAllister has our backs. It's going to be fine. We tell the truth, do the interviews, and everything will work out. I'll prepare some mock scenarios for us to run through just so you feel prepared."

It'd better be fine, because Mina loved this job, too.

Lee looked confused, but that was better than looking rattled. "Mock scenarios?"

Mina settled a hand on his back, steering him out of the semi. "Yes. I'll be the interviewer, and you'll be the interviewee. Now let's go talk to McAllister so we can help Norm. That's our top priority right now. Try to put this out of your mind."

He owl-eyed her. "You're kidding, right?"

Chapter 11

Mina elbowed Lee. "There's Harmony. Have you asked her to your recognition ceremony yet?" Harmony and Kaylee stood on the roof, waiting for a craft. "If not, now's your chance."

"Um," Lee replied.

She urged him forward. "Go do it. Both our drones will be here in a few minutes. You're not to get another chance in person. No time to waste. Shoo, shoo."

Kaylee turned, spotting Mina and waving. Harmony hadn't seen them yet.

Mina made a hand gesture to signal that Kaylee should move to the side and meet her, then pointed at Lee. Kaylee had no idea what Mina was talking about, but she took the cue—because great agent—and leaned over to say something to Harmony before she excused herself.

"What's up?" Kaylee asked. "That was quite the arm swirl. I hope whatever secret you're going to tell me is stinky and delicious and doesn't involve a panther-scratched bot."

"Stinky and delicious? Those two do not go together. Who hopes for stinky secrets?"

"The stinkier the better. That means they have *flavor.* Which also makes them delicious."

Mina chuckled. "Potent or juicy. Or literally any other word other than stinky."

"If they have a good layer of stink on them, they're always potent *and* juicy."

"I give up." Leave it to Kaylee to have her laughing in two seconds flat. "This secret is not stinky or particularly delicious. I just wanted to give Lee a little privacy so he can invite Harmony to his recognition ceremony tonight."

"That is fairly stinkless information." Kaylee glanced over at the two of them. Lee had his hands shoved in his pockets, shuffling his feet, obviously taking his time. Harmony appeared to be in full chatter. "But it's kind of darling, right? The owl and the falcon going on a date."

"I'm actually not sure if it's a date. He never specified. He doesn't have any family in town, and they know each other from the hacker boards. I think he feels comfortable around her, and he could use some support tonight. I hope she says yes."

"Why wouldn't she? It's a party. It's not like she has to sign a cohabitation merger if they go together. They're friends, like you said. It's a fun night out."

Mina shrugged. "She might not want to go, or not with Lee. Either is fine. It's her choice."

Lee shot a look over his shoulder, appearing pained.

Mina waved underhanded at him, encouraging him to get it done.

"You know," Kaylee pondered out loud, "they'd actually be pretty great together. She needs somebody to tether her to the ground, because I obviously won't be around forever, and he could benefit from an occasional view from the clouds." She crossed her arms. "Look at us, just a couple of matchmakers."

"You did literally nothing but move to the side so they could talk."

"If I hadn't, the deed would never have gotten done. So does that mean you're my date tonight?" Kaylee waggled her eyebrows. "Just like old times."

"Um," Mina hedged, knowing she was doing a pretty good impression of a pained Lee. She'd been avoiding telling her friend this particular news.

Kaylee's eyes widened. She leaned forward, grasping Mina's forearm. "You didn't."

Mina tried to look away. Anywhere but at Kaylee.

"You did! Oh, thank you, oh powerful star streakers above." Kaylee dropped Mina's forearm and lofted a fist toward the sky, shaking it dramatically. "You did your job, you vast universe who works in complex, mysterious ways. You convinced my best pal to *finally* follow her heart and ask that droopy, black-hole-digging puppy dog on a date."

Mina grabbed on to Kaylee's arm, lowering it. "Jeez." She glanced around to make sure no one else had come onto the roof. "Keep your voice down. Now everyone in Government One knows what's going on."

"They don't now, but they will." Kaylee chuckled. "If you think anybody who works here is going to keep that on the down-low, think again. You show up with Kramer, and it's going to be buzz city times infinity."

Exactly what Mina was worried about. Maybe she should unask him?

"But it will stay in our circles," Kaylee said. "Civilians won't get wind. At least not from us. We know how to protect secrets around here." She mock-punched Mina in the shoulder. "You've upped the game. Now I've got to scrounge up my own date." She lofted a fist to the sky again, shaking it. "To the blessed shooting stars above, I command you to listen to my wishes. Please grant me wisdom and strength, then when you're done showering that down upon me, please, please send an adequate partner. Male, female, or anything in between. To your unlimited abilities in casting wishes, I bow down." With both hands raised above her head, she bent at the waist. "Oh, and please let them be sexy."

Mina chortled. "Your definition of sexy extends farther than the universe itself, if that's possible. I'm sure someone will be beamed down in the next few seconds. I mean, the stars have nothing better to do than grant your wishes." A craft appeared in the sky above them, coming in for a landing. Mina laughed. "I guess you'll have to settle for a drone."

"Maybe there's a hottie on board. You never know." Kaylee turned to face Mina. "All fun aside, did you get approval to look for Webb?"

"In a roundabout way, yes. Nothing official yet. We

have to wait the full forty-eight before opening a formal inquiry. But Lee and I are heading over to talk to Harri now. We need to get him out from under Bliss Corp for good and quiz him on what he may know about Norm's whereabouts. After, we're swinging by Norm's residence to see if his neighbors have seen him. Then we have a government-approved appointment to 'check in' on a guy named Wilbert Waterbury, who was freed last month. He and Norm were friends before Norm turned him in for pretending his dead mother was still alive and collecting benefits. After he was taken into custody, the authorities found out he enjoys killing, but not human beings."

"He sounds like a gem."

"Waterbury's freedom is contingent on him staying at a monitored group residence for six months. Lucky us, he was due for a check-in today. McAllister bumped the regular government-appointed counselor and put us in instead. This guy will have no idea who we are, or why we'll really be there, but he has to allow us full access. Apparently, the counselor can snoop around to make sure everything's on the up-and-up. I plan to do a fair amount of snooping."

"Sounds like a full day of investigation. So much for not having an official op," Kaylee snarked as she moved toward the craft that had just landed.

"Might be a full day, unless we get summoned to return. The audit has full priority," Mina groused, following her friend.

Kaylee shot her a knowing look. "How'd the rookie take the news?"

"About as well as you'd assume. I managed to calm him down. I told him we'd run through some probable question scenarios together. I have to get him to relax. I keep reassuring him he's not going to get fired, which actually helps me from not focusing on the fact *I* might be fired." Mina gestured to Harmony. "This is bound to cheer him up, however. I think they're done. At least they look happy."

Mina and Kaylee rejoined their partners as the drone door powered open.

It suddenly struck Mina as a little strange to think that she and Kaylee had been partners, and now they both had new ones. Kaylee had been Mina's very first. They'd worked together for almost three years, then McAllister had made the decision that splitting them up would mean two extremely competent agents could be solving two cases at the same time, therefore allowing more ops to be completed.

It made sense, but Mina missed working with her.

Harmony rushed forward, embracing Mina tightly. Mina hugged the super-rookie back, because what else could she do?

"Thank you. Thank you so much," Harmony sing-songed in her ear as she pulled away. She flexed up and down on the balls of her feet, her long, wavy, red hair dancing around her shoulders. Her smile was so broad, it made the freckles across her nose curve up and form their own mini smiley faces. "I'm so freaking happy. You changed my life the day you kicked in my stupid, sucky door. I'm going to be an agent. A *freaking* federal agent!

And it's all because of you."

Mina was ecstatic to see that Harmony had not lost an ounce of her excitable enthusiasm. She was a force.

"You're welcome," Mina said. "If you put in the work, you're going to become an amazing agent."

Kaylee made a show of clearing her throat and patting her chest. "What am I? Old tech about to be tossed into the grinder? Without me, you'd have zero, with extra o's, chance at being a great agent. You'd suck, like your sucky door. So, it's *I* who deserves the kudos for graciously granting my talents to mold you." Kaylee bent in a mock bow, her eyelids offering up a bevy of blinks, her wrist curling toward the middle of her stomach.

It was quite the dramatization. Too bad there wasn't a song to go along with it.

Harmony made an equally grand show of rolling her eyes and settling her hands on her hips, cocking one out. "Yeah, but if I hugged you, you'd toss me over the side of this building. Plus, if it wasn't for her"—she jabbed a finger at Mina—"I wouldn't be here in the first place. So she gets credit for discovering my awesomeness. You get credit for honing it, or molding it, or whatever. And that, folks, is the making of Agent Biggins. The greatest agent the world has ever seen." She took her own bow with all the flare, and more, that Kaylee had shown.

Kaylee shook her head as she guided Harmony toward the waiting drone. "It's time for me to escort the greatest agent the world has ever seen to her very first op." Kaylee winked at Mina. "We're about to get down and dirty at a maple-treat kiosk."

"How'd you manage to get an assignment at your favorite kiosk?" Mina called as they walked away.

Kaylee shrugged, feigning innocence. "The universe works in mysterious ways. Also, they love me there. I can do no wrong. And they should. I spend my weight in currency on their dreamy, sticky, sweet treats. Keep me posted on Webb. Good luck."

Harmony boarded the craft first, turning to wave excitedly back at Mina and Lee. "See you tonight, Karmaseeker!" Harmony called, using Lee's hacker handle. "It's pretty cool that you're getting a commendation so soon. Maybe we can be the greatest agents the world has ever seen together." The door closed.

Another drone was already on its way in. Usually, there were a few parked on the roof, waiting for passengers, but it seemed government staff had a lot of places to be today.

Lee stood unmoving, staring up at the sky.

"Everything okay?" Mina asked. "Harmony seemed pretty happy about being asked to the event tonight."

The rookie physically shook himself. "Yeah. She seemed excited about it. But I asked her as a friend. It's not a date or anything."

"Then why do you look like cupid just lodged a barbed arrow straight through your heart?"

"Oh." Lee seemed genuinely surprised. "It's not because of Harmony or anything. I was just thinking about the audit again. Are you sure I'm not going to be—"

"Lee, you're not getting fired. Once we get in that drone, we'll go over some interview questions." The ride over to Harri's would be short, but Mina was going to give her all to prepare the rookie for this. "They're going to ask you simple questions, ones you will answer with, 'Following the orders of my superior, Duncan McAllister, I did XYZ.' You're going to breeze through this. I promise."

The craft set down, and they got in, each placing a finger in the helix slot.

"Welcome, Agents Kane and Adams. Destination is Keely High-Rise, street-level hub. Do you wish to make any changes?"

"No," Mina replied.

"Travel time two minutes, seven seconds."

Lee sat back in his seat, looking more relieved than he had since he'd heard the audit news. "Is Harmony's first op really going to be at a kiosk?"

Mina checked her cuff. "It's not actually a real op. It's a simulation. The government brings in actors, usually other agents, and the kiosk agrees to go along with it. The entire thing is set up to see how long it takes for Harmony to put the pieces together. So essentially, it's another test. She will likely exceed expectations. When it's over, she'll find out it wasn't real, and she'll probably be disgruntled, but also happy she scored well. At least that's my guess."

"Hm. I didn't have to do anything like that. I mean, I took a few competency tests, but I didn't have any simulations."

"Not everybody does. McAllister assigned you a long, boring first case. That op had more to do with your hacking knowledge and less to do with figuring out who the bad guy was." Mina had already done that by the time Lee had come on board. "But in the end, when you took Rick the Rat down, you showed quick thinking and real, physical potential. McAllister may have been grooming you for a desk job at headquarters, but after that, he decided you might do well in the field. He was right, because here you are getting a commendation without ever having to go through a single simulation." Mina chuckled. "That doesn't happen very often, and it shows how talented you are."

"Are you sure I'm not getting—"

"You're not getting fired." If Mina thought praising the shooting stars above would get him to stop asking, she would. But she knew it was useless. Instead of complaining about his concerns, she would try her best to abate them. "Let's go over some probable audit questions."

So, in fact, he didn't get fired. And neither would she.

Chapter 12

"You want me to leave the city?" Harri stood next to one of his windows. It was a nice, panoramic view of the harbor. Mina had been in his residence a few times when they'd been dating. She'd always felt comfortable here.

It was the definition of stylish, with sleek, modern furniture that had lots of curves and the occasional accent of real wood. Harri had good taste, and she knew he loved his unit. It was hard to give him this news.

Mina and Lee sat side by side on a comfortable lounge the color of a ripe peach. "It would be for the best," Mina said. "I know it's not what you want to hear, but staying in the city places you very close to Bliss Corp's operational center. The eye of the storm, as it were. And after what you just went through, and the continued stress, I think leaving is the right thing to do."

Harri moved closer, taking a seat in a chair across from them that had springy legs and plump, scarlet gel-cush. He sat forward, elbows on his knees, hands clasped together under his chin. "They offered me my job back. They said they're going to elevate my position to senior manager. They said firing me was a mistake."

Mina nodded. "Of course they did. I explained this to you already. When my director put out the statement concerning you as our protected asset, we assumed this would be their tactic. But make no mistake, they're still dangerous, and having you back at work means they can monitor you at their leisure."

Harri's face creased with worry.

"That doesn't mean they'll do anything to you," Mina continued. "In fact, it's highly unlikely. The consequences would be too great, the media attention too glaring. But relocating would remove you out from under their direct radar. The farther outside you stay, the better."

They believed Bliss Corp was testing a new, harmful pharma on unwitting people without their permission. The side effects could render some users extremely sick. Mina had seen a severe reaction once already in Quinn's friend Daphne. So far, no other cases had come to the attention of the media or anyone else, but it might be only a matter of time before news of widespread incidents broke to the masses.

"To help the relocation process along, I was able to secure you a virtual interview at a biodome in New Mexico. The government has an aqua gardener position listed as open. Quinn said you enjoyed your time in New Mexico, so I figured it wouldn't hurt. Interviews are hard to come by, so I wanted to facilitate the process as best I could."

"Really? An aqua gardener?" Harri seemed both relieved and sad.

"Yes," Mina said. "And I'm sincerely sorry it came to this. I feel responsible for placing you in this position. If I hadn't come to talk to you about Daphne, you'd still have your old job and your old life. If I could, I'd go back and approach the situation differently, first of all by conducting an interview off-site, where there would've been no ears. That would have ensured your identity stayed cloaked. I apologize for my lack of foresight."

Harri shook his head. "They would've found out no matter where you talked to me. They're crazy like that. And if you hadn't come to investigate, then Bliss Corp would have kept doing what they were doing without consequence. Things would only get worse. At least now they know the potential for being exposed is out there. Maybe that will force them to think twice about putting more of that dangerous new pharma out into the world. I care about Quinn *and* Daphne. I've had time to reflect on things and calm down a little. You were trying to help the people you love. I not only appreciate it, I support it." He rubbed his face, sighing. "I've been unsteady and hard to deal with. I apologize. My nerves, up until last night, were completely fiber-thin and worn to the breaking point. I honestly thought they were going to find me and kill me. You stopped that from happening. You saved my life. Maybe getting out of the city is the right thing to do." He stood and paced back to the window. "I did enjoy my time in New Mexico. It's a nice place to live."

"There's a chance, once things calm down, you could come back," Lee offered. "More stories about Plush are bound to become public, and Bliss Corp will start feeling the heat even more. They won't have time to worry about you, because they'll be too busy putting out fires."

"He's right," Mina agreed. "This doesn't have to be a forever relocation. There's a chance the public will find out sooner than later. So maybe go to New Mexico, allow yourself to get away from all this stress, and enjoy life a little bit. Then, when the time is right, come back to the city."

"It's going to be hard to give all this up," Harri said, motioning around his residence. "I've worked on refurbishing this place for nearly six years. The borrows are still very affordable because of that. I love it here."

Mina nodded. "It's amazing. Again, I'm so sorry it had to end up this way. If New Mexico isn't the right fit, I also secured a couple of interviews for you in Ann Arbor, Michigan. They don't have many biodomes up there, but they do have some printed restaurants looking for air breathers. I know you have family up there, and I wanted to give you options."

"That's kind of you. Even though my family's in Michigan, my preference is New Mexico. The heat makes it almost impossible to live there year-round unless you work in a biodome. But they're really cool." His eyes regained some of the light Mina knew hadn't sparked in a while. "They're really lush, almost like a jungle. They grow real food from dirt and raise live animals. I loved doing that work."

Mina hadn't remembered him talking about that when they'd been together, and maybe he hadn't, but she was happy to hear it now.

"The domes are enormous," he went on. "They house thousands of people. It's a true community." His head bobbed up and down as he seemed to get used to the idea. "Yeah. I could do that. Which biodome did you contact?"

"The one you worked in before outside Santa Fe," Mina said. "Quinn actually tracked it down and left me a message. I sent the request in this morning to inquire about a position. I'll airmeld you the name of the contact and the callback address, cuff to cuff."

"Okay, that sounds good."

"If for some reason they don't offer you the job, let me know, and I'll help you track down another interview. These positions are held for government affiliates, which you are now. Since you've had experience doing the same kind of thing, I don't see a problem with them hiring you. But just in case." Mina cleared her throat as she stood. "There's one more thing we need to discuss with you." Now that Harri was calm, Mina didn't relish winding him up again. He'd spent a lot of time with Norm over the last few days and would be affected by the news that the spider had gone missing. "We're having trouble getting a hold of Norm." Mina had tried him again in McAllister's office. No answer, no message back. "Did he share anything with you while you were together? Possibly about a case he might be working on, or that he'd worked before? Or about anything that was bothering him?"

Harri gave Mina a quizzical look. "Are you sure he's missing? Maybe he's just taking some time off. That was quite a ride we went on over the past few nights. It certainly wore me out."

Made sense that a civilian would be worn out, but not someone like Norm Webb. He was an ex-marshal. Those guys kept on ticking. When he wasn't working a private case, he worked out with the young ones at a superdome or did something physical.

He had to keep those golden fingers in shape.

"That could be," Mina hemmed, not wanting to increase Harri's fear. "But as long as I've known him, which has been several years"—almost since Mina had joined the agency—"we've had a good rhythm together. If he doesn't answer my call, he usually responds with a message or calls back within an hour. I haven't heard from him since yesterday evening, when we all left the safe house in Pormal. He said he was going to accompany you home, which he obviously did, but we don't know what happened to him after that. We're going to check his residence next. Did he say anything to you about what his plans were after he dropped you off? Did he seem worried about anything?"

"Not really," Harri replied, "though I don't think he would've necessarily said anything to me. I was pretty much a mess the entire time we were together. He was patient with me, even though I don't think I deserved it."

"You spent a lot of time alone together at the pay-a-day and then at the safe house," Lee encouraged. "Think back to some of the conversations you had. Maybe an offhand remark he made? Specifically about an old case of his, somebody who might've been released in the last month or so. It would really help us if you could remember something."

"Do you really think he's in trouble?" Harri rubbed his chin. "He just seems so...competent, like he could get through anything. Hard to imagine somebody getting the jump on him. During our time together, he told me stories, mostly from his glory days when he got out of a lot of sticky situations. He was trying to make me feel better. It worked." That was Norm. "I don't think he mentioned anything specific that was bothering him."

"Did he ever mention the phrase code teal?" Mina asked.

Harri nodded. "I overheard him say it when he was talking to you. After he hung up, I asked him about it. I was worried it had something to do with me and my situation. He assured me it didn't. He told me he was giving you a heads-up."

Mina moved forward in her seat, eager. "What kind of a heads-up? Think back. I need his exact words when you asked him about code teal."

"*Hmm*." Harri shut his eyes as he tried his best to recall what he'd heard. "He said, 'The code teal has nothing to do with you, kid. I'm just giving that smart agent pal of yours a heads-up. My future is trending toward teal, and I want someone to know about it.' So I asked him what the phrase meant. He said, 'Teal is a kind of duck.' And I said, 'So your future looks like a water bird?' Then he quacked. I laughed. He told me it was 'more water berry, than water bird.' I had no idea what that meant." Harri's eyes opened. "He waved away my questions after that, and we got ready to meet you at Biters. He didn't seem worried at all. He made it seem like he was only talking about ducks, which was weird, but not alarming."

"Waterbury," Lee said. "He didn't say 'berry,' like a fruit, he said 'bury,' like putting someone in the ground." He shot Mina a look. "You were right."

"Now we just have to find him and prove he was taken against his will so we can secure a warrant." Mina walked over to Harri. "Thanks for your time. I'll notify you when we find Norm safe and sound, and we will. I don't want you to worry." She placed her cuff next to Harri's wrist and ordered, "Airmeld biodome job description and details to Harold Hampburg."

A small beep sounded.

"Thank you," Harri said. "I wish you well. I mean, you know, if I don't see you again." He blushed. "I appreciate you keeping me safe and alive. I'll never forget it."

"I wish you well, too, Harri. I hope you enjoy your time in New Mexico." Mina nodded to Lee. "We'll see ourselves out."

CHAPTER 13

"DESTINATION OAK LANE Care Residences, communal landing pad. Travel time two minutes, sixteen seconds. Do you wish to make any changes?" the sim asked once Mina and Lee had swabbed in.

"No," Mina answered.

"Do you think we're going to find any solid evidence in Wilbert's transitional-housing residence?" Lee asked. They'd just finished interviewing Norm's neighbors. No one had seen him. They couldn't enter his residence without a warrant, which the residential bot in charge had helpfully reminded them, and they didn't have a warrant because this wasn't an official missing-persons case yet.

Mina sat back in her seat. "It's not likely. Nor do I think we're going to get a confession. Wilbert is only allowed out of his residence a few times a day, for an hour or two at most." The requirement of transitional housing was determined by prison officials. It was actually rare. The order meant that the people around Wilbert weren't convinced he was ready to live on his own yet. According to what Mina and Lee were uncovering about his leap right back into crime, they'd been right to place him here. It was also much more likely that a guy like Wilbert would do something drastic rather than go back into a box, so if he was prepared to harm Norm, he could harm others, or himself.

They had to tread softly.

"If Norm knew this guy might be a threat," Lee said, "he would've been on the lookout. How do you think Waterbury got to him, if he did?"

"I have no idea," Mina replied. "I'm hoping we get a solid indication from this guy, one way or another. Then we'll consult with McAllister. There's not a lot we can do without a warrant, which is frustrating. And once a case is opened, we won't be able to take lead. The marshals will want it. So this is our one shot to help Norm before it's too late."

It was not lost on Mina that Norm had told Harri he'd been giving her a heads-up with his use of the phrase code teal. If something happened to him, he'd wanted her on the case.

"It would be cool if we just found evidence lying around," Lee mused. "Then we could for sure get a warrant."

Mina chuckled. "It rarely, if ever, happens like that. A psychopathic animal killer is not likely to leave details lying around. But it's possible. According to the report I read about him before you arrived at headquarters, he liked to toy with the animals first. They didn't all die immediately." It was so disturbing to think about. "If he blames Norm for his seven-year incarceration and wants revenge, he would absolutely want to make Norm suffer before ending his life. He'd want him to experience some of the pain he went through emotionally while trapped in that stifling, sterile environment."

"Where would he stash him?" Lee wondered out loud. "He obviously can't keep him in this one-room transitional residence. It has to be somewhere where he has access to. And he'd have to have tools and tech to keep Norm restrained and, um, to do the torture stuff."

"That's true. It means that Wilbert has a hidey-hole of some kind. He could've stashed some of his favorite toys there before he went in a box. It's hard to know. The report stated that he and Norm were friends, but didn't say how close. I'm assuming they knew each other well, because you're right. In order to get the jump on Norman Webb, you'd have to know his habits and be three steps ahead." That would be hard for a civilian, but maybe not for someone with laser focus and hard-core issues.

"I hope he's okay," Lee said. "I really like him."

"Me, too." Mina sighed. "Norm is one of a kind. He's so loyal he'd peel the skin off of his back if he thought it would help you. He's cut from an old-fashioned fiber cloth. The world is not ready to lose a guy like him yet."

"Landing in thirty seconds," the sim announced.

"Once we're inside, let me take lead," Mina instructed. "You inspect as much as you can without arousing suspicion. We're government-appointed counselors making a routine checkup. We don't want to give away that we suspect Wilbert did anything wrong. If he thinks we're something other than counselors, he could decide to finish Norm off before we can secure a warrant. This is going to take finesse. If you don't feel like you can play along, you're welcome to take a look around the grounds while I go in on my own."

"No, I can do it," Lee said as they got out of the craft. "I'm not as great of an actor as you, but I can make it work."

Mina nodded, pleased with his decision. "I know you can. Come on."

They walked across the public landing pad, which held a few private drones and one small airbus, which likely transported residents to and from official meetings. The red-brick building was nothing to look at. Refurbished from years ago. Aged, rectangular, no specific attributes. Ten stories tall, roughly seven or eight residences per floor.

Inside the main entrance sat a bot in a white uni with black trim.

"How may I help you?" he asked. His dark red hair was cut short and serviceable, just like the entire building. It looked like he'd been designed exactly for the space.

Mina popped her generic government badge, rather than her agent badge, up on holo.

"I'm Mrs. Kaplan, and this is Mr. Anderson. We're here from government services to check on Wilbert Waterbury."

The bot dutifully scanned Mina's badge, then leaned over to scan Lee's. Thankfully, he'd selected the right one.

"You're cleared to go up," the bot instructed. "Take the tube on the left to the eighth floor. Residence number 802. I'll inform Mr. Waterbury you're on your way."

"Thank you."

The ride was short. The tube door slicked open, and they stepped into a bare hallway with white walls and a worn fiber floor covering that once could've been brown, but was now more dirty gray. Since these were government-subsidized buildings, there wasn't much to them. No decoration, no added comforts.

Before she could knock on Waterbury's door, it swung open.

Mina had to stifle the urge to take a step back. The man was enormous. She'd seen his stats, but hadn't adequately factored in his height and girth. This man was half Norm's age and nearly a meter taller. Seemed that his prime activity inside his box must've been exercise. His ability to get the jump on Norm now seemed less unlikely.

"Who are you?" he questioned, his voice a solid baritone. He had thinning, brown hair and looked much older than the image they'd seen of him. Since he'd just been released from a box, where no enhancements were allowed, he was bare of any upgrades, his face lined and a little saggy around the jowls.

"I'm Mrs. Kaplan, and this is Mr. Anderson. We're here for your check."

He narrowed his eyes. "Let me see your badges. I know most of the counselors, and you don't look familiar." This guy was shrewd.

Mina remained undaunted. She held up her wrist. He didn't have a scanner, but he made a show of bending over to read her badge. He could technically ask for something to be sent to a computer or to his cuff so he could look it over, but he didn't have either.

Once he was done with Mina's, he turned to Lee.

Satisfied by his own scrutiny, he stepped back and allowed them inside. The accommodations were teensy. She imagined they made Lee's residence look like a palace. The room was five meters square, if that. It contained one well-worn sleep pod, extra long to accommodate his height. A small meal area was built into one wall, with a fold-out table that would barely fit a plate and a chair she wasn't sure would hold this man's bulk, but likely did because he'd been there a month, all next to one of the smallest meal printers Mina had ever seen. The portions would be on the small side.

Mina assumed the only other door in the room led to a waste room.

The man swept a beefy arm around the space. "Have at it." He wore a standard black government outfit. Not a uni, but two separate pieces. But they had no form or style and draped around his body like a smock.

Mina flashed him a genial smile. "No problem. I'm sure it won't take us long. You've been here for what, a month?" Lee went to look inside the waste room. She knew he would scrutinize it, using the mini lidar wand hidden in his pocket.

"The date I arrived is in my files," he said, lips pursed.

Mina walked over to the solo window. It contained

regular, paned glass that was only a centimeter thick. Not solar catch, which was five centimeters thick and made of cells of clear conduit that efficiently transformed the sun's rays into energy.

This was an old, severely neglected building. It must feel like an insult after seven years in a box. It was just another jail cell.

More to be angry at Norm about.

"After your six months are up, where are you planning to move?" Mina asked casually as she made her way toward the tiny meal-prep area, glancing inside the grinder, which was smaller than the printer, which seemed impossible. They were both secured to the wall and couldn't be removed. At least the building had elemental valves. No cooling unit that Mina could see, though.

"Not really your business," he quipped, becoming more annoyed with her.

Mina turned, giving him a look that said she actually didn't care, but was just making small talk.

"It actually is my business, since you have to get approval from us before you can relocate. If you let me know where you're interested in going, I can submit inquiries ahead of time and see if we can get you a match. That way, the data stream can be started." Because of his incarceration history, this man would be forever limited in what residences he could and couldn't secure.

"Approval won't be necessary," he grunted. "I'm going back to my family's residence. I've been paying for it for these last seven years. It's mine by rights. And by law, you can't kick me out of my continuously contracted home. I've already gone over this with another counselor. Not quite sure why you're asking." Suspicion laced his words.

"I'm asking because someone hasn't done their job," Mina answered in her best prim, exasperated voice. "There's no information logged into the system about your next steps. And if you don't want any hassle or holdups, it's better to have it all squared away well before you're ready to be released from this...inhumane hellhole." Mina made an exaggerated sniff, frowning as she glanced around. "I hate these places."

The man snickered.

Mina was relieved to see her choice of descriptive words had garnered the effect she'd been hoping for. It could've gone either way.

"You and me both," he said. "I can't wait to get back home." Something in his eyes sparked. It could've been excitement or possibly anticipation. "I never should've been put in a box in the first place, much less for seven years." His statement held anger, but also clear focus. He was a man on a mission. "Once I get home, things are going to go back to the way they were."

Mina hoped not. "Seven years was completely unfair. I read in your report that you were ratted out by one of your friends. Just for accumulating a little extra currency? That's a tough way to go." He darted a look at her. She shrugged, feigning indifference. "Mr. Anderson and I don't usually oversee what I would call *petty* criminals." Killing and torturing animals wasn't considered petty, but she was working an angle. "We see major offenders."

She made a sweeping gesture, spreading her arms to encompass the small space. "In my opinion, you should be out already. You did more than your fair share of time on the inside. This is a waste of *our* time and a total waste of government resources. You should go home *today*. A crime like yours should've been a year in a box, tops." She shook her head sadly. "You were robbed. And you're never going to get that time back. For what? Because someone was *jealous* of you?"

Anger flitted across his face as he dropped his hands, fisting and unfisting them. "That bastard had me locked up. He took my life away from me."

Mina, satisfied she was making progress getting this criminal to talk, was a little worried about why Lee hadn't come out of the waste room yet. That room couldn't be more than a meter square. Pretty soon, Wilbert would notice.

At the same time, she hoped Lee was finding something incriminating.

"*He's* the one who should go to jail," Mina murmured, assessing Wilbert.

"He's in for more than—" Wilbert shook himself, realizing he was saying too much. He flashed Mina a cool smile. "I mean, he's in his eighties and has one foot in the grave already. He'll get his final ending soon enough."

Soon? That meant Norm was still alive.

Wilbert glanced toward the waste room. "What's taking the other guy so long?"

At that very moment, Lee exited, appearing apologetic. "Sorry about that. I actually had to use the facilities.

I hope you don't mind." He glanced down at the flooring, which was the same worn fiber covering as in the hallway. "I overheard your conversation." He glanced up shyly, putting his full youth and innocence on display, the kind you couldn't really fake. "The walls are really thin. I agree with my co-counselor. Checking on guys like you is a waste of our time. You barely did anything wrong. If you give us your family's address, I'll make sure it's cleared within the day and gets appropriately entered into the system. That's my specialty." He leaned in like he was about to give Wilbert a stinky secret and lowered his voice. "Maybe we can even negotiate an earlier release for you. Six months is way too long." He jabbed an elbow at Mina. "She's been doing this a long time, and she's got *sway*, if you know what I mean." He winked.

The rookie actually winked like they were all in on a secret together.

Mina guessed they were.

Go, Lee!

Chapter 14

"THAT WAS *INCREDIBLE.*" Mina nearly squealed once they reached the walkway outside the residence. And Mina was not a squealer. But Lee had just pulled out a pitch-perfect performance. "You got that criminal to *talk.* You guys were *buddies* in the end. Seriously, Lee, that was fun to watch."

They chose not to use the community landing area upon exiting, in case Wilbert was watching and the other counselors had arrived in a different style of craft. They didn't want to arouse suspicion in the man who'd seemed convinced they were on his side. Mina had summoned a drone to pick them up at a nearby public landing pad. They headed down the block on foot.

There wasn't much traffic in the pedestrian lanes. A few airchairs, a few jetties. They boarded a people conveyor.

As it whisked them down the street, Lee blinked a few times. "Thanks. I don't know what came over me.

I just kind of fell into a groove."

"Well, it was an excellent groove. I totally bought what you were selling, and he did, too. Now we just have to check and see if the address he gave us matches the one on file." Mina lifted her cuff. "I'm going to contact McAllister and let him know what's happening. If Wilbert's taken Norm back to his family residence, he'll want to check on him during that free time he told us he has coming up in the next hour. That's my guess, anyway. I don't think he's restricted from visiting a residence he's been paying for." She addressed her cuff. "Contact McAllister, voice only."

"Report," McAllister said five seconds later.

"We were able to get Wilbert Waterbury to discuss Norm in a roundabout way. I just forwarded you the audio. He didn't confess, per se, but there is a ninety-nine-point-nine percent chance this is the guy we're looking for. Apparently, he's paid for his family's residence throughout his incarceration. Not unheard of, but a little strange. It didn't come up in his release data, and it should have. His room at the Oak Lane is not big enough to stash a human being out of sight, so the family residence as a hiding place for Norm is a good guess. Just to be sure, we checked the public spaces here before we left, as well as below ground. The bot was a little perturbed, but allowed it. They have vid surveillance in all the public areas. We don't think Wilbert would risk doing anything where he could be recorded. His tiny, one-room unit didn't offer up any clues, although Lee found a hollowed-out area behind one wall. It was empty.

Wilbert has some free time coming up, and I think it's appropriate for us to follow him or simply head to his family residence and wait until he arrives. Norm is going to be his top priority. As you'll hear in the audio, he told us that Norm's time was coming soon. 'Soon' could mean today. I think we made him feel comfortable, no hint of us being federal agents. Lee actually made friends with him. If he's not stressed or thinks somebody's about to figure this out, he won't be in a hurry to change his plans."

Mina didn't want to think about what he'd been doing to Norm during the time he'd had him. She just knew they had to locate Norm soon.

"You have my permission to check out the family residence and wait for him to arrive. I can approve access at the hub level, but you'll have to figure out how to get around the high-rise on your own," McAllister said. "At this point, we cannot engage unless irrefutable evidence is uncovered. Even though he may have talked about Norman Webb in a roundabout reference, that doesn't make him guilty of a crime. We are still bound by the time frame of forty-eight hours to report Norm as missing."

"Got it."

Everything her director said was the truth. But she'd known after five minutes with Wilbert Waterbury that he'd taken her friend, and she was going to do everything in her power to get him back. Norm had had an inkling that this would be a code teal if Wilbert got a hold of him, that bodily harm would be imminent.

And Mina was determined to save him today, not tomorrow.

Her brain was busy working on formulating a plan. She would get McAllister's agreement once she had the evidence they needed.

"We'll head there now," Mina told her boss. "I'll report back once we find something new."

"Agent Kane, I know how you feel about Webb. I concur. If this perpetrator has taken him, we'll get him back."

"With all due respect, sir," Lee interjected, hearing everything on Mina's open cuff, "going by official procedure might cause ex-marshal Webb undue pain. From what I understand, antisocial sociopaths who commit these kinds of crimes enjoy it for a while, but their ultimate goal is to kill. If we're forced to wait forty more hours before we can make a move, Norman Webb could be dead."

"You are correct, Agent Adams," McAllister replied. "That's why you're going to procure the needed evidence first. Proceeding without it would go directly against my orders. I'll talk to you in a few hours."

He clicked off.

Lee blinked a few times, glancing at Mina. "I think I missed something."

"You did, but that's okay." Mina hopped off the people conveyor at the corner. Lee followed. "McAllister is going by the rules on this because that's his way and also because of the audit." McAllister was known to bend on things when it was absolutely necessary, and he would likely find a way to do so this time as well, if needed. "If we find Norm and break him out, there will be media coverage. Whoever's investigating us will find out if we don't follow protocol. You weren't wrong to question McAllister, as saving Norm's life is of the utmost importance, but you have to tune in more carefully. The very first thing he said to us was that we can't do anything without 'irrefutable evidence.' He didn't, however, put limits on how we can go about gathering that evidence. Only that he wouldn't okay anything but getting us through the hub door until we have solid evidence." She guided Lee by the arm, directing him across another pedestrian path toward the public landing pad. Mina pulled up her holo keyboard and typed in the address Wilbert had given them. The location was less than a kilometer away. "Lee, cross-check this address on your cuff with the one on Wilbert Waterbury's lifecheck file. The info isn't in his release file."

Lee got busy doing that. The results came back instantly. "It's the same place. The Meridian. Fifty-second floor. Four rooms." A sound resembling a gurgle erupted from his throat.

"What?"

"I just did a quick search of government data on the building. Reno on that unit was just completed, but it doesn't say what was done."

"Does it say by who?"

"Yeah, Reliance Renovators."

"Super. Now you just have to hack into their system and pull up the schematics of the unit, along with the high-rise schematics, so we can formulate a good plan to see what Waterbury is up to."

"I can't do that without my compucase." Lee frowned. "I left it at home."

Mina didn't have hers either. If they took the time to go back to her residence or Lee's, they could risk missing Wilbert.

"I have an idea."

"I can't use the drone's computer," Lee preempted. "I have to have a Level I supercomputer or higher to complete the hack."

"I know. We could have one delivered from head-quarters, but I think it might be faster for a certain some-one we know, who is not doing much of anything these days, to meet us at the high-rise with his."

"Who?"

"Vincent Kramer," Mina answered.

Props sounded overhead, and the craft she'd ordered set down. They got in.

"What is your destination?" the sim asked.

"The Meridian, hub level ten," Mina said.

"Travel time is less than one minute," the sim announced as the craft powered upward.

Instead of using the drone's comm system, Mina tapped her cuff, pulling up the appropriate tag. She didn't want to use a voice command to order the call, because that could confuse the sim. Sometimes voice activation was tricky to work around.

"Hello," Vince said, his voice floating up from Mina's wrist. "I didn't expect to hear from you so soon."

"I didn't expect to call you again so soon," Mina confirmed. "My partner and I have found ourselves in a bit of a bind. We're short on time, so instead of waiting for a supercomputer to be delivered to us from head-quarters, we're hoping you're free."

"Are you telling me I'm your most hassle-free option again?" Vince chuckled.

Lee's eyebrows shot upward. Mina hadn't filled him in on Vince's participation earlier in the day.

"You are," Mina said. "This is actually a personal mission, not an approved op."

"I'm listening." Hearing the seriousness in Mina's tone, Vince responded in a grave voice, all playfulness gone. He was in full colonel-in-arms mode.

"Norman Webb is missing. We're pretty certain we found out who's responsible. Everything is a hunch so far, but it feels like a pretty good one. We're going to watch this guy, a perpetrator with a grudge and fondness for cruelty, and hopefully secure some needed evidence that he has Norm. There's a high likelihood, in my profes-sional opinion, that Norm could lose his life if we don't find him in a hurry. Waiting the full forty-eight to file a missing-persons is not an option."

Vince had spent time with Norm last evening and had admitted to Mina that he'd heard about the ex-marshal's exploits in France.

"I'll be there," Vince said. "When and where?"

"The Meridian. The high-rise is two blocks from The Bella. On foot would be easiest. We're due to touch down in thirty seconds. Our suspect is getting an hour-long break soon. That gives us time to find a place to set up the supercomputer you're bringing and to hack into the cams before he arrives. I want to know the moment he walks in and the second he leaves. We're landing at the hub on ten. You're likely going to have to sweet-talk your way up there without authorization. Any other tech you have handy is appreciated, and please leave your tail at home." Ambrose's watchdog was not invited.

"That won't be a problem. I'll see you in three." He clicked off.

Lee owl-blinked at her.

"What?" Mina shifted in her seat. "As an agent, you utilize the resources at your disposal. Vincent Kramer just happens to be one of my resources." She shrugged. "He's pretty much salivating for something to do anyway, and he met Norm last night. He has a personal connection to this, and he's literally two blocks away."

"True." Lee fidgeted. "I get it about the resources. I'd do just about anything to save Norm's life, but getting used to Vincent Kramer helping us out with our cases is just a little...weird."

Mina couldn't argue. "It's completely weird." This would be the third case in a row he'd been involved with. "I can't help it that my childhood friend grew up to be a capable, intelligent colonel. He's here, so we use him." He could've said no. "He's got a supercomputer and fancy French tech that we might be able to use. It's a win-win."

She didn't feel one gram of guilt. She was on a mission to save Norm, and Vince, with his tech, would be an asset. One they sorely needed.

The craft set down at the hub, door rising.

"People are going to recognize him," Lee pointed out

as they exited. "I'm not sure if this is going to run as smoothly as you think it will. I mean, the guy is really brilliant, but if everybody here mobs him, that will tip Wilbert off that something's amiss or, at the minimum, scare him away. We need proof that Norm is here and that Wilbert is responsible. That won't happen if gossip hits a fever pitch that the colonel is in the building."

The rookie was speaking the truth. Damn Vince for being so recognizable and heartthrob-y.

Mina tapped her cuff. Before Vince could get a word in, she said, "Change of plans. Drone over and land on the roof."

Without so much as a sputter, Vince replied, "On it."

Now Mina and Lee had to get to the roof to meet him.

Chapter 15

MOST HIGH-RISES WERE equipped with landing pads on the roof. They were used for medical emergencies, rescuing people during a fire or some other natural disaster, and things like international military colonels coming to the rescue.

"How are we going to get up there without authorization?" Lee asked as they entered the hub.

"Pay attention," Mina instructed. She marched up to the head of transpo, relieved to see that this particular hub was overseen by a bot.

"How may I help you?" The bot was a male twenty-something with shaggy brown hair and an affable smile. A good choice to calm people down who were in a hurry and stressed out.

"We need access to the roof," Mina said. "Do you handle those requests, or do we need to find a concierge or security guard?"

Without batting an eye—because why would he?—the

bot replied, "Only approved personnel of the Meridian are allowed on the roof."

"What about PPF or federal agents?"

"PPF or federal agents are allowed on the roof if there is a building-wide emergency declaration."

"What about a medical emergency?"

This bot saw nothing extraordinary about Mina's line of questioning. He was required only to answer each individual question with whatever was preprogrammed in his data bank. He wasn't programmed to be suspicious.

"If one of our residents has a medical emergency, PPF, Meridian personnel, and agents will be allowed on the roof."

"Check your system."

"I have not been alerted to any such emergency."

"Check again," Mina instructed. "There should be something coming in—"

"A medical emergency drone has just been cleared to land on the roof." The bot cocked his head like he was listening to instructions, which he might be. Mina couldn't spot any canal phones, but communication could be airmelded right into his core, which was certainly a benefit to placing bots in these positions. "Agent Kane and Agent Adams are cleared to meet Mr. Raphael on the roof and escort him down to his residence on level fifty."

Mina popped her badge on holo and elbowed Lee to do the same. "Scan these, please."

The bot was quick and efficient. "You're cleared to go up. Any tube will get you there, just swipe your DNA. Have a nice day."

They turned and headed to the modest wall of tubes, four to a side, unlike the fleet of tubes at The Bella.

"How did you know Vince was coming in as medi?" Lee asked.

Mina stuck her finger in a helix slot. A tube door opened, and they stepped inside.

"There are limited choices when you have to land in a no-access zone. Medical emergencies are the easiest."

"Yeah, but…" Lee was genuinely confused. "How did Vince find a resident in this building so fast? And get it approved so quickly?"

"The man is a top-grade military official," Mina offered. "This is not his first foray into the medi-landing-on-roof strato."

"Yeah, but…" Lee continued to sputter. Then he shook his head. "Okay. But it's kind of cool. You knew what he was going to do before he told you. Then you prepped the bot for it because you *knew* it was coming. It's like you two share a brain." Lee gazed at her like she had transformed into something extraterrestrial. "It's a little freaky."

"It's not that strange," Mina scoffed as the tube door whooshed open, and they stepped into a small room that held a single door. "We've known each other almost all our lives. We used to play holo-seek games together and solve puzzles. We both know what it means to take the easiest path."

"It's more than that," Lee pressed. "If you two were partners, there'd be no stopping you."

"Don't sell yourself short." Mina pushed open the

door. There wasn't a DNA swipe on the inside to engage it, but she knew there'd be one on the outside to get back in.

A generic drone, likely a private transpo unit from The Bella, was in the process of landing, so Mina stayed in the doorway, which was covered by an awning. She propped her back against the door to keep it open, just in case a mix-up from the bot downstairs prevented them from swiping back inside.

Lee lamented, "I know I'm not close to being like Vincent Kramer, so you don't have to—"

"You're an excellent partner, Lee. Without you, I wouldn't have been able to solve the biggest ops I've ever been assigned in my entire life. When it comes to hacking, you're the best of the best. You're the one who's going to help us catch Wilbert. Vince is just bringing the tech we need."

"Yeah, but—"

"No more buts. Get your head in the game." Mina turned her attention on Vince departing the drone. He had a compucase in one hand, a small bag in the other. He came forward with his head down so he wouldn't be recognizable from satellite images. Smart. "Thanks for coming so quickly."

"Of course," Vince said as he neared. "We're cleared to use Mr. Raphael's residence for setup and surveillance."

Mina didn't question the announcement, but Lee made a noise that sounded a little like a wounded kitten.

Lee blushed. "Sorry. I'm just wondering how you located someone in this residence so quickly and convinced them to let us use their personal space."

Vince flashed Lee a genial smile as he clapped him on the shoulder. Mina swiped for the tube.

"The Bella employs a lot of air breathers," Vince explained as they all stepped inside. Vince swiped for the correct floor, because he'd been authorized by Mr. Raphael. "Many people like working within walking distance of their employer. I simply asked the concierge to locate an employee at The Bella who lives at the Meridian." Mina had no doubt the cooperative concierge had been Helen, who simply *adored* Vince. "I was connected to him immediately and politely asked for his permission to make a medi landing and utilize his residence. After a brief negotiation, he agreed."

Mina didn't want to think of what this was going to cost Vince, but she was grateful he'd done it. They were one step closer to helping Norm.

"But you did it in, like, one minute," Lee countered. "He had to call in a medical emergency himself to get permission to land on the roof."

"It was part of the negotiation." Vince winked.

Was there anything this man couldn't do?

The tube opened on level fifty.

Vince didn't know it, but this put them within two floors of Wilbert's residence.

"Knowing what to do and how to do it comes with experience," Mina told her partner as they exited. "Keep your head down so our faces stay off the cams." She didn't want there to be any proof yet that they were investigating. If they were wrong about Waterbury, and anyone cared to check out the building feed from the day, she didn't want them to be readily identified. "It also helps when you have currency at your disposal and a face adored by the masses."

"Not entirely fair," Vince commented, leading them down the hallway. "I could've negotiated this as a civilian."

Mina left the snark unsaid. He was ridiculously charming, so it was possible he could've pulled it off on his own. Not to mention, wealthy people were the only ones who had access that high in The Bella. Rich snobs got what they wanted most of the time. So unfair. "Maybe. But it would've taken you more than an hour and some creative bargaining. Winning over Helen would've taken at least fifteen, and you would've had to promise Mr. Raphael much more than I'm sure you did."

He came to a stop in front of one of the four doors along the corridor. Two units per side. "That remains to be seen. But I'm in agreement that people knowing me can be a benefit, as well as a deficit. Arranging to land on the roof was a benefit. Sneaking around the Meridian is a deficit."

The door clicked open, and they went inside.

A polite female sim intoned, "Welcome home, Phineas."

"This is Vincent Kramer. I have permission from Phineas Raphael to be here, with company, along with full access to screens and tech."

"Checking permissions," the sim said. "Permission granted. How can I be of service?"

"Stand by until summoned," Vince commanded.

He and Lee headed to the table while Mina took a look

around. In buildings like these, the units were nearly all identical for ease of infrastructure. Elemental lines, sewage lines, recycling, and everything else it took to run a building had to be streamlined.

"This is nicer than it seems from the outside," Mina murmured, pacing through the small living area.

"Screen on, compucase link to Vincent Kramer," Vince told the sim. "Activate airmeld to local satellite for connection." Once his compucase powered up, he said, "Approve use for Agent Lee Adams, civilian settings only, voice and key. Standard blocks remain in place."

"An airmeld won't be necessary," Lee said. "I can set up my own connection through a government-secured satellite. That will keep us cloaked better. Just give me one second." He began typing. Not twenty seconds later, he announced, "I've hacked into the reno company."

Data blinked on the only wall screen in the residence.

The logo in the corner consisted of two R's intertwined around some sort of tool Mina didn't recognize. Below it read Reliance Renovators.

"It should only be a few more seconds until I locate Wilbert's account."

Vince came to stand next to Mina. "Fill me in on the plan."

"Plan is loose until Lee nails down the schematics for Wilbert Waterbury's unit, which is two stories above us. Apparently, when he was released, he was able to secure a reno of his family's residence. He paid for that same residence while he spent seven years in a box. It's all a little sketchy."

"You think he brought Norm back here?"

"I do." Mina gave him the quick version, concluding with, "When we tracked Waterbury down today, he admitted he still holds a grudge against Norm. He basically mentioned Norm by age, not name. Said he would get what's coming to him *soon*."

Lee added, not pausing to look up from the supercomputer, "Harri also overheard Norm tell Agent Kane about code teal and told Harri that his life was about to get more water bury—bury, like digging a hole, not berry, like a fruit—than water bird."

Mina cocked an eyebrow at Lee as Vince struggled to follow along. "What my partner means is that Norm confirmed the name Waterbury, in an indirect way, when he spoke with Harri. Never mind. Are you familiar with the phrase code teal?"

He nodded. "I've heard it before. It's mostly American, used during the Global Climate War. But it's been thrown about here and there in Europe. Means things will get bloody." That cut to the heart of it. "I haven't heard it said in a long time."

"I'd never heard it before," Mina confirmed. "Norm mentioned code teal when I talked to him yesterday morning, before we went to Pormal and everything took flight. He dropped it without explanation, and I didn't bring it up again. I should've."

Mina would've known if Norm had been holding something back if she'd quizzed him on it when they'd been together.

"He's a hardheaded guy with a lot of experience. He

probably decided to give you a quick heads-up just in case things fell apart, but felt he had it all in hand. Until he didn't."

"I'm in," Lee announced. Three-dimensional room renderings popped on the screen, along with text. Mina moved closer to inspect them. "Looks like the whole unit was soundproofed with specialized panels. They also did some work on the utility room, but the specifics aren't here, which is weird. Otherwise, most of the reno is standard. Upgraded meal printer, new grinders, one of them oversized, an extra-large platform, new color on the walls, updated screens. The cost was high, but it was paid promptly."

"Look here." Mina pointed to some small print as Lee pumped up the view. "He added extra cams." She paused, glancing over her shoulder at Vince. "Twenty can't be right. Who needs twenty cams in their residence?" Mina had three in each room, which was more than plenty. Triangulation gave you a 360-degree view and holo if desired.

Vince joined her next to the screen. "Someone who wants to watch from afar. There are six alone in the utility room."

"I wish this was enough evidence to get us in there," Mina lamented. "But hoarding cams won't secure us a warrant." Lee made a gurgling noise. Mina whipped her head toward the table. She knew that sound. "What? What do you have?"

"More than half the cams in the residence are linked to a private satellite owned by Travis Blade. The only reason I have this information is that Waterbury had the reno place set up the cam-to-satellite link, which was dumb. It left a trail."

"I'd say it was super of him. Can you hack into it?" Mina asked.

At the same time, Vince said, "Travis Blade is a boss of the Syndicate."

CHAPTER 16

THAT'S WHY THE guy's name sounded familiar to Mina.

Thirty seconds longer, and it would've rung for her. "He's not just a low-level boss," she said as she began to pace. "He's one of the Syndicate's main bosses. Right along with Marcus 'Mad Money' Coin and Steve 'Boom-Boom' Hydro."

The Syndicate wasn't known for their casual identity chips, or anything mundane, for that matter. They were all about the flash. They'd been in the business of organized crime for hundreds of years, evolving their practices so they stayed steadily above the atmospheric fray, making it extremely hard for any charges to ever stick. They covered their tracks better than wolves on the hunt, and they knew it. They gloated about it. They rubbed it in.

It was widely speculated that the amount of currency used to pay off their adversaries was in the trillions a year. Getting people to say a bad word about them was nearly impossible. Over the last fifty years, they'd peppered ninety percent of their enterprise with legitimate business.

Arresting someone connected to the Syndicate was a hard thing to do. Getting charges to stick was even tougher. But even so, a few individuals got boxed up every year.

"Travis 'T-Sharp' Blade is a notorious pharma dealer," Vince said. "But since he owns four legitimate pharmaceutical corporations, worth a combined thirty trillion a year, it's almost impossible to trace anything back to him." He began to pace right along with Mina. "The Syndicate, as you know, has ties all over the world, including France. We've been investigating them, as well as fighting them, for years—long before I joined the Protectorate. They're extremely dangerous and have business interests in even the most mundane places. It's how they've stayed so strong over all these years."

Mina sat on one of Phineas Raphael's loungers. She wanted to settle her head in her hands, but she didn't. "This is about to become another high-profile case. No wonder Wilbert Waterbury was able to keep his residence during incarceration and has borrows stacked in the bank. He has ties to the Mafia. Nothing about this was flagged in his criminal data file. It should've been in there."

This information also explained how a guy like Wilbert could overtake someone like Norm. He probably had years of experience as one of the Syndicate's fixers, something Norm might or might not have known. Mina guessed Norm knew about Waterbury's connection to the Syndicate, but had deliberately kept quiet about it when Waterbury was arrested.

Since Wilbert's criminal activity hadn't been connected to the Mafia in any way, they didn't do anything to help him. Which also might prove that Waterbury could be considered disposable or below their care.

It'd been a smart plan by Norm, but it'd turned out to be a very dangerous game.

Wilbert hadn't even been out a month, and he was already well into executing his vendetta against the man he blamed for his incarceration.

Mina didn't want to think about how Norm had already paid for it. She just hoped they weren't too late.

Lee glanced up from the keyboard. "The reason it wasn't in his data file is the Syndicate has hired—or, more accurately, forced into service—the best hackers in the world. They clean up everything. I avoided them like a murky hot lava flow on the boards, because even talking to them once can link you to the organization. They use an imprint in their display names that's meant to identify them to other hackers in their sphere, but it also works as a warning to everyone else to stay away. The imprint is a little anchor with blades on either end of the curved sides."

"If they'd given Wilbert Waterbury Babble seven years ago," Mina pondered, "they would've uncovered all this. He would've been boxed for life, and we wouldn't be sitting here right now." She ran her hands through her hair, feeling frustrated. "He might've killed his mother to get her benefits and probably a ton of others on Blade's orders or for the other Syndicate bosses." There was no way to know who Waterbury had taken orders from, but there was an excellent chance that they'd used huge, menacing Wilbert to do their dirtiest work. "Killing animals must've been a favorite pastime, but his *real* job was torturing and killing human beings. He was just smart enough to not do it anywhere that could be linked to him."

Mina stood and walked toward the unit's modest windows. Since they weren't incredibly high up, the view was mostly just urban sprawl. The city certainly had a lot of buildings. "I have to contact McAllister. This is too big for us to proceed on our own. Saving Norm now involves the Syndicate." She turned toward Lee. "If you hack into Blade's satellite, can you see what's on Wilbert's cams? What are the chances it pings back to this location if you do?"

"Extremely high." Lee confirmed what Mina had assumed. "Like I said, the Syndicate employs—or forces—the best hackers in the world to cover their tracks. If it were me, and I was tasked to protect that satellite from hacks, I would build multilayers of complicated blocks, a few completely undetectable. And while the hacker was trying to get in, I would be homing in on their location. With a satellite, that's an easy thing to do. If I try to break in, somebody could be outside this door in less than ten minutes. If a hack is connected to the Meridian, they're for sure going to alert Waterbury."

That would not work well for Norm. Or them.

"What if you mirror everything on that satellite," Vince asked, "and beam it to the media outlets like you did on the Tedesco case? Think of what they're storing up there. It would be a breach of epic proportions and would give us all the evidence we need to get into that unit and help Webb."

Mina's eyebrows rose. It wasn't a huge surprise that Vince knew Lee had been the one to create the pixel mirror. He'd been debriefed by McAllister after they'd stopped Veritus from launching a missile into the city. Mina glanced at Lee, who was in the middle of some critical thinking, judging by his closed eyes and wrinkled forehead.

"I'm not sure a mega breach is what we're after here," Mina finally said. "We have to save Norm without exposing the entire federal government to retribution by the Syndicate." She crossed her arms. "Even though blowing that satellite's data wide open does sound extremely satisfying. Causing an organization that large to fall, even if it's just Blade's enterprises, would be incredible."

Lee nodded, opening his eyes. "I can't do a pixel mirror anyway. It wouldn't work because I'm not already inside their database. And Agent Kane is right, exposing everything on that satellite could be catastrophic to so many people. It's too big of a risk to take. But you're on the right track. I just have to think about it for a bit. Something should hit soon."

In light of this new Syndicate connection, they were going to have to fast-track Norm out of there, even if

Mina had to go in and kick the door down herself. She wasn't leaving Norm alone with a cruel killer for one second longer than she had to.

"I'm contacting McAllister," Mina said, making up her mind. "This situation has officially been elevated." Past strato, straight into meso.

Operation Free Norm was going into effect.

"This could circle back on us in more ways than I'd like to count," McAllister contemplated. "Even if we had sufficient evidence, Wilbert Waterbury could end up getting off because we didn't pause to secure a proper warrant. More than that, if he's truly connected to Travis Blade and the rest of the Syndicate, they could seek retaliation, particularly if we don't have the law behind us."

"We might have to risk their retribution," Mina argued. "We can't leave Norm in there. The threat against his life is too great. Now that we know this Wilbert guy is much more than we thought, he will be harder to nail. And if we do successfully bring him in, he could still slither out of the charges. There's no choice but to act. We have roughly ten to fifteen minutes before the anticipated arrival of a person we now believe is a fixer for the Syndicate. That's barely enough time to get up there ahead of him, break into the unit, and rescue Norm. We need an order now." Mina blew out a breath. "On the plus side, Wilbert is not going to press charges, especially when we have a solid connection between him and Travis Blade. He's going to be angry his prey is gone, but it's not like he's going to call the PPF to come and investigate where his missing torture victim went."

"Reliance Renovation is a Travis Blade subsidiary," Lee called from his place still hunched over the compucase. "It took me time to trace it because so many of his corporations are interwoven together. But it looks like Blade owns the reno company who installed all the cams."

Mina addressed the holo of her director floating above her wrist. "The connections are only getting stronger and stronger. There's no way Wilbert Waterbury is going to let Norm go. We need to move now."

"I agree with your assumptions, Agent Kane. The evidence, even though it's circumstantial, is compelling," McAllister said. "But we must do this thoughtfully. From your report, there are twenty cams installed in that unit. If you go storming in, everything you do and say will be recorded and beamed directly to the Syndicate via that satellite. The Syndicate bosses will have proof that you were in that unit, and they will retaliate. We cannot risk that. They also have powerful lawyers and regularly pay off magistrates. We have to find a way to enter without being seen, since getting a warrant will be next to impossible with what we have so far."

"That means disabling the cams," Vince said. "We can handle that."

"We can," Lee agreed.

McAllister had noticed Vincent Kramer in the room,

but had made no other comment. Mina would make her report later. She wasn't relishing it. She hadn't asked permission to include Vince, as she'd thought he'd just be providing a quick compucase and some tech. But here they were.

"Can you disarm twenty cams and kill audio in the next ten minutes?" McAllister asked.

"Unlikely," Lee answered, his desperation clear. "But I could do it in thirty."

Mina gritted her teeth. "Thirty's too long. That would give Wilbert time to harm Norm, or possibly kill him."

"How about we get the transitional residence to call him back early?" Vince suggested.

After a moment, McAllister answered, "I can make that work with little or no connection to this department. I am personal friends with the director of counseling services, who is an upstanding individual, and can have him personally flag the empty hidey-hole Agent Adams found in the waste room as suspicious. That's how I was able to get you as substitute counselors so quickly in the first place. Waterbury will have to obey the summons, or risk going back into a box for a month."

Mina nodded. "I wish there was some way to take Wilbert down for this at the same time. Freeing Norm is the most important item on our agenda, but if we fail to connect the kidnapping and assault to Wilbert, this guy will just keep coming after Norm. The fixer has resources."

Lots and lots of powerful resources.

"At this moment, we can't have it both ways,"

McAllister said. "That means we save Webb, but Waterbury goes free for now."

"Knowing that old goat," Vince said, "he'll be happy to offer himself as bait for next time."

Mina shot him a look. "Next time?"

"Norm is going to want Waterbury back in a box as much as we do," Vince replied. "He will help us net him. I've been thinking that if we can make it look like Norm broke out of the residence himself, then Waterbury might not suspect the feds are on to him. He'll be angry, but not suspicious. Then, when he goes after Norm again, which we all know he will, we can come up with a way to catch him and do our best to make the charges stick. They may only be for breaking and entering or aggravated assault, but that might lead to more, based on this guy's past history. The best possible scenario is, once he's incarcerated, we petition that Waterbury get Babble. Then we watch the Syndicate take a huge, painful hit. That's a hard thing to do, but it would be satisfying to almost every country in the world to watch Waterbury spill on all the killings he's done on their behalf."

There was a lot of *wc* going on in that plan.

Mina ignored it for now, thinking. Vince definitely had a knack for covert operations.

It seemed McAllister agreed. "That idea has merit. Making Waterbury think that Norm broke out himself leaves the federal government out of this for now. As Agent Kane pointed out, it's highly unlikely that Wilbert Waterbury will call in the PPF or anyone else. He will take it to the Syndicate, but without audio and vid, they will have to assume Norman Webb was wily enough to slip out of that situation on his own."

Norm *was* wily. He just happened to have been taken by surprise this time.

"I like it. I like it a lot. Lee," Mina ordered, "hack into the Meridian's surveillance. We need to know when Wilbert arrives, which could be very soon. Let's make sure he gets into his unit and sets eyes on Norm for at least a minute or two before we call him off. If we make it look like a bust-out, and Waterbury is angry he had to leave before he had any fun to do some damage, he's more likely to think he left something unlocked or made a mistake."

"Got it," Lee said.

"Then you're going to have to disable everything in that residence," Mina said. "I'm not quite sure how you're going to do that, but it's necessary."

"A power outage would do the trick," Vince offered. "They likely have generators here, but it will take some time to get them up and running. Most of the generators in a place like this are old-fashioned and have to be manually started. When's the last time there was a massive outage in the city?"

Mina had never experienced one.

The entire world ran on clean energy. The city's power grid consisted of batteries that were protected from any sort of natural or manmade disaster.

"That won't work." Mina shook her head. "A targeted power outage would clue in Waterbury that Norm had outside help. We need something else. Looping the feed on the cams would work better. Then we turn them back on so they can record Norm making his dramatic exit." She asked Lee, "Will a cam loop work? Like we did at Tedesco's?"

"It should," Lee confirmed. "Most cams are susceptible to our tech. But the reason it worked so well at Tedesco's is that he had his security set on low inside the residence, because he was old and forgetful"—and thought he was untouchable—"and it wasn't continually monitored. If someone had been paying close attention, they could've seen the blip when we started the loop. But we don't know who's monitoring Waterbury's cams. If they're marked as in-house, it won't be an issue. But it's impossible to know what setting he's on until we've hacked in. They could be monitoring it closely, particularly a vid feed that's piped into the satellite. If it was my operation, I'd have a dozen hackers watching. The Syndicate has currency to burn, so why take chances?"

"Okay, so looping might not be the best option." Mina walked toward the windows and back again. "What else have we got?"

Lee cleared his throat. "I can come up with something, but it would work faster if I had some help."

Anything for Norm. "What kind of help?" Mina asked.

"Harmony. She's the best of the best. Between the two of us, I know we can find a way to get in there without anyone noticing. It's the quickest way we can help Norm. We can focus in on Vince's plan of making it look like he broke himself out."

"Done," McAllister said. "I will have Harmony Biggins

and Agent Poston gather up whatever technology you think you'll need to aid you in this endeavor. They will arrive within ten. Link me in with the surveillance feed to the Meridian. I'm calling the counseling director now. The call will be in place to order Waterbury back two minutes after he enters the residence." McAllister's voice was grim. "As you've been debating this, I've been considering the best approach for the agency, and I've come to a decision. I want Kramer to run point on this."

"What?" Mina was dumbfounded.

"I do not have the authority to sanction this as a government mission without vid proof of Norm being inside that residence. We don't have enough evidence as it stands. We have speculation and opinions, and we have a renovation company with ties to the Syndicate."

Mina began to sputter.

"That doesn't mean I don't agree that Norm Webb's life is in grave danger," he continued, ignoring the sputter, "but we have a means to protect the agency if Colonel Kramer takes lead, and that's my preference. If he agrees to run this, and if information about it spills into the public, which we would like to keep from happening, it will play as a *civilian* happened to get word that Norman Webb was in trouble. Then said civilian broke into the unit on his own. Once he found Norm, he alerted federal agents, who then came to his aid quickly and efficiently, thus saving Norman Webb's life and exposing Wilbert Waterbury. None of this will have to play out if the media doesn't get a hold of it. It's just precautionary."

Mina tried to get her brain on board. Vince was technically a civilian in the US, as he was not a member of the military or law enforcement here. But no one actually considered him a civilian. "Vince posing as a regular person will hardly fly with anyone, much less the Protectorate. If he gets involved in this publicly, they could fire him, or worse. Not to mention what the Syndicate would—"

"I'll do it," Vince cut in. "I'll sign whatever you need me to that says it was all my idea. If it comes out in the media, I'll manifest a workable backstory for how I found out about Norm. My guards will support me. It will hold."

"You can't do that," Mina protested, her mouth continuing to open and close with no intelligent sounds coming out. "It could mean the end of your career. The Syndicate could hunt you down—"

"I'm well aware of the stakes, but a man's life is on the line. There is no way I'm saying no."

"I'm inside surveillance at the Meridian," Lee said excitedly. "They have cams on every floor. Not every high-rise does." He gasped. "There he is. Waterbury just entered the building."

Chapter 17

THERE WAS NO time to argue with Vincent Kramer over his possibly ill-advised decision to accept lead. Mina appreciated that he was willing to risk his career, but at the same time, she was worried for him. She didn't want him to lose his position in the Protectorate. She didn't want the Syndicate to think he broke Norm out.

It was a lot to gamble on.

So, in order to combat that, they had to make sure they did everything correctly and that it stayed out of the media. If the news didn't break to the public, it should be okay.

No pressure.

McAllister had popped off to make sure everything ran smoothly on his end. Mina and Vince were perched over Lee's shoulders, watching cam feed of Waterbury making his way down the hallway and entering his unit.

Once the door was shut, Mina began to pace, hands on her hips. "I'm not going to rest until he's out of there."

Vince announced, "I have some things to go pick up. Now that the Syndicate is involved, I need more high-powered tech. Too much is at stake. I'll be back in ten."

"Wait—"

He was already out the door, probably on the phone with Phineas Raphael to secure permission to regain entrance upon his return.

"We're going to figure this out. Try not to worry," Lee told her. "I've got a few ideas. Once Harmony gets here, it'll all come together."

"I know." Mina sat back down on the lounger and blew out a breath. "I just hope we're not too late. Tell me the minute Waterbury comes out of that unit."

"Will do."

Mina set her head in her hands for what felt like the hundredth time, allowing a moment to herself. Her mind was racing. She needed to slow it down and refocus. Having the Syndicate out for vengeance would be a very bad situation. Having Vince take lead meant he would go in first and find Norm, shouldering the burden. If Waterbury found out it was him, he wouldn't be safe, not even in France.

She rose suddenly. "He needs an alt."

"Who needs an alt?" Lee asked, not taking his eyes off his screen.

"Vince. He's not thinking about protecting himself right now. He's lasered on getting Norm out. But he can't enter that apartment looking like...well, him."

Mina walked swiftly back into Phineas' sleep room.

She knew nothing about this man. His age, size,

anything helpful. But everyone wore clothes. She felt a little bad going through his things, but Mina would make sure the government gave him excellent credit on anything they used.

As she opened his closet, his sim intoned, "Is there anything I can help you with, Phineas? The weather today is sunny with a small chance of rain. Temperature is seventy-three degrees Fahrenheit, about twenty-three degrees Celsius."

Mina kept quiet. Hopefully, he didn't have any locking mechanisms attached to anything, like Mina had in her own home. If Veronica didn't receive a response within thirty seconds, she would repeat her question, then she would shut everything down.

The closet door opened smoothly, no locks that Mina could see.

The man didn't have a whole lot and seemed to be a conservative dresser, judging by the simple designs hanging in there. His pants were much too short for Vince, but there were a few overcoats and some hats.

She pulled out a coat printed with a flashy design, squares in different primary colors, the base of it dark blue. A wide-brimmed hat sat on the shelf above in a two-toned fiber that made it look like it had ridges. That would work if it fit low enough over Vince's head. She moved to another door. Sleep clothes. She shut it and went to a drawer. It required a fingerprint to open, so she moved on.

In the connected waste room, she opened a mirrored vanity. Inside, she found a pair of enormous sunshades.

The lenses were large round circles with a reflective sheen the color of steel.

"All the better to conceal that pretty face," she murmured quietly.

"He's leaving!" Lee cried from the other room. "Waterbury's leaving the unit. He's got something in his hand, but I can't see what it is. I'll track him down to the lobby and follow him out."

Mina rushed out to the living area with Phineas' clothing draped over one arm. She leaned toward the screen, watching Waterbury board a tube.

A minute later, he arrived in the lobby.

"He doesn't look happy," she said, feeling satisfied. They'd gotten him out of there in time. "One of his hands is fisted. We aren't going to see what's inside." Mina's cuff beeped. "Kane here."

"Hiya," Kaylee said. "We're outside the Meridian. McAllister wanted us to wait to enter until the perp was clear."

"He's heading out now," Mina said. "Over two meters tall, dark, thinning hair, wearing a basic black two-piece government-issued outfit. He's got something in his hand. If you're close enough, try to see what it is, but don't give yourselves away."

"Got it. We're concealed across the street behind a parked airbus." Mina heard some shuffling, and then Kaylee ordered Harmony, "Don those macros. See if you can see what's in that guy's hand. The tall one who just came out with the grim look on his face." To Mina, she said, "He's moving fast. Oh, wait, he stopped. He's turning in a circle. He's slamming his huge fists against his legs. He's walking. Wait, stopping again. He's pulling out whatever it is to look at it."

Mina heard Harmony in the background. "It looks like a small dagger," Harmony said. "The blade is so sharp it's glinting in the sun. That asshelmet is wiping blood off of it. Right onto his pants. Gross! His hand is bloody, too. Either from the knife, or he cut himself. There's not a ton of blood, though. It's not dripping or anything."

"Keep eyes on him for a short distance," Mina instructed. "We don't want him circling back. Tag me back when you're out front. We need Harmony up here fast."

"Gotcha. Back in two." She clicked off.

Lee turned from the compucase. "I have some ideas about the cams. Instead of looping the feed, because someone could catch the blip, and the feed would still technically be running, which would record us breaking in, we pop in a static image as a kind of blocker. Cams record continuously, but they can also snap images. Doing so doesn't make them hitch. We have all the cams snap an image at the same time. We lock in the images, and then we pause the entire feed."

"Won't someone catch the pause?"

"Not likely. Pauses can happen for a lot of reasons, including connection interruptions, power inconsistencies. A lot of things. As long as the feed *looks* the same to anyone viewing it on the other end, and it seems like nothing's changed, they shouldn't be suspicious. If they become suspicious after Norm 'escapes,' because they are of course the Syndicate, there would be dead space between when we took the image and when we unpaused. But there's a way around that."

"Which is?"

"We stack the feed with as many still images as the time we took inside. Snapping an image takes zero-point-zero-one millisecond. I know that for certain, because I use stills all the time. So we just multiply that by how long we're in the residence and adjust the timing. They will run like a vid if they're stacked."

Lee seemed proud of himself for figuring that out. He should be. Mina was impressed, as usual.

"Have you ever done anything like this before?"

"Not exactly." Now he looked sheepish. "There's a possibility Harmony has. But between the two of us, we can produce the code to do it. I believe this way is the only foolproof plan we have."

Mina liked the sound of foolproof. That could be the key word of the day.

Behind them, there was a click.

The door opened, and Vince came in, an important-looking briefcase under one arm. He'd managed to do a round trip in under ten. He brought it over and set it on the table, settling his thumbs into the grooves, waiting.

The top eased open slowly, revealing what was inside.

"*Oooh.*" The sound Lee made upon seeing the contents was a cross between a standard moan and some kind of ecstasy Mina didn't want to name. He got up from his chair. "Is that a multifaceted tech wand with a fiber-optic point and three-level variation?"

Lee began to reach for it, then snapped his hand back.

Vince chuckled. "It is. Go ahead and touch it. It won't bite."

The gurgle that came out of Lee's throat next was a little embarrassing as he reached for the wand once again, taking it out of its special place inside a bunch of cushy gel-foam.

While the rookie was elbows-deep in the treasure trove of tech that was more sophisticated than Mina had seen in a long time, she pulled Vince to the side, handing him Phineas' clothing. He took the stack without comment. "Lee thinks he has a way to manipulate the cam feeds," she told him, "but he's waiting for Harmony. Waterbury just left the building with a blade in his hand. It was bloodied, and he was clearly frustrated. We need to get into his unit as soon as possible. Who knows how long the Oak Lane residence can hold Wilbert, especially if he's agitated? We just took his prize away for the time being."

"Agreed. Getting in there quickly is imperative." Vince set the clothing down. "I assigned two of my guards to the outside of the building. They will alert me if they see the suspect come back."

"Are you sure you want to involve the Protectorate in this?" Mina questioned. "That doesn't exactly help us keep the profile low."

"I had to give them something. I've been gone too long. If we want this to stay cloaked, I have to keep them apprised, or they'll report back to Ambrose that something is happening. The story I gave them is the story I'll give to the media if word gets out. A friend of mine might be in trouble, and I'm checking it out. My guards will keep their mouths shut to the public, but the Protectorate is a different story. I'm not exactly...a fan favorite at the moment. It seems everyone is suspicious of my motives these days."

Mina frowned. "Sorry to hear that. It doesn't seem fair. We're living in an era of greed and power, and it shifts as quickly as the wind. You just happen to be caught up in a gust, but I'm sure it will settle soon. We're appreciative of your help and your skills." She gestured to the table. "And your tech. As soon as Kaylee and Harmony arrive, and the hackers get the cams figured out, we're on the move. I'm going to schedule a medi-unit to be waiting on the roof."

Vince nodded. "Have the drone park as close to the entryway as possible and have them erect a screen to block visual access of the door."

Mina nodded her agreement. "If the Syndicate looks into who landed, the name will be unavailable. We can't use Phineas Raphael's name for Norm's exit. Just in case. And, just to be safe, we should relocate this nice man until we know how this will play out. I think Phineas will be happy with a vacation on the US government, don't you?"

"He will. I'll arrange a room for him at The Bella in the meantime," Vince said. That was very generous of him to offer to do that. "I don't want him to be caught in the middle of this either. The guard force at The Bella makes it difficult for anyone without authorization to enter."

Mina had encountered that herself just today.

Vince continued, "Each unit in The Bella has its own emergency button, so that will be an added layer of protection for him."

Too bad Petra hadn't enacted hers when she'd taken too much medication.

"The government can't cover such an expensive offer, but we can give you the standard rate toward a safe house for this man for a day or two. When he agreed to this, we didn't know we were up against the Syndicate." If they'd known, they never would have embroiled a civilian. "My director will make it happen."

Mina's cuff beeped.

She answered with a question. "Where are you at?"

"Outside the Meridian," Kaylee said. "Harmony is advising that we kill the cams before we enter. Your floor, tubes, and lobby. Not sure if that's possible."

Mina heard Harmony in the background. "Of course it's possible. I'm sure Karmaseeker's already inside surveillance. It's a flick of a couple switches."

"I'm not going to kill it," Lee confirmed. "It's just another thing for the Syndicate to find. I'm looping. It's the best we can do. If someone is monitoring it, they may see a millisecond of a glitch, but only if they're highly trained. They probably won't notice. Security here is weak, nowhere near hacker level. Just give me a second."

"You said the Syndicate might be able to override a loop," Mina cautioned.

"They might be able to with their *own* cams, linked to their *own* satellite, with their *own* hackers. It would be much harder with hacked or borrowed feed from the Meridian. From what I'm seeing, the software that controls the surveillance in this place is at least ten years old. It's not connected to any satellite. They had someone in here to repair it"—Lee leaned toward the screen, scrutinizing—"at least twenty times in the last two years. Nothing the Syndicate would get from here would be worth their effort."

"Do it already!" Harmony hollered from Mina's cuff. "You're wasting time. We gotta get that sweet old man out of there!"

The young super-rookie was right. Harmony wasn't one to second-guess herself. And Norm was going to get a kick out of being called a "sweet old man."

"Done," Lee said. "Bring them in."

Chapter 10

MINA STOPPED PACING, but only to check her cuff. "It's been ten minutes. He could be bleeding out by now." She was frustrated this hadn't gone faster.

"We understand. I'm worried, too," Harmony said from her position at the table next to Lee. "But this is fragile business. Karmaseeker came up with a brilliant plan with the static images, but implementing this kind of thing takes time. We can't go through the mob bomb satellite, so we're forced to control the cams from the home sim, which we have to infiltrate through the power grid at the Meridian. We're almost in. Once there, we have to give the sim orders through code, which we can erase once we're done so if someone decides to check, there's no trail. We're almost done. Give us another two."

Kaylee met Mina's gaze. "Webb is alive." Mina had to believe that. "Waterbury didn't get to have any fun this time. He still wants Webb to suffer. It's too soon for all the excitement to end." She gestured to Harmony and

Lee. "We have to trust them to get us in and Webb out safely. The Syndicate is a heavy-duty crime family who love to get even. I don't pretend to understand what the two of them are talking about. When Harmony speaks like that, it sounds like a foreign language I like to call Geek Agent, and we're not proficient. But they'll get it done in the next two, like she said."

"You should be thankful I speak Geek Agent," Harmony countered as she typed furiously on her own compucase. "I tracked down that fake kiosk criminal in less than sixty seconds. By the way, next time you throw a make-believe case my way, make sure it's a challenge, wouldja? I was bored outta my mind."

Mina's eyebrows rose. "She tracked down the kiosk thief in sixty?"

"She did," Kaylee confirmed with wistfulness. "She's a weird little hacker wizard. The air breathers at the kiosk reported what happened. She took over their surveillance and located not only the thief's address, but she also homed in on his cuff. I've never seen anything like it. We watched the pretend criminal run down the street from a satellite feed she hacked into right above him in the next thirty."

"But if the pretend criminal was an agent playing a part," Mina said, "his cuff should've been encrypted."

"Encrypted *emshmipted*," Harmony huffed, still typing, her eyes not leaving the screen. "He used his cuff in the store, which is a petty-thief no-no. It pinged a server nearby. Time stamp in the vid surveillance gave me a time stamp for that server and a location triangulation.

The encryption was garbage. You guys really should do something about that. *Oooh*, I'm inside the creepy killer's sim. Its name is Manson. *Rude.* I'm going to trigger the cams to take a still image in the next twenty secs. Read this code back to me just to be sure," she instructed Lee. "This is a triple-check op."

"Looks like we're a go in a few minutes," Mina said with relief as Lee began to read the code aloud, which was the height of Geek Agent. Nothing he said made any sense to her. "It's time to don your alt," she reminded Vince.

He obliged by picking up the coat and threading his arms through it, choosing not to comment on the vibrant pattern. It was tight, but it would work. Then he pulled the cap down low on his forehead. He then plucked a small spray bottle out of his tech briefcase and proceeded to mist his fingers, coating them in a flexible silicone adhesive that would cover his prints and prevent the skin from shedding DNA.

Kaylee looked over some things inside the case. "Pretty fun trinkets, Kramer." She lifted something long and shiny, inspecting it. "I've never seen one of these before, but I'm assuming it's a spectrometer of some kind."

He nodded. "It specializes in recognizing molecules, particularly in poison." He shook his hands out to dry them, then he grabbed another tool from inside. It resembled the lock disengager, but it had a prong on one end. "This should get me inside his unit without ruining the locking mechanism. It's a good thing you're controlling the sim," he told Harmony and Lee. "A guy like Waterbury would have his home system controlling his locks and alarms."

"Yeah," Lee said. "We've blocked the sim from any aural or visual feed. I wouldn't, you know, make a lot of noise, just in case. But it won't recognize what's happening. If Waterbury asks it if anybody broke into his residence, it will answer no. We can turn it back on when Norm is ready to break out, so it will catch all of that and give an accurate recounting."

Harmony added, "I have a tool that would've worked just as well. My very own creation. I call it the Skewer Extraordinaire, because it skews sim programs perfectly. It specifically integrates into the software that ninety-nine percent of dumb humans use on their home sim systems. If you didn't already know, there are only two manufacturers of home sim systems. And they buy all their software direct from the same company. The smarter—bordering on serious orbital intelligence—one percent of us create our own software, which is impervious to my Skewer Extraordinaire. This guy went with the Meridian's system, though he did enact a few safety protocols." She scoffed. "As if. The protocols are still manufactured by the same company. There really shouldn't be a monopoly on home systems, but since there is, I was able to create my own weapon against any sim. I can literally get inside anywhere."

Mina glanced at Kaylee, who shrugged. "What do you want me to say? She's an evil genius who creates evil-genius tools. It's a good thing she's on our side."

Harmony snorted. "Now I am. Okay, just one more sec. When I say go," she instructed Lee, "start the clock. In order for this to work, we have to be down to the milli on time inside." She shot a look at Vince. "Sexy Protectorate Man—who knows my dad and lied to me, but I've forgiven you—you have to signal us the moment you turn the lever of that door. The *moment*. And then again the second you leave. I want exacts. We're not leaving a gap in this thing for anyone to find. Gaps are a group of sulfur farts that will stink up this mission and set the goons on us."

"Will do." Vince shot a wistful look at Mina that said, *Can you believe a child is running this op?*

Mina copied Kaylee's shrug. "We do what she says. I'm linking our cuffs now so everyone's on the same open line of comm. Kaylee and I will be watching from the stairwell while you're inside. I want a verbal play-by-play. Everything you see and hear."

"I'm no stranger to giving play-by-plays," Vince said. "Is the medi-unit ready?"

"It's on standby," Mina confirmed. "Hopefully, he can make it there on his own."

It chafed Mina that she couldn't be there for her friend, but she would see him soon after.

If he was unconscious, then plan B would be enacted, which was basically haul him out of there and figure out a cover story later.

That's all they had time for.

Vince donned the sunshades. They looked completely ridiculous, but the effect was perfect. He wouldn't look like himself, especially not through a cam mounted on the ceiling. Not that anyone would see that feed, but if they did, he would be unrecognizable. "Let's get Webb out of there."

"Three...two...one," Harmony called. "First images taken. There...they're in place. We're a go!"

Mina's cuff beeped.

"Agent Kane, you and Agent Adams are needed at headquarters." McAllister's tone was raw.

"What you mean? We're right in the middle of freeing—"

"I realize that. I can extend you fifteen to twenty. No longer. As I told you before, this must take precedence. That's enough time for you to get into the residence. Agent Poston, Harmony Biggins, and Colonel Kramer can take care of the rest. Waterbury is back at his transitional residence. He won't be leaving anytime soon. Webb will be in capable hands." McAllister was being covert about the topic, because he knew more ears were listening, and was leaving it up to Mina to let everyone know what was going on if she wanted to.

"Thank you, sir," Lee said. "Fifteen should be fine. Agent Kane and I are absolutely necessary for the success of this op. We're at a critical stage of hacking this residence. Any mistakes could lead the Syndicate to discover Colonel Kramer's involvement. There's no way we can leave right now."

McAllister paused. "Understood. Get the job done and get back to Government One. Contact me immediately when you've finished freeing Webb."

With relief, he signed off.

Mina said, "Okay, you heard him. We have fifteen minutes to do this." Vince gave her a questioning look. He was wondering what could possibly be more important than springing an ex-marshal from the hands of a fixer for the Syndicate. "Lee and I are involved in an audit. I'll explain later."

Kaylee herded them toward the door. "Let's go."

The three of them rushed into the hallway and toward the staircase. They ascended two stories quickly.

On the landing for level fifty-two, Vince turned. "If I run into problems, I'll let you know. From what we've gone over, the utility closet is the best guess. If my disengager doesn't work, I've got a couple of other things to try, along with some pry tools. Using tools will be messy, but it'll get the job done."

They all knew they weren't leaving without Norm.

"Sounds good," Mina said. "Good luck."

The landing door had a small window, and they watched Vince take off down the hallway. He stopped at Waterbury's door, his tool up against the lock.

His voice came out of their cuffs. "Turning lever now. Start the clock." They watched him duck into the residence. The door closed behind him. After a brief pause, he reported, "It smells bad in here." Kaylee tapped her cuff off to cut down on the echo. "Strong scent of blood and human waste. So far, the living area is clean. The furniture doesn't look lived in. It's very spartan. Coming up on the utility closet now. The door's closed. I'm settling my ear against it." They heard him call, "Norman Webb, are you in there?"

A soft moan erupted.

"That's him!" Mina exclaimed excitedly. "I'd recognize his voice anywhere."

She didn't comment on how drained it had sounded.

"Verifying Norman Webb is inside the utility closet," Vince said. "My first try with the lock disengager didn't work. A rotary lock has been installed on the outside of the door. Might have to use my pry tools."

Mina swore under her breath. A rotary lock required a combination to unlock. It was meant to keep hackers out.

Vince asked, "Norman, are you near the door? Is there any way you can get to it?"

Mina held her cuff up so she and Kaylee could both hear Norm's weak response.

"No," Norm replied.

Lee said, "Colonel Kramer, place your cuff against the combination lock. We'll amplify it on our side. Rotary locks make small clicking noises when they hit the right number. Turn the dial right two full turns. Then move it to the right slowly. Stop immediately when we say so."

They waited not so patiently for Vince to start turning the combination. The clicks were barely audible through the cuff for Mina and Kaylee.

There was lots of relief when Lee yelled, "Stop! Okay. Now you're going to go left at the same speed and stop when I tell you to."

It took a painful two minutes to finish the process.

There was a louder, more audible click, and Vince said, "That's it. Going in now." The next sound was one that Mina hadn't wanted to hear. Vince swore, loud and viciously. "He's here. He's alive. There's blood all over the floor. There's no way he can make it out himself. I'm putting him over my shoulder."

Mina's hand shot out to open the stairwell door, but Kaylee stopped her.

"We're staying right where we are," she reminded Mina. "Vince is coming to us. Then he's going to carry Norm to the tube on level fifty so we can get him up to the roof. We don't need your image, your fingerprints, or your DNA anywhere near this scene." Her expression was compassionate. "I know he's like family to you, but we're not making this messier than it already is. As of right now, the Syndicate is going to know somebody broke him out of there. They're going to hunt for that person, and there's nothing we can do about that. But what we *can* do is keep this as clean as possible."

"You're right." Mina ordered Vince, "Get out as fast as you can. I just alerted the medi-unit. The drone will set down in less than one."

Vince grunted, then swore again. "I just found something to stanch the bleeding. He's bound with e-restraints. There's no way to get them off without shocking him. If I don't, they'll shock us both when I move him. No way to keep him steady enough. I'm sure these are juiced up, so it's going to be a heavy hit."

"Just do it, kid," a very tired, very groggy Norm said. "Get me the hell out of here while I still have breath left in my body. I can handle the shock. Hopefully, it'll knock me out. Pretty sure both of my legs are broken. I can't feel 'em any longer."

"Holy hell bats of Hades," Kaylee murmured. "He's a mess."

"Shock him," Mina ordered, "and get him out of there."

Norm screamed once. Then there was silence.

NORM WAS BLESSEDLY unconscious when they placed him in the craft. The medi-workers were on it, pumping him full of painkillers and running their assessments.

"Go with him," Vince ordered. The overcoat borrowed from Phineas was covered in blood, as was the side of his face where he had settled Norm over one shoulder. Hat and glasses were still on. "See that someone is guarding him at all times." Spoken like a true colonel. "We'll do what we can here to make it look like a civilian found him and called it in." His grim expression mirrored the emotion swirling inside Mina.

Lee stood behind Vince. He'd rushed up to see Norm off safely, while Harmony was adding up the time on the cams. "I'll head to headquarters and inform them you're on your way," he said to Mina. "Harmony can take care of the rest."

She nodded as she boarded the drone.

As asked, the medi-unit had erected a privacy screen

from the craft to the door. No visibility from above.

"We're going to the medical unit at Government Four," Mina told the crew. McAllister had already okayed it. She nodded toward her partner. "Lee, you can do this. Just tell the truth. If anything seems fishy, hold your ground. I'll be right behind you."

Lee saluted as the door closed.

Mina took a seat at Norm's head as the drone took to the sky. He was beginning to come around.

"You have clearance to land on the roof of Government Four," Mina instructed as she popped her badge on holo. "Scan this for approval."

An attendant brought out a thumb scanner, and once it signaled green, she gave the order to the pilot. These drones were flown by air breathers to mitigate any issues due to panic or an unruly patient.

"Is he going to be okay?" Mina asked the woman.

"He's pretty beat up, but his vitals are good. Doesn't look like there's any internal bleeding." The attendant ran a wand up and down Norm's side, while two others did the same over the rest of his body. "As of right now, he's got multiple fractures—both legs, elbow, three fingers—a few bruised ribs, a mild concussion, and a small puncture wound on his side. The blade didn't hit any internal organs. He's a lucky guy. Lost a lot of blood, but we're transfusing him now. We just gave him an adrenaline booster to help with the process. He should be waking up any second. He's got enough pain blockers in him now, so he won't feel much."

Norm began to moan.

"Hey, you took quite a beating," Mina said, close to his ear, her hand settled on his shoulder, "but you're going to pull through."

Norm coughed. "Good to know." It sounded like rocks were tumbling around in his throat.

"We're taking you to the medi-unit at Government Four," Mina said. "Your release was messier than we would've liked, so McAllister is tapping some of the marshals to meet us. They're going to keep you safe while you heal."

The spider blinked a few times, shaking his head, his gaze landing squarely on Mina, his eyes going wide. "Damn, I was hoping this was a nightmare. I guess it's not. You know who he is, right?"

"We do. We're taking care of it. There might be some blowback. We'll deal with that tomorrow, once you're healed. Right now, just focus on getting through this." Mina was careful not to give away too many specific details in front of the medi-workers.

"I wasn't careful enough," Norm murmured, closing his eyes. "I let him get too close."

Mina knew Norm would take this hard. The ex-marshal prided himself on being able to outmaneuver almost anyone he came in contact with.

"You can't blame yourself. He got the jump on you because he had a lot of resources behind him."

Norm shook his head, then winced. "He didn't jump me. Waltzed right up to me like he didn't have a care in the world. I went with him willingly."

Mina tried not to gape. "Why would you do that?"

Norm opened his eyes, focusing on the ceiling of the craft. "The kid. He said he'd get the kid. He found out who I was guarding. He was waiting right outside of the kid's residence when we arrived last night. He threatened to slice and dice him. I couldn't let that happen. He disabled my cuff and threw it in the grinder before I could send out the Mayday I had ready to go."

Mina's expression was grim as she brought up her cuff, ordering, "Call McAllister."

"Report," McAllister said.

"The perpetrator threatened to harm Harri and knows where he lives. We need to get him out of his residence immediately."

Mina heard some shuffling, then some tapping. "I'm summoning two agents to his door now. Hang tight, Agent Kane. The suspect is still at his restricted residence. He won't be able to leave again until tomorrow afternoon. That will give us time to do some much-needed cleanup and get Mr. Hampburg to safety." McAllister paused. "I just received confirmation not ten minutes ago that your friend did in fact accept the job you arranged for him. I will have the agents escort him across state lines and give him the option of a new identity chip, on us, effective immediately."

Mina blew out a breath of relief. "Thank you. We'll be landing at Government Four in the next minute or so."

"See Webb handed off to the marshals, then take the tunnel to Government One. Report to my office immediately."

McAllister clicked off.

"I'm sorry," Norm murmured. "I was trying my damnedest to keep you out of it. I knew he'd be gunning for me once he got out. I had plans in place. I took precautions. But when you called me for the job of protecting the kid a few days ago, I thought I could do both. Turns out, I couldn't. I put you both, along with everyone else involved in this fiasco, in the crosshairs of a very powerful organization. I promise I'll make it right. I'll do everything within my means to make sure nothing happens to anyone else. I must be slipping in my old age. I'm going to retire after this with a blotch on my record. I'm clearly unfit to do this job any longer."

"You're not going to retire," Mina informed him. "You may need to take a few lessons in how to alert your friends if any serious problems arise in the future. That would be helpful. I believe you took precautions. You had no idea when this guy was going to make his move. He surprised everybody."

"I thought I had a month or two to finish the plan while he got organized," Norm continued. "I've been keeping tabs on his temporary residence. I have someone on the inside. He had limited time to wander, less than fifteen minutes per day, but that suddenly increased a few days ago. I had no idea he was maintaining another residence. There was nothing on file. It was stupid of me not to dig deeper."

"We didn't know it either, until he told us. Lee informs me that their hackers are greater than super," Mina said, leaving out the Syndicate by name. Norm knew who she was talking about. "You did all the right things. You even gave me a code teal heads-up. Next time, I want the details in person, or at least an automatic vid recording if you go missing."

"There won't be a next time," Norm replied stubbornly.

"Hopefully not like this scenario," Mina countered. "But work will be coming your way in the next day or two. We're putting a plan in place to nab him. He needs to go back into a box indefinitely."

Norm angled his head to face Mina. "You're not going to take him on alone, are you?"

"I won't be alone," Mina said. "You're going to help me."

"Sir, I need you to calm down," an attendant said. "Your heart rate and blood pressure are soaring." To Mina, she clucked, "I need you to stop interviewing him, or interrogating him, or whatever you're doing. He needs to remain calm. We're hoping the pain blockers won't wear off before we can get him into a medi-pod. But stress can cause that to happen quicker."

Mina nodded, sufficiently chastised. "Fine, I'll stop. You and your team are going to need to sign some nondisclosure paperwork once we arrive."

The drone began its descent.

"That's standard procedure when we set down at Government Four," another attendant chimed, clearly unhappy that Mina had riled their patient. "We know how to do our jobs."

Mina kept her mouth shut until the door opened.

Medi-drones had a wide door in the back, and when it

rose, a ramp extended so they could easily roll or air-carry the patient off.

Settling a hand on Norm's shoulder, Mina said, "You're going to be fine. Those golden fingers will be back in action in no time. I'm going to talk to the marshals waiting for you over there." She gestured to one female and two males. "Everything's going to be fine. I'll check in with you later tonight."

Before she could exit, Norm grabbed her forearm, holding her steady.

"Thank you. I wouldn't have lasted much longer. I knew if I disappeared, you would put the pieces together. I owe you my life. I will make all of this right. I swear I will."

"I know," Mina said. "Just focus on healing."

She departed the craft and spoke with the marshals. They would take care of their own. Norm had a room waiting. A medi-pod was open. There wasn't any more she could do. He was safe. At least for now.

After swiping into a tube, Mina took it down to the tunnel where mini mag-lev trams connected all four government buildings.

She swabbed and retinal-scanned, then boarded one of the waiting trams. They were two-seaters, but she was alone.

"Please connect your safety harness," a sim intoned. "Time to Government One is twenty-seven seconds."

Mina had a moment to try to center herself for this audit interview.

Depending on who these investigators were calling in

to interview, the story could go a number of ways. Veritus was the biggest issue, the one where their process could be questioned the most. They'd gone after Franco Tedesco the Third on the sly. He'd been caught shipping chemis illegally. They'd had a warrant for a quiet entry in order to airmeld sensitive data out before Tedesco could destroy it. A standard warrant would've given a guy like Tedesco too much of a heads-up. Storming a protected castle in the sky would've been tricky and could have backfired. Tedesco had a long reach.

It turned out, in addition to shipping chemis, he was the head of a serial-killing ring that had been in operation for over twenty-five years. Veritus had killed Lee's father nineteen years prior. That meant her partner had an emotional, personal connection to Tedesco. He was subsequently allowed to continue with the op.

That personal connection had affected Lee in the beginning. When he'd created a pixel mirror of Tedesco's supercomputer to beam incriminating evidence straight to the media, he'd started the process without author-ization, and several agents in the room had disagreed with his actions. But McAllister had been running lead, thank goodness. He'd ultimately given permission, so *technically* no rules had been broken.

Depending on who you asked.

Then there was Vincent Kramer's involvement when Tedesco's minions had decided they were going to launch a missile full of poisonous gas into the city. Mina had allowed Vince to participate in the takedown and then had discovered he'd omitted serious intel about the French Protectorate coming to his rescue.

It'd been a debacle. But luckily, everything had turned out fine in the end. No one had been harmed, and all the Veritus members had been rounded up and jailed.

It *could've* massively backfired, and a lot of people could've been killed. The auditors could focus on that. Mina felt responsible, even though she'd been in contact with McAllister, and he had given them the authorization to go ahead.

She rested her head against the gel-cush as the tram took off, whooshing through the tunnel on a bed of smooth, fric-free air.

Now that Mina had more clarity to think about it, the audit didn't make a lot of sense. Why would anyone question such successful outcomes? It wasn't like evidence had gone missing or something was off.

Kaylee had to be right about this being based on fear in the upper ranks. The infiltration of the government by criminals was rampant. Several Veritus members had held government positions. They'd been conducting illegal business right under everyone's noses. Same with the Nesbit case. Seventeen bankers and brokers had been brought in. The BB&C was in charge of ensuring that the banks were free of corruption, but the Nesbits had been able to plow ahead with their scheme. There was a strong possibility that some people inside the BB&C had wanted the alias scam to move forward, as they would've benefited from it.

If powerful people wanted Mina and Lee to stop

investigating high-profile cases, they could lose their jobs on a technicality. The auditors could find some way to keep them from investigating in the future.

She had to tread lightly.

First thing on the agenda was to confer with McAllister about her suspicions. She would follow his orders, and she was certain he would have something to say.

Chapter 20

"Good afternoon, Agent Kane. Thank you for joining us." Mina took a seat across from two individuals who resembled federal agents but weren't. They had the same look and feel, with formal outfits and ordered appearances. Not that Mina wore formal outfits and always looked perfectly put together, but there was definitely a federal-agent look, and they had it.

On purpose.

One female, one male.

Upon discussions with her boss before she entered the interview, Mina had discovered that they'd been cagey about their agency affiliation when McAllister had asked, and he'd been none too happy about it. He'd assumed, when he'd gotten the order, that it'd come directly from the committee he reported to.

But once they'd arrived on the scene, he'd found it hadn't. Another committee or agency had ordered the audit, which was curious. Other committees weren't supposed to even have knowledge about the CIU or its agents.

It was secret for a reason.

Because of that, McAllister had ordered her and Lee to answer questions vaguely until he sussed out the origins of the audit, which would take him some time. He'd also left it up to their discretion how long they would sit for questions. Since this audit had been ordered by someone outside of the CIU, McAllister believed they didn't have the authority to initiate any disciplinary action against Mina or Lee, such as firing or suspending them.

Regardless, Mina was determined to figure out what was going on here and gather as much information as she could about the situation.

The female, who hadn't introduced herself, said, "We're going to ask you a few questions about some of your recent cases. There's nothing to worry about. Just answer them honestly, and we'll be out of your hair in no time." She chuckled, giving off an air of calm, even though she was fidgeting, continuously smoothing her shirt and shifting in her seat.

Mina didn't reply. She simply waited.

The male investigator leaned forward. "Is that...is that blood on your sleeve?"

"Yes," Mina replied. "I was clumsy today and cut my arm. I haven't had time to step into a pod yet, as I was summoned here before I could do so." Mina pulled up her sleeve to reveal the gel-skin bandage she wore. The blood on her sleeve was indeed Norm's, but luckily McAllister had caught it. She'd been running too late to change, so she'd slapped on the bandage to make it look like she'd been injured. She and McAllister had decided to keep what had gone down today completely out of the discussion.

Not a whiff.

Thankfully, McAllister had told Lee the same thing before he'd gone into his own meeting. If these investigators got wind that the CIU had just had a run-in with the Syndicate and was now in a position to bring down one of their fixers and possibly expose the organization, Mina wasn't sure who would get this top-secret information or what they would do with it. Everyone agreed it wouldn't be a good thing.

"Sorry to hear that. Accidents do happen," the man said. "By the way, I'm Investigator Dunn, and this is Investigator Linette. We're representatives of Government Internal Affairs." He cleared his throat, coughing into his fist.

Hm. The lie coming out of his mouth wasn't agreeing with him. That likely meant he had a conscience of some kind.

"I've never heard of an agency called Government Internal Affairs," Mina quipped. When neither of them responded, she continued, "The PPF has an Internal Affairs Department. But as far as I know, federal agents are overseen by their directors, who are overseen by government committees. Those committees have the authority to launch an audit, but neither my director nor I were aware that an undisclosed audit, ordered by a separate committee, was possible."

"We aren't allowed to elaborate," Linette answered primly, sitting a little straighter. Her lips were pursed. Apparently, this wasn't going according to plan. "Just know that we're authorized to conduct this interview and that everything you say will be on the record."

It would be on more than one record. McAllister was running full audio and vid in this conference room.

Mina crossed her arms, leaning back in her seat, assessing the two of them. "Feel free to proceed."

Dunn reached over and picked up something that looked a lot like Vince's tech briefcase. He set it on the table and made a show of opening it.

He pulled out a stack of paperwork. Actual paper.

"This is your file," he commented as he placed the several-centimeters-thick bundle next to the case. "You've been very busy these last six years. It's impressive."

That was the only thing he'd said so far that held any truth.

Mina made a move to pick a piece of paper off the top. She was curious about what it would say.

He slid the stack closer to himself, out of her reach. "Oh, the file's not for you. It's just for our reference."

"I can't read my own file?" Mina asked, surprised.

He chuckled nervously. "Well, you see, there are notes in here and things that are confidential."

"Confidential notes?" Mina quirked an eyebrow.

If that was true, why bring them in and set them on the table right in front of her? Mina grinned as she came to the conclusion that this was an extremely small, very inadequate attempt to intimidate her. Which made her precisely aware that this was Dunn's first gig investigating a federal agent.

What a shame.

"Um, yes." He shuffled the papers, clearly disarmed by her smile, before he pulled one sheet from the top to read. "This is a recounting of your most recent escapade."

Escapade? No intimidation, just incompetence.

"You discovered a large bank-and-borrows scam before it got off the ground. Good work. This enterprise stemmed from the outskirts." He made a weird clucking sound in the back of his throat, then coughed into his fist again. "The outskirts, as you know, are beyond the watchful eyes of the federal government." He set the piece of paper down. "How many connections do you meet with regularly in the outskirts?"

"None," Mina answered immediately.

They waited for Mina to elaborate.

She didn't.

"That doesn't make any sense," Linette countered. "If you were able to uncover such a huge operation, you had to have intel. Agents utilize intel often."

Did they, Linette? How very insightful of you to think so.

"Surely you have a few moles. Informants? People who are down on their luck and willing to sell you information for a fee?"

Yes, Mina knew what an informant was.

"It makes sense," Linette went on, "given what happened. We just need to know how entangled you are in the outskirts and the names and locations of your informants."

Mina almost laughed out loud.

Like, a heaving belly laugh accompanied by thigh slapping.

Their techniques—if she could call them that—weren't honed or practiced. They were just going for the ram effect.

As if.

"I'm not entangled in the outskirts," Mina answered with a straight face.

"Who are your informants?" Dunn asked in all seriousness.

"I don't have any informants there." She lowered her voice to a conspiratorial whisper. "Even if I did, it's illegal for you to ask me who they are. And I certainly wouldn't give out their names and locations. But I'm positive you already know that, and you're just asking for kicks." She ended with an exaggerated wink, including a side mouth cock.

Federal informants, like Harri, were protected by law. They were read their rights, paid for their time and information, and their identities were kept cloaked on purpose.

These two pretenders were not authorized to ask Mina for names. If they wanted that information, they'd have to take their request to a high court. The judge would side in favor of the informant, if he or she wasn't dirty.

The fact that they thought Mina didn't know the law

was shocking, yet that felt on par for what was happening here. Their own lack of knowledge was glaring, and it showed.

Oh, how it showed.

If they had any affiliation with the federal government, Mina would be surprised. If McAllister had been angry before, he was going to be apoplectic now.

"If not by informant, then how did you find out about this banking operation?" Dunn asked, trying a different tactic.

"Through an ex-marshal and a vid star. It should all be right there in my file." She bobbed her head toward the stack of paper she wasn't allowed to look at.

If that was actually her file at all. Mina was having her doubts. That's probably why Dunn wouldn't let her see it.

Every time Mina gave her director an official report, it was recorded. That report was transcribed by intelligent software, then sent to an air breather at headquarters, who read through it to make corrections, then it was sent to Mina's director for approval. It was a voice-to-digital process. No paper involved.

McAllister then read over it, added and subtracted anything he deemed necessary, and only then was it filed as *official.*

Dunn picked up another sheet from the pile. "Yes. I see. Petra Pebbles and an ex-marshal by the name of Norman Webb. He met you at a place called Biters on the edge of the outskirts."

They definitely had accurate information. If they did have official files, how had that been authorized outside of their department? It felt like something McAllister would have to sign off on, and clearly he hadn't.

"Correct," Mina answered.

"That's where he informed you of this scheme?" Linette asked, clearly greedy for a single, solid tidbit.

"No," Mina said. She had no desire for these investigators to make a trip to Pormal. Though, envisioning how Suli and Beastly would deal with them made Mina incredibly joyous. "It was common knowledge around those parts that Dominic Nesbit had an operation, and he was looking to expand outside the outskirts. Nobody at Biters knew what that operation was, only that he was planning something." The people of Pormal had ideas, they had gossip, but what Mina was saying was the truth. They hadn't known exactly what was going down. "Before we were assigned the Petra Pebbles case, my partner and I did a run on Dominic Nesbit, based on these rumors. The name Shauna Nesbit popped. And it just so happened that the same Shauna Nesbit tried to kill Petra Pebbles in an attempt to assume her identity. Once we had those facts, the cases came together. We were actually investigating what we thought was a DNA alias scam. We were unaware until right before we went in that banks and brokers would be involved. It was just one of those lucky coincidences, I guess."

"I guess." Dunn coughed again. Maybe he had a chronic condition. "Do your cases often come together by lucky chances?"

"Not usually."

"What about the case against Franco Tedesco the

Third?" Linette asked. "You were investigating him because you received a lead he was shipping chemis? Is that correct? And then you just *happened* to discover he was the head of a serial-killing ring?"

It was hard to ignore where this line of questioning was going. Mina steadied herself. She would continue to provide answers, but only because she was curious what these two would end up revealing about themselves.

That, and they'd already read through her cases, so she didn't feel she was divulging any information they didn't already have access to.

If this had been a fishing expedition, she would've gotten up and vacated the premises already.

"It wasn't just a lead," Mina said. "We had solid evidence. One of his ships was searched by the authorities in Greece, and enough chemis were found on board to create a hive bomb. We had a warrant to enter Tedesco's residence on the sly. As you know"—*or don't because you're not in this business*—"those are hard to get. It was procured because a hive bomb can kill thousands and is considered a Class AAA threat to humanity. And as warrants go, they often uncover more evidence." Or in this case, it had allowed Mina to get close to a thug who'd broken during an interview. That thug, Andy, had been installed by Tedesco's son, Frankie Four, whom Tedesco the Third had murdered in cold blood in front of Lee. Andy had tried to grope Mina. She'd brought him in for questioning once she'd discovered he was a plant. He'd ended up sharing much more than any of them had bargained for.

That's how Mina had uncovered Tedesco's link to Veritus.

But it was all in the file. No need to go over it in detail.

Dunn and Linette continued to watch Mina, so she added, "Criminals tend to enjoy participating in illegal activity. They're not bound to just one wrongdoing or one wrong deed. In this case, Tedesco was chock-full of wrong deeds just waiting to be uncovered."

Linette's expression became pinched. Dunn thumbed through a few more papers, finally plucking up one he liked. "It says here that your partner, Agent Adams, had a personal connection to the Tedesco case—"

"It's the Veritus case," Mina corrected. That's what it was called in the official report, and it was a pleasure to remind them that she had brought down a Planet's Most Wanted.

"Yes, of course. The Veritus case. Even though he had a personal connection, he was sent in to bring down this notorious killer, Franco Tedesco the Third, on his own. Isn't sending in someone who could be emotionally compromised a no-no?"

They were definitely looking for things to hang on Mina and Lee.

"Agent Adams was the only agent qualified to hack into Tedesco's system. Since we didn't want Veritus to kill any more innocent people, it seemed like the obvious choice," Mina countered. "Director McAllister made the call, not me." Well, *technically*, it'd been McAllister, but with Mina's blessing. "Without Agent Adams, Veritus would still be operational today, and many more people would've died." Mina had to grit her teeth to get through the last part. She had the sudden urge to punch a no-no right into this guy's face. "If hive bombs are Class AAA threats to humanity, then Veritus was a Class AAAA." Was there even such a thing? It didn't matter at this point. "I'd like to think *any* director would make the same choice if presented with identical options. If you have an issue with it, I suggest you take it up with him."

Linette frowned.

This was obviously not going as she'd intended. Apparently, they'd figured Mina was a pushover. Someone hadn't done their homework.

Do better, people.

"Do you feel it's a little odd that you've been in charge of so many important cases recently?" Linette asked. "Up until now, your path has been fairly mundane. I mean, the Cullen case took you a long time to solve. You were after a hacker who worked in the semi next to yours, and it took you more than a year to nab him."

Ouch. Thanks for the reminder, Linette.

"Then suddenly"—she brought her hands together, then flared them outward like an exploding starburst in front of her—"you're bringing down a Planet's Most Wanted, busting a sex ring with ties to the government, and ending a wide-ranging banking scam before it even began."

Wait until they find out about the Syndicate.

She continued her roll. "Other than one highly charged case in the outskirts at the beginning of your career, you haven't seen much action in, well, *ever.*" The investigator, if Mina chose to call her that, ended with an arched eyebrow, inclining her head like the fact that there had been *two* outskirts cases on Mina's record meant that Mina had deliberately kept details from them, such as all the informants she'd obviously gathered up the first time around.

It was time to put an end to this.

"I don't assign myself operations," Mina clarified. "And if you've read what's in those *confidential* files, you know that both of my recent cases started as one thing and turned into another. We actually like it when that happens. We tend to catch more criminals that way. You don't have a problem with us catching crooks, right?" Mina moved forward suddenly. Linette didn't blink, but Dunn startled. It wasn't a surprise. "I have a feeling you're not here to see if these cases were investigated properly, which obviously they were. You're here to investigate me specifically. I don't know why, as I've done my job to the best of my abilities, and bad guys have been boxed. Unless, of course, whoever you're working for is *not* interested in catching criminals and would rather they go free." Mina met both of their gazes individually. Slowly. "If there's something in those files that points to the fact I'm crooked or have one foot in the outskirts, by all means, let me know." She shoved back her chair. The polycarb scraped against the floor. "If not, this interview is over." Mina stood.

"You can't just leave," Linette sputtered, incensed. She'd come in thinking she was in charge. She'd been mistaken. "We're not done here."

"Oh, yes, we—"

The door opened. McAllister stood in the doorway, arms crossed, his black suit immaculate. "This interview is over."

Chapter 21

"THEY HAD ALL my case files dating back to the beginning." Mina paced by McAllister's desk. Lee sat in a chair, and McAllister was in his usual spot. "How did they get a hold of confidential CIU case files if they don't have ties to the committee that runs this agency?"

"I'm trying to uncover that, as well," McAllister said. "It's unclear who they are and where they came from. They completed several DNA swipes to get into the building. Their identities have been verified. But they're not affiliated with any government agency or department that I can see." He glanced down at the superboard in his hands. "Both were previous litigators with private firms, but neither specialized in criminal cases. Dunn practiced real estate law, and Linette specialized in tax evasion. It's not unheard of that a committee would hire litigators to conduct these meetings, but this feels off in a way I can't identify."

"The two who interviewed me were nice enough," Lee

added, "but they were completely inexperienced in federal law. I was able to evade most of their questioning because they didn't understand that what they were asking me to reveal was illegal. Such as what my affiliation was to Jordan Maybach, who's now a protected asset. It was a little strange."

Mina nodded. "They asked me similar questions. They assumed I had informants in the outskirts and was just going to hand over their identities. They had weak intimidation tactics and tried to shame me for doing my job. When that didn't work, they were irritated and surprised. They clearly had no experience doing this kind of investigation, particularly not with a federal agent. They had to have been rounded up, in what, less than a day? I mean, we just ended the Nesbit op yesterday evening. What time did you get the audit order?"

"Midmorning," McAllister replied, his voice clipped. "Normally, I would have asked more probing questions, and something like this would not have gotten by me. Audits, as I said before, were common when I was a young agent. But they're rarer now and usually crop up when a case has gone wrong, not right, usually when the criminal has either escaped, or someone was injured or killed during the arrest. In other words, they investigate cases that were unsuccessful, not cases that were successful." McAllister tapped his fingers on the board, then looked up. "I will be getting to the bottom of this, have no doubt. I've already contacted my committee members. There's a meeting scheduled for tomorrow morning. After they're finished discussing it, they will send me a report. I'll have more information then. As of right now, you're both excused. That should give you an hour or two to get ready for the ceremony tonight."

Mina moved in front of McAllister's desk. "I'd like to accompany Agent Adams to his bank meeting first. Lee is supposed to be moving in the morning and needs to make sure all of his borrows are in order. If we leave right now, we can get there before closing."

"Thanks," Lee said. "But I missed my appointment. It was half an hour ago."

"No, you didn't miss it," Mina contradicted.

"I did—"

"Lee, they want their currency. As long as the bank is still open, they will see you." She nodded at McAllister. "If we discover criminal activity going on"—which was an incredibly high likelihood—"using some persuasion will be necessary to get Lee out of his situation."

McAllister asked, "What exactly did they tell you was the issue, Agent Adams?"

Lee worried his fingers together like he did when he didn't want to talk about something. "That there was some sort of mix-up at the bank. Honestly, I'm not sure. The man I talked to at the Parkay Group, which owns my building, was pretty vague. He was also pretty intense. Told me I had to get my account caught up quickly. Then, when I reached out to my bank, they wouldn't give me the information I asked for over the call. They said I had to come in. I spoke with my mother, and she said everything was supposed to have been taken care of with my dad's death benefits. She didn't have any more information than that. Talking about my father is painful for her, so I didn't press her."

"While I summon a craft," Mina told Lee, "go get a hold of someone at the Parkay Group in charge of your residence and have them meet us at the bank. Then call the bank and tell them you're on your way. Where do you bank?"

"Colossal. Um, my mom said Dad had the best death benefits package at the time." Lee got up from his chair. "What if they refuse to come?"

Mina didn't even feel like rolling her eyes. They weren't even twitchy. She was Lee-teaching. She didn't mind it. "Your landlords want their borrows. And if they want them badly enough, they will meet you at the bank in the next five minutes. Main location. If not, tell them you'll see them in high court. That ought to get their attention."

"Court?" Worry creased his forehead. "Do you think this will go to court?"

Mina settled her hand on Lee's elbow, guiding him to the door. "No. I don't. But there's nothing greedy businessmen dislike more than having to appear in front of a magistrate. If you say 'high court,' they will send someone." She opened the door. "Go give them both a call. I'll be right behind you." As Lee walked out into the hallway, Mina turned back to her director. "I'm not an expert on how death benefits work, but legally the residence group has to give an account record to the resident once or twice a year if there are any issues or oversights. Demanding years of back borrows is illegal.

This smells rotten, which is unsurprising." Way too many people would end up exiled in the outskirts if this happened on a regular basis. "I don't expect either of these individuals to admit willingly to any illegal activity, but we we've both seen this kind of corruption for years. I've personally brought in enough dirty bankers to fill a mag-lev compartment. I'm hoping, with enough persuasion, I can settle this tonight so Lee can attend his ceremony feeling relaxed and excited about his move tomorrow. Death benefits run nine years. Lee's father was murdered when Lee was three, so they would technically be up when he was twelve. But his mother could've delayed them so they would cover Lee when she left him at sixteen. Or thought she did. I'm assuming the transaction was mishandled, which would also point to illegal activity. Either way, these guys are dirty. The best angle may be to go in strong, leave no wiggle room."

Bankers knew how to wiggle. They were masters at it.

McAllister nodded. "I agree. This reads as a standard borrow swindle. While you're in the air, I'll do a Level VI search into it. I'll send whatever I find to your cuff as I receive it. You have my authorization to go in tough and knock them off their guard." It was really the only play with these guys. They were smart and wily. "If we've mistaken this, I'll see to it we make amends. If you can't find an adequate solution by the conclusion of this meeting, let them know that the federal government will be sending a litigator on Agent Adams' behalf to deal with the rest. If they threaten to put a hold or a block on his bank borrows or block his ability to move out of his residence, they will be held in contempt. Read them their rights and let them know that they can and will be held in a box, at our expense, until this case is thoroughly investigated."

Mina was loving the sound of this. She'd figured McAllister would take this route, but had had to be sure before she went in and pulled out her big lasers and swung them around.

"When his mother left him, he was a minor," McAllister went on. "Because of that, he remains covered under the Minor Protection Act of 2085, which was established to protect underage children from unscrupulous borrow reassessment and being kicked out of their homes, for this very reason. Remind them of that."

"I plan to." Mina opened the door. "And thank you. Lee will be grateful. Using your time and departmental resources to do the digging and putting your muscle behind this means a lot. Plus, we get to net a couple of bad guys. I'm certain it will be solved, at least on Lee's end, in less than an hour." If Mina had anything to say about it.

"No need to thank me," McAllister said. "Oh, and, Agent Kane?"

"Yes?" She ducked her head back around the corner.

"Lee is lucky to have you as part of his family now. That is all."

"Loosen up," Mina instructed her partner. "You need to appear relaxed and confident. Your banker was happy to extend this meeting to accommodate you, so that means we're going to get to the bottom of this right now."

Mina had listened in on the call on the flight over, and the banker had been extremely jovial. *Too happy.*

"I don't feel relaxed and confident." Lee frowned.

"You need to act the part." They were midpoint across an enormous lobby at the main branch of Colossal Bank. It was opulent and ornate, a puke-inducing display of greedy borrows gleaned from people who didn't have much to begin with. "You nailed it with Waterbury. This is the same technique. It's an act, so put on your *op mode* face."

"But this is not an op."

"It's likely to turn into one very quickly, in, like, under a minute."

"It is?"

"Yes," Mina confirmed. She hadn't wanted to alarm Lee on the flight over, so he was just getting the high-lights. "McAllister gave me permission to read these guys their rights and let them know we can and will hold them in contempt if we find out they're being unscrupulous. Which, I feel at this point, is almost a certainty. We'll know if this guy's guilty within seconds."

"How will you know—"

"You must be Mr. Adams. I'm Alden Richards." An older gentleman, who had iron-gray hair and augmented enhancements that made his seventysomething visage appear fifty, held out his hand. You could always tell when older people had these specific enhancements, as their skin was now unnaturally smooth. He wore a stylish eurosuit with a crisp white shirt underneath, like most of the other bankers here. "I recognize you from the image in your file, although it was taken many years ago. I'm happy that you could meet today after all." Lee shook his hand. He turned to Mina. "Are you his significant attachment?"

"No," Mina answered, shaking his outstretched hand. "I'm Agent Kane, and I'm here to assist Agent Adams in figuring out why a bank would suddenly demand years of accumulated borrows from him. We're happy you could find the time to meet with us today." She flashed him a wide smile as she popped her badge up on holo. "That will help us along."

The banker immediately became flustered by her credentials, smoothing his shellacked hair back with one hand as he glanced over his shoulder and then toward the door, likely hoping somebody might shuffle through and help him out.

No one was coming.

His body language signaled to Mina everything she needed to know about his motives in this situation. Now she just had to wait for McAllister to send the proof to her cuff. She knew it would come momentarily.

"Please step into my office," Alden offered graciously with a sweep of his arm. "I'm sure we can expedite this issue." The door to his fully enclosed glass cubicle powered open with a touch of his fingertip.

More unnecessary, expensive tech put in place to impress and intimidate.

A *colossal* waste of currency.

Once inside, he strode behind a very sleek desk made out of a single smooth, continuous piece of high-sheen bent metal. Several superboards were seamlessly integrated into the top.

There were two chairs. Mina and Lee sat.

"We'll be needing an extra chair," Mina informed him. "Agent Adams is expecting a representative from his residence ownership group to join us."

Alden cleared his throat, but refrained from coughing into his fist, like Dunn had, while managing to look just as uncomfortable.

"That won't be necessary," Alden replied. "We work very closely with the Parkay Group, which owns the building that, um, Mr.—I mean—Agent Adams occupies. I will inform Mr. Pippen of everything we discuss here today."

So even though Mr. Pippen had assured Lee he would be there, he had not planned to attend. *Interesting.*

Mina checked her cuff. It was time to take this to the next level.

"Judging by your reaction, Mr. Richards, I take it you didn't know that Lee Adams was a federal agent." She sat back in her seat. She was going to enjoy the hell out of this.

It wasn't going to take an hour. If it took even ten minutes, she'd be surprised.

"No, I did not." He addressed Lee. "Congratulations on your new employment. That's very impressive—"

"I mean"—she interrupted to purposefully throw him off—"he basically went from being an orphaned minor to a federal agent in just a few years. Not many people can climb a hill that steep, am I right?" She flashed him another genial smile.

Stuff like this shouldn't be so fun. But it totally was.

Lee glanced at Mina, his eyebrows slightly elevated. He was catching on to the game, but was still worried.

"I've worked very hard to get where I am today," Lee offered, his voice growing stronger as he went on. "I was told by Mr. Pippen, and then it was confirmed by a secretary at the Parkay Group, that I owe years of back borrows on my residence agreement. I don't understand why I wasn't notified before this."

Mina piped in before Alden Richards had a chance to answer. "Just in case you were thinking of lying, don't. Everything you say from this point forward can and will be used against you. I'm happy to read you your rights now, if that would expedite things?"

"No. That won't be necessary." Alden forced a small chuckle that sounded like a dry leaf disintegrating inside his trachea. "I will answer any and all of your questions truthfully."

That remained to be seen.

"We enjoy hearing the truth." Mina smiled. "So the question, just as a quick refresher, is why is Agent Adams being charged for years of back borrows and only now that he's given notice to end his residence contract?

Saying it's an oversight is unacceptable. As you and I and everyone else who works at this bank know, you're required to give borrowers, your valued customers, updated reports on any outstanding payment owed. Banks must do this quarterly, and landlords must do it twice a year. Since you have admitted to having a very close relationship with the Parkay Group, which signals that you are both shared cosigners on the documents that have enabled Agent Adams to live in his residence for the past six years, you are in this together. Agent Adams was under the impression that his father's death benefits were covering his residential fees during this time, which is why he didn't inquire about it. Can you tell us why that doesn't seem to be the case?"

"Certainly." Alden tapped on his superboard. "Just give me one second to pull up Agent Adams' file."

He'd already had the file up, since he'd admitted to recognizing Lee's image and had been waiting for him.

This was one of the easier cases Mina had ever had to solve. This banker had been hoping that a sixteen-year-old out-of-work kid would never amount to anything, and when the time came to cash in on these "late" borrows, Lee wouldn't have a leg to stand on, much less have both legs propped up by the federal government.

"Oh, here it is." Thankfully, he'd located it. "Langley Adams' death benefits were enacted in 2092 when Mrs. Adams submitted her claim." That had been thirteen years ago. "They ran out in 2101." Four years ago.

"They conveniently ran out the year Lee turned eighteen and was no longer a minor," Mina confirmed.

"We had nothing to do with that, I can assure you—"

"You had everything to do with it," Mina refuted. "Have you been Mrs. Adams' banker for long?"

"Well, yes." He trailed his fingertips along his desk, then skittered them to his collar, where he tugged on the curved edge. Must be a little too tight for this conversation. "I was their banker right after Mrs. Adams and Langley Adams entered into a cohabitor agreement. I was the one who wrote it up."

"Then you're the one who Mrs. Adams would've consulted on any major move involving currency or anything else. When did she tell you she'd be leaving the state and setting her only son up with a residence of his own?"

"I don't remember. I'd have to look it up."

"You can just guesstimate for me," Mina encouraged. "Several years before she did it? Or a few months?"

"Again, I am unsure."

"My guess is you had a hand in guiding her from the very beginning, certainly after her husband died. She would've been overwhelmed. From what I understand, she was unsteady and spent time in-residence at a Medi Center after the death of her beloved soul mate." Mina was bummed she had to bring this up in front of Lee, but they needed to finish this. "What you overlooked when you printed up this excrement cake of a scheme with the Parkay Group, hoping to nab Agent Adams with back borrows that would've netted you quite a bit of pocketed interest, is that since all this began when he was a minor, he was and still is protected by law."

"I assure you there was no scheme—"

"Of course there was," Mina challenged. "Don't insult us with things that are so crystalline. What we require from you now is that you zero-out the borrows owed relating to Agent Adams' Parkay Group residence. After that's finished, I want a direct data link authorization sent to my cuff verifying the adjustment to his account."

"I don't have the authority to do such a thing—"

Mina drummed her fingertips along her thigh. "You have the right to procure representation of your choice. You have the right to continue in silence. You have the right—"

"Wait!" Alden lunged up out of his seat. "*Wait.* That won't be necessary." He was breathing heavily. When he realized he was still hunched over his desk, he sat back down, running his fingers along the smooth surface of his desk. He must do that a lot. "I apologize for my outburst. You are correct. We were negligent in not informing Mr.—um, Agent Adams when his father's death benefits had reached their conclusion and that he was responsible for payment of his residence borrows."

Mina nodded along. "Yes, you were. Not doing so is a criminal offense. I believe the box time is one to three years. Not to mention your oversight that Agent Adams is protected by the Minor Protection Act of 2085, which states that anyone under the age of eighteen entering into a binding agreement with a corporation or entity requiring bank borrows and currency fees is not liable for any damages in any legal dispute. Back borrows would be considered damages, particularly when they were *not* reported as required for years on end."

"Yes. You are correct." Of course she was. "That is the law. It was an oversight on our end."

"I already told you that claiming it was an oversight is unacceptable." Mina stood. She took her time pacing behind his desk to peer over his shoulder, glancing down at the superboards. Lee's file was open in front of him. The back borrows balance was astronomical. Mina hoped Lee didn't see it. Having to pay it would have wiped out future credit approvals for him for years. "You screwed up with this one, Mr. Richards. Four years ago, when the death benefits for Langley Adams expired, you should've invited Agent Adams here to renegotiate his residence agreement. At that time, being prone to corruption as you clearly are, you could've found a way to overcharge him and pocket some of the gain. But you didn't. You bet that he wouldn't amount to anything based on the interactions you had with his mother. You waited four years for his borrows to accumulate so you could take advantage of him, knowing that when the time came, he wouldn't have the funds to hire a litigator. And if he tried to fight back, you would simply shut down his account, leaving your client without a bank, borrows, or any means of regaining them. As federal agents, we know you bankers all talk to each other. Particularly individuals from big banks who are usually the most corrupt and take the most pleasure in blacklisting innocent people." He began to sputter. "Did you know that at least half of our cases involve bankers?" She was stretching, but they did investigate *a lot* of banks and bankers. Way too many. "You could say federal boxes are literally *buzzing* with bankers. The only thing left now is to make this right." She startled him by leaning over and speaking into his ear. He jumped like she'd tasered him. "Or we take you in right now. I'm more than happy to finish reading you your rights."

"I... I...can erase the borrows. Just give me a second." He began to tap on the board.

Mina crossed her arms and took a step back, still keeping her eye on what he was doing. "When you're finished, I want the remainder of Agent Adams' positive borrows to be transferred into this government account." Mina tapped her cuff, gathering the information that McAllister had sent. As her airmeld connection reached out to meet the banker's connection, a soft beep sounded, signaling the two had linked. "Send a data link confirmation to the same address. And just so everyone in this room is clear, a federal litigator, as well as one of our accountants, will be contacting you to go over all of Agent Adams' records to make sure every last borrow has been transferred. If anything, and I mean anything, is out of line, you will be taken in for questioning. Do you understand?"

"Yes. It's done." Alden's voice held more than a tremor. His fear had become bone-deep. Poor man. He knew a federal inquiry was going to turn up things he didn't want anybody to see. "And there's no need for anyone to go over this. I'm sending the confirmation to your cuff right now, as well as transferring all of his borrows to the Government Currency and Handling branch of Genesis Bank."

The government dealt with its own borrows for its employees. But employees had to opt in. Lee was so new that he hadn't yet and likely hadn't been properly advised. Everything involving government bureaucracy took time, including having a counselor go over bank account options with new employees.

Mina walked back around the desk, satisfied.

She gave Lee a quick nod. He scrambled out of his seat. He looked dazed, but also incredibly happy and relieved. Just as Mina had hoped.

At the door, Mina turned. "Let Mr. Pippen know a litigator will be knocking on his door next. Unfortunately for you, you chose the wrong target. But don't worry, I'm certain your box time will pass quickly."

Chapter 22

"THAT WAS...COMPLETELY amazing." Lee's mouth was gaping, and he wouldn't stop staring at her. "I've never seen anyone do anything like that before. You had him backed into a corner before he knew who he was dealing with. It was masterful."

"Gee, thanks, Lee," Mina said, tapping her cuff to summon them a ride. "But it wasn't as masterful as you think. What they did to you was highly illegal. I just expedited a process that might've taken someone else a week to deal with. You never want to give these guys the upper hand or too much time. With time, they can gather confidence, cover their tracks, bunch up their resources, and make it harder to get the end result you deserve."

"I knew what they were doing was wrong," Lee said, shaking his head. "But they made me feel like I was the bad guy for thinking that what they were doing was illegal."

"That's exactly how they get away with it." They

headed out of the bank and began walking down the street. "Once Alden gets his wits about him, he's going to be angry we bested him, and he'll use whatever resources he has, which are considerable, to fight this in court. They're masters at evading the law. It's what gives them confidence to continue to conduct their criminal activity. That guy's probably been successfully chiseling people out of interest and pocketing it for fifty years. They've got back deals with residency groups all over the city and beyond. And that's just one of their schemes. The corruption is vast and varied. But it won't work out for him this time. He's a lock."

"A lock? Are you sure?" Lee asked as he hurried to keep up with Mina.

"Yes. McAllister accessed your account during a quick Level VI search, and immediately obtained a warrant. It went through instantly. As we speak, all Mr. Richards' files are being uploaded, without his knowledge, to a secure government server. What they find in there will probably box him up for three to five, maybe longer. That's my guess, anyway."

"Wow." Lee was incredulous.

Mina chuckled. "I didn't have time to brief you on everything as it was happening. McAllister sent through the confirmation he was dirty right as we sat down."

"They wouldn't even let me *see* my account when I requested to go over it this morning."

"Of course they didn't. Once they alerted you to their scheme, they weren't going to let you view it. However, you being the industrious hacker you are, you would've accessed it in time. Instead, McAllister did it for you. He sent the information to my cuff, and I had it scrolling the entire time. I couldn't catch everything, but I got the main bits and knew he was dirty."

"You know"—Lee was wistful—"you're what I aspire to become. Confident, self-assured, and intimidating when necessary."

"You'll get there," she assured him. "In less time than you think. Some of it is knowledge, some of it is intelligence, which you have a great deal of. But the greater portion is confidence. At no time in that office did Alden Richards think I didn't know what I was talking about. Even when I wasn't sure, I acted like I was. It makes all the difference." Mina clapped him on the back. "It just takes time to build up that level of confidence. You have great instincts, Lee. Not everyone does."

"Thanks."

"You were in the zone with Waterbury today. He shouldn't have given you his address, especially when he was harboring Norm, but you made him trust you. You convinced him you were telling him the truth."

"Like you did with Mr. Richards."

"Kind of the same, but I *was* telling the truth. What you did with Waterbury was something else. You finessed him. You fed him tone and emotion that he related to. There's a difference. You played your part convincingly. You believed it. He believed it. That's what counts. Trust your instincts. We won't have all the details every time we engage with a perpetrator. You simply use what you have in front of you to get the job done."

As they approached the landing pad, a government drone dropped out of the sky, setting down. They boarded.

"What is your destination, please?" the sim asked.

Mina gave the address by Lee's residence, and the sim confirmed travel time.

"Your big recognition ceremony starts"—Mina glanced at her cuff—"in less than ninety minutes. That's pretty exciting. It's going to be a big night."

"Yeah, I guess."

The drone rose into the sky.

"Aren't you looking forward to it?"

"I am," Lee said. "It's an honor. I'm just…"

She waited for him to get his thoughts in order.

"I'm a little nervous," Lee admitted. "I've been kind of by myself, doing my own thing, for so long, this doesn't feel real. Being on the hacker boards every day is a lot different. Now, all of a sudden, all this stuff is happening. I'm still trying to process it. What am I supposed to wear tonight? Do I pick up Harmony? Do I have to make some kind of speech?" His face flashed panic for a quick second. "It's overwhelming."

"I get that," Mina said, conveying her sincerity. "I really do. I'm sorry I didn't realize you were feeling over-whelmed. I should have."

Lee looked shocked. "Why would you?"

"Because I read people for a living. But I'm here to help. That's what I do now." Mina chuckled. "First of all, wear something a step up from casual. It doesn't have to be flashy, but a nice pair of pants and an upscale shirt. If you don't have anything like that, I'm sure Jeni Crisfold could get you in. I can make some calls on your behalf."

"No, that's okay. I have something that will work," Lee replied. "There's a memorial for my dad every year. I've been wearing the same outfit for a while, but it's nice enough."

Mina nodded, sad that Lee would have to wear his mourning outfit. It was an oversight not to have asked him about this earlier. But it would do for tonight.

"After you get settled into your new high-rise, you should make an appointment with Jeni to get a few new permanent pieces for your wardrobe. Now that you have an influx of credit and a steady borrow line from this job, it's important to have options for whatever case we're called in on. Sometimes you have to get new things printed, like I did on the gardening job. After a while, you'll have a bunch to choose from in your closet. It's kind of fun."

"That will be nice." Lee nodded.

"As for Harmony, once you get home, tag her. Ask her what she wants to do." Mina had to do the same thing with Vince. She had to admit she fully regretted asking him to the ceremony. She didn't want this night to turn into a hassle. It was Lee's night. "Harmony will have no problem letting you know what she wants to do. Since you're going as friends, meeting her there might be the easiest. But I have a feeling Harmony will make the decision for you."

"Okay."

"As for a speech, there's no pressure to perform. The entire thing is pretty low-key. McAllister will get up and say a few words about why you're getting the commendation. People will clap. You're presented with the commendation. Then you can simply say, 'Thank you.' If you're moved to say something more, you can. But it's not required. I think on the whole, agents are just happy to be out doing something for the evening. Our last few cases have been pretty extreme. That's not typical for this agency. We take out corruption for a living, but we usually play a smaller role in other departments' cases." She smiled. "This is really great, Lee. You deserve it. Going up against Tedesco was a big deal for a rookie. And hey, after tonight the term 'rookie' will not apply to you. You'll be a full-fledged federal agent with a commendation."

"Thank you." Lee flashed a tentative grin. "Honestly, thank you for everything. This has been the greatest gift for me. And you're really good at teaching. I'm learning an incredible amount."

That hadn't been Mina's strong suit up until now. She felt a little shame creeping in as she thought back to how she'd iced out Lee on their first op together.

She couldn't make a trip back in time, so moving forward she had to ensure she did everything in her power to make him the best agent he could be.

"Setting down in thirty seconds," the sim announced.

"I'm the lucky one," she told him. "Having you by my side makes me a better agent. In this job, you never stop learning. You're teaching me as much as I'm teaching you."

Lee blinked and turned away.

She gave him a moment.

The drone set down, the door rising. Lee exited.

"The main thing about tonight is to have fun," Mina called. "I'll see you in a few."

Lee turned and gave her a three-finger salute, grinning.

***

"You're not dressed yet," Kaylee helpfully pointed out from Mina's sleep room wall. "The fun starts in T-minus forty-five minutes. How do I look in this?" Kaylee twirled around, showing off her lavender minidress covered in sparkles. She looked amazing, as usual. Her hair was in an updo, and her lips and nails matched her dress, as did the careful application of color around her eyes.

"Fantastic," Mina said. "You always look like a vid star. No, wait, now that we've met one, you look *better* than a vid star."

Kaylee snorted. She stopped midtwirl, bending over to take a closer look at the screen.

"What's up? I already sent you a report about what happened at the Meridian. I think we found a way to fool Waterbury into thinking Norm escaped on his own— well, Vince found a way. That sad puppy is highly intelligent. We won't know until the perp gets out and checks on things tomorrow. I also called in to see how Norm was doing, knowing you were tied up in that black-hole-sucking audit, and he's great. Full recovery expected. He going to be released soonish. By the way, how did things go with the aforementioned sucky audit?

Certainly looks like they audited all the fun out of you."

Mina ran a hand through her hair, blowing out a breath as she flopped onto her platform, landing on her back, arms splayed. "There's a high probably that this wasn't a formal audit. Seems like you were right, and someone at the top is nervous that we're bringing down too many top-level criminals. McAllister is checking it out."

"Huh. Not unexpected. Crime reaches all levels, including the very tippity top. I mean, overall, ordering a fake audit was a stupid thing to do. They'll probably end up exposing themselves in all the wrong ways. Then we can figure out what they've done wrong and box 'em up tight."

"Yeah, I can see that happening."

"Okay, you're starting to freak me out. What's going on? What am I missing? You saved a guy who's like family today, you cracked the audit case, your super-smart hacker-geek-cutie-pie-rookie is getting an award, and we get to attend a fun party. Why do you look like you have an appointment to clean out a grinder filter and go to sleep hungry?"

Mina struggled up on her elbows. "I'm going to cancel tonight with Vince. I'm not looking forward to telling him. I must've been temporarily out of my mind when I asked him to come with me. Can you do it for me? He'll take it easier if he hears it from you."

Kaylee's growl was mixed with a huff. "Like hell he will. And I don't need to, because you're not canceling."

"Yes, I am."

"No, you're not. And here's why." Kaylee settled her hands on her hips, her face stern. It was a good rendition of her *don't mess with me* look. "You want this, he wants this, you're doing this. That's all there is to it."

Mina leaped up out of her platform, which meant she rolled out, but she could do it much easier now because she'd raised the interior with help from her best pal, who was now clucking at her from her wall screen.

She began to pace. "I can't do this. I can't lead him on. There's no hope for this to develop into any kind of relationship. I'm a *secret* agent. I rely on *not* being picked out of a crowd. I want my face to remain going unnoticed. Secret agents can't have relationships with high-level, completely recognizable, known-around-the-globe-and-beyond colonels from France. There's no place for this to go. It's been fun reconnecting with him. He's a great guy. But going out tonight is a *date*. We can't have dates. We can only meet up as friends once in a while. That's it."

"Says who?"

Mina lofted her arms toward the ceiling with dramatic flair. "Says *everyone*. How in the world can I have a relationship with someone who's so easily identifiable? So for the rest of our lives together, we have to go out in disguise? That's crazy! I *love* my job. I plan to keep it. Dating the colonel-in-arms of the French Protectorate is not a way to do that."

"You just have to think out of the box."

"This isn't an in- or out-of-the-box situation. This is me being realistic. Whoever dates or enters into a cohabitor agreement with Vincent Kramer will be flashed around every media outlet across the globe." Mina winced as she thought about who that might turn out to be, since it wasn't going to be her. "If my face is flashed around, I cannot do my job. You know how this works. We pretend to be other people for a living. Sometimes we're required to wear moderate or semiperm alts. And the reason I had a semiperm in the first place is that I'd been seen out with Vincent Kramer. Are you telling me to throw away my career for a guy?"

"No," Kaylee huffed. "I just know you can have it both ways."

"How so?"

Kaylee stamped her foot. "I don't know. I just know."

Mina shook her head sadly. "There isn't a way. I've been going over and over it in my mind. The only solution is to stay friends. Staying friends means not going on dates."

"How about just this once?" Kaylee countered. "You're going to an event that is completely cloaked. Most of the people who are attending already know that you and Vince are intertwined. There won't be any talk, no media coverage. How about just enjoy this one night together? Have fun. Lose yourself in it. Then you have something to take with you in the future when you need it."

"What do you mean intertwined? And that's not exactly fair to Vince." He'd been clear about the fact that he wanted more.

"Well, he's been involved in your last few cases. There were enough witnesses on that marshmallow boat to see how he feels about you. People talk." She shrugged. "And it's perfectly fair to Vince. The man has a brilliant mind. He understands how the world works. He understands that if you have a relationship, it will jeopardize your career. You canceling tonight will not convey anything he doesn't already know. And honestly, you might not ever get a chance to see how it feels to be on a date with this man who so clearly is absolutely craze-craters about you. My advice, enjoy it. Revel in it. Then, if it doesn't work out for all those reasons you've already stated, tuck it away."

Mina knew what *tuck it away* meant.

There would be times in the foreseeable future where she would want to reflect on this memory. It would sustain her, at least somewhat, in the sad moments when she might've wished things had gone a different way.

"Fine. I'll go. With him. On a date. But this doesn't change anything. And I know you." Mina scrutinized her friend, moving closer. "This is not going to sway me, and it's not going to change anything."

"Whatever you say." Kaylee chuckled. "So whatcha going to wear? Let's blow this thing out of the water."

Chapter 23

"YOU LOOK BEAUTIFUL," Vince murmured as she boarded the craft.

"Thank you," Mina replied. They'd decided it would be better if Vince picked her up and remained inside the craft so no one would see him. Kaylee had decided that Mina would wear her black sheath dress with silver accents, because, as her friend had put it, *It's your mega la-la dress, and you need some mega la-la tonight.*

She wore her hair long and loose. Actual enhancements had been applied to her face. There weren't very many, but her already long eyelashes had been darkened. She'd accented her eyes, added lip cream, but stopped at the hyperglo. That stuff took too much time to get off.

"You don't look too bad yourself." Mina settled in opposite him. The drone door closed.

"I figured wearing my uniform would be too much. So you'll have to settle for basic Vince." He flashed her a wide smile.

"Well, basic Vince looks just as good as Colonel Kramer."

That was an understatement.

Vince looked as good in his black eurocollared suit as he did in his uniform any day.

"I'm glad you think so."

Mina shifted in her seat uncomfortably. Even though she'd agreed to go on this date, she wasn't feeling entirely great about her choice. She wasn't looking forward to hurting Vince in any way.

"Your destination is Government Four, roof landing. Do you wish to make any changes?" the sim asked.

"No," Vince said.

"Travel time one minute, seventeen seconds."

"Kaylee filled me in on what happened at the Meridian," Mina said, feeling more comfortable talking about work stuff than personal stuff. "She said you came up with something that might fool Waterbury into thinking Norm escaped on his own. That was a pretty big ask. That's impressive. I hope it happens."

"I can't take all the credit for that," he said. "If Harmony wasn't so ridiculously talented, we couldn't have pulled it off. We had no way of getting vid of him leaving the residence, so I had an idea of making our own vid. Kaylee had the marshals in charge of Norm take some images of him before he was out of his clothing. Then Harmony was able to take those images and animate them, using a program she came up with herself. She included interior shots of the residence from the internal cams, then pieced it together. It took her less than thirty minutes. She's astounding. Then she fed it into Waterbury's vid system at the right time slots, replacing the still images the cameras had taken. She even added audio for the sim to catch. It's not going to play back extremely smoothly. Waterbury will understand that something has happened. He'll see the evidence, but might question whether or not the vid was real or tampered with. That's fine. It will remain a mystery, but hopefully, he won't think anyone went to the extent we did to make it appear like Norm escaped on his own." He shrugged. "It has as good of a chance of working as any we had. Either way, Waterbury is going to be extremely pissed off. That will work to our advantage. I've been thinking about ways we can have Norm lure him in—"

Mina cleared her throat. "We'll have to wait and see what McAllister says. Now that Norm is no longer missing, the op could change significantly. If there's threat of blowback from the Syndicate, precautions will have to be taken. It's going to take time to formulate an appropriate plan."

"Yes, of course." He smiled, a little shyly this time. "I certainly don't intend to take over your case. I'm happy you included me in the first place. Doing media all day every day has taken a toll on my brain. It was nice not to have to think about it for a while."

"What did you end up telling Ambrose's guardsmen?"

"That my friend was in trouble, and I helped him get to a medi-unit. That was enough for now, particularly since this won't be breaking anywhere in the media."

Mina was extremely relieved about that. "There's no

way Waterbury is calling anybody but his friends and bosses in the Syndicate. There won't be a whiff anywhere else."

Their gazes locked for a few heartbeats.

Mina gulped.

She finally looked away.

"Mina, I—"

"It's a good thing—"

They both laughed.

Mina desperately tried to relax. She was ridiculously tense. It would probably be better if she just told Vince how she was feeling. It was just hard finding the right words.

Surprising her, Vince leaned over and grabbed both of her hands, scooting forward on his seat. "I know what you're thinking."

"You do?"

"Yes. Because the same thing is running through my mind." His voice was earnest, soothing in its intensity. "Us being together would be very difficult. In a sane world, it would be the insane choice. What you do for a living needs to be kept carefully under the radar. What I do is at meso level, so high above it can be seen from space. Literally. They tell me my image is beamed into the space station science colonies on a regular basis." He blew out a breath. "All I'm asking is for a chance. Just to try it. I have no magical fixes. No answers to all the questions that are pinging around in both of our minds right now. Life together would be difficult—if not impossible—out in public. But I'm hoping you give me a chance—*us* a chance. I've loved you since I was a little boy. Those feelings weren't romantic then, but they were as close as you could possibly get. I'm not a little boy anymore." His eyes smoldered, making her instantly feel hot and tingly. "The love I felt for you then has never evaporated. It's even stronger now. The woman you've turned into is beyond amazing. She blows me away. Just like she did when we were kids. I feel lucky to know you. Just one chance." He held up a finger, letting go of one of her hands. "Let's agree to give it a try to see if maybe—*just maybe*—we can figure something out. If we don't, that's okay. I'll feel better knowing that at least we tried."

"Vince, I—"

"Please, Mina. No promises. No expectations. We just get to know each other again as adults, enjoy each other's company, and see what happens. We deal with the day-to-day as it comes. Nothing more than that."

"Landing at Government Four in thirty seconds," the sim intoned.

She closed her eyes, trying to steady herself.

"Okay." She opened her eyes. "But we have to take it slow. No rushing. I can't seem to get my emotions in order when it comes to you. I'm not sure if they're tied up with feelings of friendship and love I had for you when we were younger, versus new feelings I have now. Because of that, I believe it means we should give it a try. But I'm going to hold you to no promises. I don't want you to feel like I'm leading you on, and if I decide to call it off, I don't want you to be angry with me. There's a very high likelihood you and I won't work out. We have so many things going against us. Not to mention you live in another country."

"A country that's much less media-conscious and easier to get lost in. A country that takes less than three hours to get to." Something flittered across his face Mina couldn't name. Uncertainty? The craft landed, and the door of the drone rose. He disembarked first, reaching back to grab her hand as she stepped out. "Let's make a deal with each other for tonight, at least. It's an evening to enjoy and hold on to."

She smiled. "Have you been talking to Kaylee?"

"She's a smart woman."

Mina swiped into the sky screen entrance. Vince had been cleared by Mina's director, so his skin scrape passed with no issues. They boarded a tube that would take them directly to the entrance of the Gala Room, which took up an entire floor.

The ride would be brief.

Mina began to feel anxiety creep back. She was second-guessing herself once again. Was this just going to lead to inescapable heartache? Did she want to go through that?

Startled, she felt Vince's arm encircle her shoulders. She tilted her head up, and he gave her a sweet smile, his eyes twinkling.

He leaned over and whispered, "It's going to be okay."

The tube door whooshed open.

He let go of her.

They walked out. The mood was festive, the ultras dim, lots of people already mingling. Upbeat music was playing. Lights from the city and beyond twinkled beyond the enormous windows every direction you looked.

Mina spotted Kaylee by the bar. "Do you want a drink?"

"Sure," he replied.

They headed toward the bar. Vince settled his hand on the small of her back, guiding her, nodding and saying hello to people as they passed.

She didn't hate it.

Even though she felt like the agents were showing them way more attention than they needed to, having him next to her actually made her feel calmer and somewhat invincible. That was weird. But not unwelcome.

Kaylee squealed when she saw them, clapping her hands. "Well, don't you dress up nice?" She play-slapped the agent standing next to her with the back of her hand. "Doesn't she dress up nice?"

Agent Wentworth nodded. "Yes, she does indeed. Hello, Agent Kane, Colonel Kramer."

Mina nodded a hello. When she got close enough, Kaylee embraced her, whispering, "I almost thought you'd be a no-show. Glad you made it. Sad puppy looks like a happy marmot. So that's good anyway." She pulled back. "What would you two like to drink? Since the federal government is picking up the tab, might I suggest something frothy and bubbly with lots of alcohol?"

Mina chuckled. "Anything is fine. I'll have whatever you're having." She looked to Vince. "What would you like?"

"I'm easy. How about a bottle of champagne?" He

smirked at Mina's surprised expression, winking. "Only joking. Any rye over ice is fine."

Kaylee put the orders in with the air breather tending the bar, then grabbed Mina's hand. "I saved us a booth near the stage. I thought a booth would be less conspicuous for your super-shiny date. Agents don't talk, but we can gawk." She pulled Mina forward, stopping in front of a semicircle with broad gel-cush seats in soft, velvety gold. "Have a seat. I'm dateless for the evening. Go figure. I'm going to go let McAllister know you're here. He didn't want to start before you showed. Then I'm going to grab Harmony. She's been chatting it up with just about every agent on the floor. She's sopping up all she can get. If I don't stop her pretty soon, her brain is going to inflate to an unmanageable size." Kaylee arced both hands around her head. "Then she won't have any room left in there for the real knowledge I plan to stuff in there."

"Where's Lee?" Mina asked.

Kaylee glanced around. "I'm not sure. He was here a second ago." She shrugged. "He'll turn up. I'm going to go grab the drinks and my super-rookie. I'll be right back."

Before Mina could check to see if Vince had followed her, he leaned in and said, "Go find him. Give him my best. I'm sure he's nervous."

Mina gave him a long look. "You have to stop doing that."

"What?"

"Knowing what I'm going to say before I say it."

Vince laughed. It was full-throated. It sounded like heaven. "I can't help it. I know your tells."

"I don't have tells."

"You do for me." He brought his finger up to her temple, then slowly dragged it down to her chin, his eyes focused on her lips. "And I enjoy them very much." His fingers lingered for a second or two.

Mina's mouth fell open a little, and she maybe forgot to breathe for a second.

She recovered quickly, or so she'd like to think. Time was now an abstract concept. They could've been standing there for a minute, or eight years. She had no idea what was going on anymore.

"I'll be back in a second." She darted off, enjoying the low, raspy sounds coming from behind her.

Since he could read her tells so easily, she felt a soft blush flare across her cheeks. What she'd been thinking as he'd been stroking her face and staring at her lips hadn't been for a general audience. Even the audience it was meant for would blush. She had to get her head in the game. This was Lee's night.

"Agent Kane, glad you're here," McAllister said as he strode toward her.

"Sorry I'm late," she said. "I encountered a few... issues." Mostly emotional, but she would leave it there. "I'm looking for Lee. Have you seen him?"

"Yes, I just briefed him. He's in the adjoining room on the left. I'm sure he'd appreciate a few words of encouragement from his partner."

"Is he holding up okay?" she asked.

"He is. A bit overwhelmed still, but that's to be expected. My belief is that he is struggling with his self-worth. It will take some time for him to adjust to the fact that he's contributing to this department and making a difference. Events like tonight will help validate that aspect. After you speak with him, bring him out, and we'll start the ceremony. It will be brief."

She had one more thing to ask her director. "Is it okay that I brought Vincent Kramer tonight? I'm feeling like it might be too much exposure, and it was a mistake."

He assessed her for a second before answering. "Agent Kane, my advice to you is this—live your life. Being in a relationship with the colonel-in-arms of the French Protectorate will bring its own issues, but you're both intelligent adults." He was kindly leaving out the fact that Mina had made a mess of her first outing with Vince. "I expect you, as one of my best agents, to keep this relationship undercover for the time being. But the good news is you're talented in that regard and work undercover for a living, so it won't be that much of a stretch." He gave her a nod. "Enjoy your evening."

She watched him walk away.

For the time being?

That was something to chew on.

Would there ever be a time when she could be in an open relationship with such a public persona? Best not to worry about it right now. After all, she'd just promised Vince she would give it a chance.

Now she had to find Lee.

Chapter 24

"HEY THERE," MINA said as she walked into the annex room. It was tastefully decorated just like the rest of the Gala Room, with a table and two chairs, a small lounger, and a few decorative lamps. This was where people prepared speeches, got ready for events, or took private calls. "Are you ready?"

Lee glanced up from his seat at the table. His hair was nicely ordered, his outfit suitable for the evening—a black eurocollared button-up with basic black tuck pants. His shoes had been glossed.

"I think so."

Mina moved closer. "Any reason you're hiding out in here?"

"I was just taking a few minutes to get my mind set and give thanks for everything that's happened in my life."

That was a nice sentiment. "I just spoke with McAllister. He's not going to drag this on. He'll say a few words, pin the commendation on you, and that's it. Whenever you're ready, we can head out."

Lee stood. "I'm ready." He flashed Mina a smile. He looked more sure of himself than he had in the craft. She felt relieved. "Thanks for coming to find me."

"You're my partner. What else would I do?"

"I keep asking myself how I got so lucky." They made their way toward the door. "For so many years, I felt unlucky. I lost my father, then my mother. Now it's turned around. It's kind of hard to believe."

"It was a very sudden change in your life. It's going to take time to get your head around it," Mina said. "It's natural for you to feel unsure."

"It's like Mr. Richards thought today," Lee said. "I shouldn't have amounted to anything worthwhile, and here I am, a federal agent getting a commendation."

Mina stopped at the doorway, settling her hand on his forearm. "What Mr. Richards thinks does not resemble any kind of normal reality. He's a con artist who takes pleasure in ripping off the vulnerable. Plenty of people work hard, and that hard work pays off. Look at Harmony. She was in the same place you were just a few days ago. It happens all the time. You can't let that criminal skew the view of what the world is really like. Hard work and talent elevate many. You're an amazing agent. Tonight, you lose your rookie title. You earned it. And you're only twenty-two, which is incredible. I didn't get my first commendation until I was three years in. You've managed to get it done in half that time."

They exited the room.

Chatter had fallen away. People had taken their seats. Mina and Lee stood in the back as McAllister took the stage, ultras beaming down, highlighting their director, making him look regal. He spotted them in the back and inclined his head before starting his speech.

"Tonight, we gather to honor one of our fellow agents, a new recruit hired into the agency a year and a half ago. He was *recruited* because of his exceptional hacking skills, but has proven to have much more than high-speed computer efficiency zinging around inside his brain." Low laughter rolled through the audience.

Recruit was a universal term reserved mostly for hackers. When they were arrested, they were given a choice between the box or a job. It was always their first offense, and whatever they'd been caught for was innocuous. Mina hadn't looked into Lee's case file, but she assumed that it'd been a low-level offense.

"We're honoring him for his intelligence, quick thinking, and bravery while bringing down Franco Tedesco the Third, head of the Planet's Most Wanted serial-killing ring, Veritus." Rampant applause. Hoots and foot stomps. Agents could go their whole career and never participate in a case that big, much less have a chance to solve it. "Agent Lee Adams not only kept calm in the face of a direct threat to his own life, he was able to build a complicated pixel mirror to expose incriminating files that were necessary for a conviction, as well as disable security protocols inside Tedesco's residence that would've killed myself and dozens of other agents if enacted, which Tedesco tried to do."

Mina had suspected Tedesco had gone that route, but she hadn't heard the final on that. It seemed Tedesco, after he killed his son, had been willing to die and take as many agents as he could with him. His final act of glory.

"That, in and of itself, deserves this commendation. But he managed to do it all, which is why I'm presenting Agent Adams tonight with the Gold Standard."

Another agent delivered a small, sleek, black box to McAllister. There were lots of *oohs* and *ahhs*, as well as enthusiastic clapping.

"Wow, Lee." Mina leaned over, whispering, "That's incredible. Gold Standard is the highest commendation you can get, and I believe it comes with an increased borrow account. Congratulations." That meant Lee was getting a pay raise. When he didn't respond, Mina settled a hand on his shoulder. "You can do this. Everything the director just said is absolutely true. You did all that. You deserve this."

"I know." Lee's voice broke. "I just... I wish both my parents were here to see it." Before Mina could respond, he turned to her. "But I'm glad you are. It wouldn't be the same if you weren't. I mean, I'm only here because of you."

Before Mina could correct him, McAllister announced, "Agent Adams, please come forward and join me on the stage."

Surprising Mina, Lee turned and embraced her. He whispered, "Thank you for everything."

Lee broke away and wove his way through the tables.

As he passed, agents stood, continuing to clap.

Mina headed toward the booth where Vince, Kaylee, and Harmony were sitting. She slid in next to Vince as Lee stepped onstage, taking his place next to McAllister. Vince's hand found hers under the table. He gave it an encouraging squeeze, then continued to hold it.

Kaylee flashed her a smile and held up a drink in a mock toast.

Mina grabbed hers and did the same.

"Isn't he spectacular?" Harmony hissed in the quietest whisper she could manage, which was more of a yell. "So. Damn. *Incredible.* He looks cute up there, too. Like a deer about to be shot between the eyes by a guy holding a double-barrel laser."

"Shush, you," Kaylee murmured, holding back a laugh. "Look, McAllister's pinning it on him." Kaylee cupped her hands around her mouth and shouted, "Go, Lee!" Then she turned toward Mina, excitement sparkling, fueled by the cocktails. "That's our Hacker-Lee right there." She gestured toward the stage. "The Wrong Lee turned out to be The Right Lee. One thousand percent. Our Babe-*Lee* is all grown up. Brings a tear to the eye." She mocked swiping away tears.

Mina chuckled, turning her attention to her partner, who had managed to mostly keep his emotions in check. His face was serene as he stepped forward and cleared his throat.

Vince squeezed Mina's hand. She squeezed his back.

"Ah, I'd like to say a few words," Lee started. He took a moment to gather himself. "First of all, I'd like to thank Director Duncan McAllister for giving me this incredible opportunity. He took a young, inexperienced hacker who broke the law and gave him a shot at becoming something more. I will be forever humbled and grateful for that. It's changed my life forever." His head bobbed toward the floor. Mina tried to will him strength to keep going. He glanced up. "I'm not sure how many of you know this, but Veritus killed my father nineteen years ago." Quiet murmurs erupted. Most of the agents hadn't known. "They took him from me and made his death horrible and painful." Lee grasped his hands together, his head bobbing. "All I have left are a few old vids and fragments of memories pieced together in my mind. He loved bacon." Laughter and some claps. Mina knew that for a fact. Lee glanced up. "I loved him. So much. When I was a child, he was my whole world. He would've been very proud of me today."

Mina held her breath, overcome with emotion for Lee and all he'd been through. The room was completely rapt. No one spoke. Mina hardly noticed when Vince let go of her hand and wrapped his arm around her, pulling her close. She leaned into the comfort automatically.

"Because of my connection to Veritus, I wouldn't have been able to succeed in this mission without the aid and guidance of my incredible partner, Agent Mina Kane." Clapping, along with a few cackles and shouts aimed her way. "When I found out moments before I was due on the scene to take the place of the superhacker Jordan Maybach that I was actually going to confront my father's killer, I could've easily compromised the entire operation. Doing so would've risked so much. Too much. People would've died. But Agent Kane believed in me. She knew I could do it, even when I didn't." He glanced around the room, finding Mina, inclining his head. "You stayed with me. You were my constant. You encouraged my every move. You counseled me, led the way, adding a few choice words in my ear"—more laughter—"and you wouldn't allow me to make a single wrong decision. Without you, there's a high likelihood I would've failed, and doing so would've jeopardized more lives at the hands of evil killers. So in my mind, we share this commendation." He smiled. Mina smiled. "Just so you know, you're more than a mentor to me. You're a gifted agent who's fantastic at her job. You have incredible instincts." Snickering and hoots from the audience. "Not only that, you're a compassionate and caring partner. With you by my side, I know I can become the agent I'm meant to be. Thank you for taking a chance on me. I will never forget it." He turned back to the audience. "Thank you, everyone."

The room erupted as agents jumped from their seats, clapping wildly. It'd been a heartfelt, emotional speech. Maybe the best Mina had ever heard an agent give. She wiped away a stray tear as she slid out of the booth, clapping for her partner. No longer a rookie.

Lee was the real deal.

McAllister stepped back onto the stage. "That concludes the ceremony portion of the evening. Meals will be served next. Enjoy yourselves. Congratulations, Agent Adams. It's a pleasure to have such an asset serving on our team."

Lee made his way toward their booth, smiling broadly, looking extremely relieved. He reached out to shake Mina's hand, and she brought him in for a quick hug, patting his back. "Nicely done, Agent Adams. Nicely done."

"Thanks," he replied shyly.

Harmony made room for Lee on the other side of the booth next to her. "Sit down, Karmaseeker. You've earned it. I brought over your drink."

Lee sat. His eyes were slightly owlish as he glanced around. "I... I didn't know I was going to say that beforehand, but it's all true. Thank you for believing in me. I really appreciate it."

"And here I thought I was the only gifted mentor in this damn room," Kaylee snarked. "Now I have to compete with *that.*" She swirled her palm in Mina's direction. "Lee just made you a legend, by the way. Greatest mentor of all time right there. I'm calling you G-MENT from now on. That's your new nickname. Live with it."

"Oh, please. That's a terrible nickname." Mina laughed. "When Harmony gets her commendation, she'll bring the house down. Then you'll be crowned the greatest. That is, until somebody else unseats you."

"Never," Kaylee said, taking a sip of her drink. "I'll be keeping that mantle, thank you very much. G-MENT times infinity."

Two agents came up to the table, Weston and Bryant. They held their hands out to Lee, then to Mina, offering words of encouragement to Lee and praising them both.

It continued like that for the next thirty minutes.

The last agent to come to their table was Agent Darian.

She reached out her hand to Lee. "Congratulations, Agent Adams. I was able to see your work firsthand, and you were absolutely amazing. Calm and cool under pressure, thoughtful and intelligent. Brilliant at code. And you're right, having a partner like Agent Kane is an amazing gift." She turned to Mina and held out her hand. "Job well done. As always, it's a pleasure to watch you work. I wish you both the very best. Enjoy your evening."

Once she departed, Mina turned to Kaylee. "We need to find Anna a mentor."

"Who's Anna?" Kaylee asked.

"Agent Darian. Her first name is Anna. She's been with the agency for four years. McAllister has offered her solo time in the field, but she always turns him down. She told me this morning if she had a mentor like me, she'd consider it. I believe she'd be an asset in the field. She's always on top of it when we work together. She has great instincts."

"Four years? Are you sure?" Kaylee glanced across the room. "That's such a long time to be at headquarters. Unless, of course, that's your vibe. Maybe that's her vibe?"

Mina shook her head. "I don't think so. She's just fearful of making wrong decisions and needs some solid confidence boosting."

"All right. Fine," Kaylee said. "Add it to the list. But for now, we're toasting Lee. And this calls for a song." Kaylee started to sway in her seat, one hand striking a beat on the table. Harmony joined with both hands. "Agent Lee's no longer a rook-*ee*, but he won't be fighting crime ind-*ee*-pendent-*lee*. His partner's smart, she's G-MENTal-*ee*. So full of *charm*, she'll do you some *harm*—"

"I will not." Mina chuckled. "Don't be scared, Lee."

"The two of them together make quite the *team*. And no, brave Lee, it's not all a *dream*. We sit here today to honor our *friend*, and if you didn't know it, you're stuck with us till the *end*."

They all cheered as they lofted their drinks in the air, clinking them together in one giant toast.

Chapter 25

"Thanks for inviting me tonight. I had a great time," Vince told Mina as they boarded his drone. "Your friends are warm and friendly and very entertaining."

"They are," Mina agreed. "Kaylee killed it at the sing-along. It's funny how nights usually end like that when she's around."

All in all, it'd been an incredibly fun evening.

Mina had spoken with a few agents she hadn't seen in a while. The atmosphere had been laid-back. The music had flowed, as had the drinks. The meal had been delicious. Now it was pushing the wee hours of the morning.

Vince chuckled as he sat down. "You weren't too bad yourself."

Mina blushed. "I don't usually participate, but after I get a few drinks in me, all bets are off. Plus, Kaylee didn't really give me a choice. When she's determined, there's no deterring her."

"It was a pleasure to watch. You have an excellent voice."

"What is your destination, please?" the sim asked.

Before Mina could give the order, Vince said, "The Spire, private hub, level four hundred."

Mina sputtered. "Wait, what? I'm sorry, but we can't land there. You have to be authorized and live on the top ten floors to use that hub." Mina knew, because she lived in that building.

"Travel time one minute and forty-three seconds," the sim confirmed.

A confirmation meant the sim had reached out to the hub, and they'd been approved for landing.

"We can," Vince said. "Suzanne, your intrepid mega rep, gave me preauthorization to use this hub in anticipation of my upcoming residence at The Spire. She indicated the invitation was open-ended, and I was to use this hub when I come and go to minimize—how did she phrase it? 'Over-the-strato female attention that would prevent easy access to my incredible future residence.' Something like that, anyway." He chuckled. "She stressed that all VIP guests, whether they're residents or not, are authorized to use this hub. So I'm not breaking any rules."

"Leave it to Suzanne to give you open access. I take it you haven't told her you're not entering into a residence agreement anytime soon."

"I haven't, no. I've indicated I still have interest, but that I'm taking a cautious approach because I'm not sure what will happen with my duties in France, and that comes first. Which is the truth, for the most part. But I'm happy she provided me with this opportunity, as it allows me to walk you to your door without being seen. Us being us, that's a necessity."

If Mina had been blushing before, she had full-on hot lava face now.

She felt a little desperate to change the subject. "I figured your presence tonight would garner a lot more attention than it did. Some agents were curious, but most respected your space and kept their distance. I didn't feel like the gossip bubbled over too much either."

Overall, it'd gone smoother than Mina had anticipated. She'd been pleasantly surprised about the lack of fuss.

"I felt the same way," Vince agreed. "So often, particularly in America, events like these can be a lot for me. I had a great time, along with some good conversations with agents about everything under the sun. Oddly, no one mentioned my role with the Protectorate, almost as if someone had cautioned them against asking me to talk about my job." He winked.

Man, he looks good when he does that.

Her heart had fluttered on and off throughout the night as she'd watched him mingle with her fellow agents. It had been strange, but it'd also been fun.

It was all new, and she was enjoying the newness.

Mina chuckled as she leaned her head back against the gel-rest, closing her eyes. "That could very well be. I didn't get that comm blast, but I wouldn't be surprised if something like that was sent out. McAllister was likely reminding all his agents to keep a lid on things and keep their wits about them, even though he doesn't have to.

It's a good, solid group who know how to do their jobs, keep quiet, and don't enter into crazy fandom."

"You're lucky to have such a strong, cohesive bunch to work with."

Entirely too soon for Mina's tastes, the sim announced, "Landing at The Spire, hub level four hundred, in thirty seconds."

As the craft set down, they both remained quiet.

Vince kept his eyes on Mina, but she flitted hers all around. The door rose, and they disembarked.

Since it was early in the morning, nobody was around. Vince took off his jacket and draped it over Mina's shoulders as they walked inside. A bot was manning the small, but elegantly furnished, transpo hub. Early-morning shifts were usually manned by bots, air breathers for when traffic increased, and people were stressed. Mina was happy to see there would be no reaction to them coming in. Just as Vince had assumed.

Mina glanced around the interior, which was covered in soft lavender tones with accents of silver and white. "This is a lot nicer than the hub on twenty. They definitely went upscale here. But it's not nearly as lux as The Bella. I hope it's not too inadequate for your tastes."

"Not at all. This is actually much more my style. There might be a lot of pomp and circumstance swirling around me, but that doesn't represent who I am. I'm still the same kid you knew way back when. Over-the-top lux is a waste, if you ask me."

"Yeah, right." Mina laughed, resting her head against his shoulder as they walked toward the tubes. She wasn't overly inebriated and wouldn't require a spin in her medi-pod, but she was comfortably woozy, tired, and very happy. His shoulder provided a nice, sturdy place to relax. "On our first dinner out together in seven years, you took me to a real, not-printed restaurant and ordered *two* bottles of grape-ripened champagne. The whole vibe there was insanely froufrou, and you looked and acted right at home. They could've built that entire restaurant around you sitting in that chair, and it would've looked perfectly right."

Vince chuckled as Mina swiped for a tube. "I was trying to *impress* you. I figured somebody as classy as you would be used to that sort of stuff."

The tube door opened, and they stepped inside.

Mina stuck her finger in the interior slot. Once it chimed, she said, "Level three hundred twenty." She glanced up at Vince. "How could you possibly want to impress me when you hadn't seen me in seven years? I could've evolved into a harpy, or been attached to someone else, or I don't know, been...generally unavailable."

"You probably wouldn't have accepted my invitation if you'd been attached," he pointed out. "And if you had, it still would've been nice for us to catch up. And I could tell by our conversation before setting up that dinner that you weren't a harpy." He grinned. "I wanted to impress you because, of all the women who have come and gone in my life, you're the only one I truly care about. Quite possibly the only one I've ever really cared deeply about. Besides my mother, whom I miss terribly."

Mina's throat felt full as the tube door opened.

What could she say to that?

They stepped out together.

The world stopped spinning in that moment. She wasn't sure if she should invite him in or not. Her heart wanted to, but her brain was arguing against it. She'd made him promise, just a few scant hours ago, that they would take this slow.

"Do you—"

"Mina, I—"

They both laughed.

She turned to peer up at him. She felt shy. Their gazes locked. His eyes were beautiful. Everything about him was magnificent.

He moved toward her, one hand running around her waist, one slipping behind her neck. She grasped his shirt, reaching as high as she could.

She guided them backward and toward the corner where she knew no cam was pointed. On this floor, the residence cam was aimed at her door.

She would rather not have a record of this.

He followed.

His lips were soft and warm. They melded perfectly with hers. She held on, her mouth moving in tandem with his. The kiss was sensual. Vince deepened it, bending over farther, his hands twining in her hair. She molded to him, loving the feeling of his body against hers.

She broke away briefly, allowing the shallow pants aching to burst out of her chest to gain their freedom, her eyes on his face, flickering to his mouth.

Their lips met again.

Her eyes slid shut.

Inside, her body transformed into one giant firework blazing in the night sky. She felt light-headed, blissful, and tingly right down to her toes.

There was no way to keep track of time.

They stood, intertwined, enjoying each other, exploring contours, whispering happy things in each other's ear for what could've been ten minutes or possibly an hour. They were quiet, careful of each other, cherishing all the firsts they were experiencing together.

Finally, Vince took a small, slightly unsteady step backward. "That was...wow." He ran a hand over his face. "Those were the best kisses I've ever had. You are...truly amazing." He glanced over his shoulder, like he was just realizing they were still in the hallway. He couldn't quite mask his disappointment, but he managed to find a smile. "I should go."

"Yes. Probably."

Should he?

Yes. Probably.

He moved forward, his hands cupping her face. His lips were featherlight this time. The kiss was sweet. It held promise. Mina was grateful for that promise.

When he stepped back again, his smile was lopsided. His hair was askew. The front of his shirt had been partially unbuttoned. She didn't remember doing that.

Mina laughed. "It looks like I worked you over. I'm sorry."

He glanced down the front of himself. "Don't apologize. I thoroughly enjoyed it." He flashed her a dazzling smile. "I hope we can see each other soon. We don't have to make specific plans—"

"I'm heading over to see Lee's new high-rise tomorrow morning. Would you like to join me? We'd have to go, you know, separately. I'm sure you could figure out a roof-clearance scenario. Lee's very excited. Once we got all the bank stuff figured out this evening, he rebooked the movers for bright and early. I want to be his welcome committee. Kaylee and Harmony are coming, too."

"That sounds great. I'll data-log it into my extremely busy media schedule."

Their eyes locked again.

Emotion, passion, and history moved between them.

A new kind of love was forming right in front of them.

Mina took a bold step forward, grabbing him by the lapels again, dragging him down to meet her lips.

She needed one more kiss.

This one was fire, not hot lava, but actual flames.

He moved closer, and their bodies pressed together once again.

This time, she took the unsteady step back.

Mina was pretty sure the kiss was to blame, not anything she'd imbibed. Before she decided to go in for one more, which would lead to a string of more because she wouldn't be able to help herself, she scooted around him toward her door.

She called over her shoulder, "See you tomorrow, Kramer."

He looked as dazed as she felt.

"Yes." He grinned, running a hand over his mouth, his eyes conveying everything she felt. "You certainly will."

DROP ZONE

A MINA KANE NOVEL
BOOK SIX

AMANDA CARLSON

Chapter 1

"HE DIDN'T ANSWER." Mina hefted up a tall, weirdly shaped vase. It had a huge bulge on the top, tapering into a spindly bottom. "I already told you. I called him twice this morning, and he didn't pick up. What is this? Does it hold flowers? Or ashes of the dead?"

It was eight thirty in the morning, and they were running late. It was Mina's fault. Getting out of bed had taken some serious effort. She'd had only around four hours of restless repositioning. There'd been no sleep involved.

Or if there had been, it'd been unrecognizable.

Now that she was up, she had a lot on her mind.

First and foremost, Vincent Kramer had brought the house down with his lips last night, contributing to the majority of her sleeplessness—to the point where Mina had been experiencing some kind of ghost-lip fixation. She would absolutely swear, to anyone who cared to ask, that Vince's lips were currently touching hers, even though he was nowhere near her.

It might be becoming a problem.

Second on her mind was Norman Webb. She was acutely aware that the ex-marshal, who was in a government medi-unit healing from injuries that he'd sustained at the hands of a Syndicate fixer, should rank first in her brain. But the phantom-kissing distraction was proving to be extremely persuasive.

She was, of course, anxious to see how Norm was doing. The main agenda, after they brought her partner, Lee Adams, a celebratory new residence gift, was to meet with Norm and figure out a way to deal with this fixer, a man by the name of Wilbert Waterbury, who'd been released from incarceration a month prior.

They needed to solve this quickly and efficiently with the least amount of blowback. It wasn't going to be easy. The Syndicate had a long reach and an even longer memory.

There was also the pesky faux audit to worry about. Mina hoped Duncan McAllister, the director of the CIU, had found out who'd ordered it. She wanted to check that off her list, too.

She yawned, halfheartedly covering her mouth with the back of her hand. She was going to have to take a dose of Jump if she wanted to remain fully functioning today.

"Here, give it to me." Kaylee took the vase, turning it upside down to inspect the bottom. They were standing in an aisle of Print It. "I wouldn't put anybody's ashes in this thing. Looks like it would topple over if you blew your nose near it." She set it down. It wobbled, threatening to fall before steadying out, which seemed like a miracle, considering. "And if you yawn like a cobra gulping down a fat, juicy rat one more time, an air breather is going to escort you over to the platform section so you can lie down." Kaylee settled her hands on her hips. "What's with you, anyway? I've been waiting to hear what happened last night with your new smoking-hot hunk of burning love since we walked into this store. If you don't spill your ever-lovin' guts soon, I'm going to dig the stinky secrets out of your body with...this."

She snatched up what could be a kitchen utensil that people had used to cook real food with years ago. Either that, or it was pet excrement scooper.

When Mina didn't respond right away, Kaylee swatted the thing, taking a few steps forward. "I want details, and I want them now." She swished the thing downward. "The only tidbit you've offered up is he hasn't answered a couple of calls this morning." She batted it upward. "So what? The man's tired. You kept him up all night." *Swish, swish* to the side. "He's sleeping in like a normal person who doesn't work full time. Or even part time." She gave up on the pooper spatula and set it back on the shelf. "Does he even work at all? I mean, what does he do all day? No wonder he's still asleep."

Mina shrugged, trying to hold back another yawn. It came out in a weird half growl. There was no good way to stifle a yawn. "I don't know. He does media interviews, but there can't be that many in a single day. Ambrose is keeping track of him with a couple of guards. Other than that, I have no idea."

Ambrose Bernard was leader of the French Protectorate and subsequently Vince's boss. The French captain of the military wasn't very happy with Vince at the moment. Vince had gone rogue without approval, and Ambrose was making him pay for it.

Kaylee puckered her lips, making kissy sounds. "You haven't asked because you're too busy sticking your face in his." She stopped, brows arching in concern. "You did stick your face in his face, didn't you?"

Mina meandered down the aisle without answering.

Her friend caught up with her in a second flat. "In case you've forgotten, we don't keep stuff like this from each other." She guided Mina around to face her. "We're best friends. I goss on everything. You know it all. From Tanya loves Tangling Tonsils to Porcupine Jones, the man who lives to creep me out. Who I absolutely never slept with." Her eyes made a slow roll toward the ceiling. "Okay, so we might've occupied the same bed together...once. Oh, never mind." She visibly shivered, rubbing her arms through her emerald-green flow shirt. "You know almost every single detail of my love life. You can't ice me out now."

Mina picked up a decent-looking lamp, stifling a grin. "How about this? Looks kind of Lee-like. It's brown and sturdy. These knobs on the sides make it look a little owlish."

"Are you kidding me?" Kaylee huffed. "We're not buying that. We're not lamp people. And why aren't you answering me? Did he break up with you? If he did, he's going to get a solid kick in the—"

"He didn't break up with me." Mina chuckled. "Stop being so dramatic. We're not even a real thing yet." Were they a real thing yet? Maybe they were. Mina sighed. "I just... I'm still trying to process everything. It's all jumbled up in my brain, and it makes it hard to talk about it. We kissed last night. It was incredible. So much so, that it feels like he's kissing me constantly. Vince's Ghost Lips won't leave me alone. And no, he didn't stay over. We're taking this slow." That decision had been debatable as she'd tossed and turned in her platform all alone. "I'm glad we are"—if she kept saying it, it would be true—"because I'm having trouble reconciling having feelings, or even allowing myself to have feelings, for this guy who was my best friend. When he's in front of me, I see grown-up Vince. But when he leaves, all these memories of us as kids flood back, and I'm"—she shrugged—"a little weirded out."

"Leave it to you to get weirded out kissing a guy with dreamy ghost lips when ten million people, and I'm being conservative with that number, would enter into cohabitorship with him, no questions asked."

Mina laughed. "Yeah, but most people didn't watch him grow up. We spent *a lot* of time together. During those years, I never felt a single romantic feeling toward him. Not a one. It was probably because we were together constantly." Mina mulled it over. "But at the same time, I can't wait to see him again and latch on to those plump, delicious, silky lips. Damn, he's a good kisser. Phen*omenal.* Possibly the best kisses I've ever had."

There was no *possibly* about it. It'd been the most romantic, highly charged interaction of Mina's life to date.

The ghost sensation tingled again.

She refrained from running her fingers over her lips like she wanted to and settled on rubbing them together. Aggressively.

Kaylee did a little jig. "See? That's what I'm talking about. More of that please." She pivoted back and forth in place, hips swaying, beckoning Mina with both hands. "*Dee-tails*. I need some of those sweet, sweet *dee-tails*. Kissing, stroking, lip-locking, nails-scraping, head-bobbing, *dee-licious dee-tails*. Feel free to get down and dirty. I'm in need of some sweet, sweet *dee-liiight*." She stopped. "Seriously, this dry spell sucks. I need to find someone with magical ghost lips. No fair."

"Okay. *Okay*." Mina giggled. "But you have to promise to stop dancing. This is honestly not the time to break into song. Why do you have so much energy, anyway? You left the ceremony at the same time we did. You should be yawning right along with me."

"Like a good girl who knows what she's doing, I downed a hyperbiotic this morning and pretty much ate my breakfast in my medi-pod. It does the body good. And don't you dare lead me off-topic. What else you got? And anytime is a great time for a song." She started snapping. "Oh, there once was a man named *Viiincent*. He kissed like he had a *biiig fat*—"

Mina grabbed Kaylee's arm and dragged her forward, laughing. "No more. We have to get serious about this. My mentorship is spiraling down the grinder as we speak.

Right now, Lee is wandering around his new high-rise wondering what to do and second-guessing if he'll be able to stay there or not. We're bringing over some printed treats and whatever we find in the next aisle."

She walked them around the corner.

The aisles at Print It were enormous—two meters wide and stacked higher than anyone could reach. Whatever was found on a shelf could be printed in any color, many in several variations. You could purchase a particular item, but the merchandise was really there to spark an idea.

Mina scanned the row. "Well, this is unfortunate. We can't really give him a gel-cush seat insert." She gestured to one side. "Or a child's plush toy." Gesturing to the other. "Why aren't they better organized? It should be groupings of similar items."

Kaylee glanced around. "I think we're in the yellow section."

"Yellow? Why would color matter?"

Neither of them shopped here often.

"I have no idea, but do you see anything that isn't the color of a drab sunflower? Or, more accurately, the color of mustard diluted with burnt carbon?"

"Hm. You're right. That's a lot of yellow. It's also the worst color. These actually look like rejects to me." Mina picked up a large urn that could be used to put a house-plant in or possibly something to keep prewash clothing in? Hard to know. "Who would buy this?"

"I'm pretty sure it's one of those decorative floor stand thingies. You put branches in it."

"Why would you put branches in it?"

Kaylee snorted. "Honestly, I've never met anyone with less of a fashion sense than you. When you move, you go with whatever decor is already inside the residence. But some people—most humans—love to personalize their space. They like to add their own planetary twist on things. And for what it's worth, I think branches are pretty. Something natural in our sterile world." She took the urn from Mina. "But this one is hateful." She stuck it back on the shelf. "That yellow color not only hurts the eyes, it offends the soul."

"I have plenty of fashion sense," Mina argued as Kaylee led them out of the land of yellow. "Just because I don't care about dotting my residence with tchotchkes doesn't mean I don't enjoy decorating. I just haven't had the time or energy to spend on it yet."

"Keep telling yourself that."

Mina snorted. "Let's get Lee some plushy dry wraps. Those are fun and functional." They walked down the much larger main aisle, glancing at the digital signage, trying to make sense of it. "Where's the fiber section?"

"Over there, I think," Kaylee said, gesturing. "And while we search for the most boring gift available in this entire, massive, sensory-overloading store, keep spilling. We're not done here."

"We might be done here. I told you about the amazing kissing. That was it."

"Your storytelling is as weak as a tot slurping fruit sauce out of a retractable straw. I like the ghost-lip stuff. Give me more of that."

"My storytelling is excellent. And there just isn't much to tell. He kissed me. I liked it. We stopped. I kind of wished he'd stayed over. He said he'd meet us at Lee's this morning, made it seem like he was into it, didn't answer my calls, now we're here."

"Proof to my point. Effective storytelling involves highly descriptive adjectives and leave-you-on-the-edge-of-your-seat cliffhangers. You just gave me bullet points. That was excrement, not excitement."

Mina yawned. "Yeah, you're probably right. I'm sorry. I'm just not all here this morning."

Kaylee stopped abruptly, turning to Mina. "Look, I get it. You're hung up on him not answering this morning. You went to bed blissed out, ready to jump into this new relationship, then Kramer gives you another setback by blocking you, which you file away as yet another possible lie he fed you. It makes sense, given what's happened recently between the two of you." She began to walk again. Mina followed. "But I can promise you that's not what's happening. He didn't answer because he's either in a kiss-bliss coma, or something came up. Something important."

"How can you possibly know that? You don't have any proof."

He could've lied again. Mina wasn't ruling that out.

"I know because every single person in that room last night saw how you guys looked at each other. There's no impersonating that much electric current. Even when you were apart, you sought each other out, giving each other silly grins and head bobs, holding hands under the table when you thought nobody was looking."

Mina made a face. "You were watching us?"

"Not like a creeper. Jeez." Kaylee laughed. "But it was hard to miss. It was also endearing and sweet and perfect and smushy. There was so much current, all the male and female agents who might've sought Vince out to, I don't know, flex their assets and give him a flyby, didn't. They didn't because they saw he was taken. That his heart was not up for grabs. So believe me when I say, the man is not avoiding you." She turned down another aisle. "And if you weren't so lovesick and paranoid, you'd see it, too."

"I'm not lovesick," Mina protested. "Or paranoid. I'm...cautious. I'm practical. I'm a realist."

"Then get real on this. Kramer is into you. He's fallen down a deep crater hole, and you're the only one in there with him. So relax. He'll call you. You'll see him again. It will be fabulous." She waggled a finger. "And if you don't give me excellent details dipped in hot buttery fudge dipped in scintillating sprinkles the size of baby elephants next time, this relationship is over and I'm moving on." She marched up to a shelf and grabbed a stack of dry wraps in a pretty aqua color. "We're getting these. Boring, but useful. Come on, let's go."

Mina trailed her best friend in the entire world. "You're never moving on. You're stuck with me. For. Life. Who's not being a realist now?"

"Try me and see."

Nothing is completed without a great team.

My many thanks to:

Awesome Cover design: Damonza
Digital and print formatting: Author E.M.S
Copyedits/proofs: Joyce Lamb
Final proof: Marlene Roberts

Head to my website to sign-up for my Book Alert newsletter to receive new release info in your inbox so you don't miss a thing!

https://www.amandacarlson.com

About the Author

Amanda Carlson is a graduate of the University of Minnesota, with a BA in both Speech and Hearing Science & Child Development. She went on to get an A.A.S in Sign Language Interpreting and worked as an interpreter until her first child was born. She's the author of the high-octane **Jessica McClain** urban fantasy series published by Orbit, the **Sin City Collectors** PNR series, the contemporary fantasy **Phoebe Meadows** series, the dystopian **Holly Danger** series, and the futuristic thriller **Mina Kane** series. Look for these books in stores everywhere. She lives in Minneapolis.

FIND HER ALL OVER SOCIAL MEDIA

Website: amandacarlson.com

Facebook: facebook.com/authoramandacarlson

Twitter: @amandaccarlson

Instagram: @author_amanda